FAIRGROUND ATTRACTIONS

'You'd do well to remember that I'm in charge here,' Corinne explained. 'I expect only one thing from those who work for me: absolute obedience. Anything less than that I consider to be a punishable offence.'

Holly swallowed thickly. The atmosphere in the caravan was so highly charged that breathing was a chore. She tried not to think of her own vulnerable nudity beneath the woman's cold, dark expression. However, the threats Corinne was making made it difficult to focus her thoughts on anything else. Meekly she asked, 'What do you want me to do?'

Holly's eyes widened as Corinne showed her the length of rope.

FAIRGROUND ATTRACTIONS

Lisette Ashton

This book is a work of fiction.
In real life, make sure you practise safe sex.

First published in 1998 by
Nexus
Thames Wharf Studios
Rainville Road
London W6 9HT

Typeset by TW Typesetting, Plymouth, Devon

Printed and bound by
Cox & Wyman Ltd, Reading, Berks

ISBN 0 352 33295 6

One

'Move faster, you stupid bitch! Faster!'

Chelsea almost stumbled in her hurry to obey. The chain between her ankles was less than ten inches long and the stilettos weren't helping on the uneven ground. She could feel herself beginning to topple and just managed to stop before a catastrophe happened. Thick tresses of long dark hair were flying carelessly about her face as she tried to maintain her balance. She shook them back with a flick of her head, trying to concentrate on the difficult task of walking. Curtis was in a foul mood and she didn't want to worsen it; not until they got back to the caravan, anyway.

'What the hell is wrong with you?' he demanded angrily. His strong voice sounded almost musical in the still twilight air. 'Why am I surrounded by incompetents and cretins?'

Aside from the heavy panting of her breath and Curtis's vicious words, the world was silent. The growl of distant traffic was faint in the faraway hills. The noise of the passing cars was drowned out by a soft breeze whispering through the neighbouring fields of long grass. Partly because of the eerie silence, but mainly because of Curtis's mood, Chelsea didn't dare murmur an apology.

Instead, she knelt down on the floor, not caring what the wet, muddy grass did to the knees of her fishnet

1

stockings. Flicking the hair away from her face again, she placed the sign against the booth door, positioned the nail and lifted her hammer.

The whip whistled through the cool twilight air.

An explosion of pain erupted on the exposed cheek of her arse. Chelsea drew breath, momentarily lost in a world of exquisite torment. The red-hot flare of the whip crack was so intense it left bitter tears stinging her eyes.

Her longing for Curtis was a burning fever that brought with it a delicious delirium. She had wanted him since the moment they first met. On those occasions when he had deigned to sate her appetite, the satisfaction had been whole and fulfilling. His swarthy complexion and cruel good looks were an irresistible combination, and his air of cold indifference only fuelled Chelsea's yearning for him. She dared to hope he had an interest in her that went beyond the joy they had already shared. The thought sent nervous explosions of joy erupting inside her stomach. The inner muscles of her pussy tingled excitedly.

'Put it higher, you stupid bitch!' Curtis growled. 'A midget chihuahua would have to stoop down to read that. Put it higher!' He followed those words with another whip crack. This time he managed to score her other cheek.

Chelsea groaned. The heated pulse of her arousal was already beating so hard it threatened to burst. This final blow only served to increase the wetness between the lips of her sex. Her nipples were rock-hard nubs that tingled with mounting excitement.

She struggled to her feet and placed the sign just above head height. As she raised the hammer, a thought occurred to her. Warily, she glanced at Curtis. It would be unwise to nail the sign until she had his nod of approval. When she saw him smile agreement, her heart suddenly felt lighter. She hammered the sign into position with three brisk blows. With the job done, she took a tiny step back to admire her handiwork.

Curtis brought the whip across the cheeks of her arse with another punishing blow. The sound of the impact echoed across the deserted fairground and over the empty fields.

Chelsea stiffened against the pain and turned to face him. Her expression was shocked and hurt. 'Isn't it right?'

He shrugged. 'It'll do.' A cruel smile twisted his lips. 'That was just for good measure.'

She realised he had moved closer. His face was only inches from hers and his lips were parted. As he stepped even closer, she knew he was going to kiss her. The prospect made her heart beat faster.

His mouth enveloped hers and his tongue pushed between her lips. She could taste his excitement like an electric charge. Dropping the whip to the floor he held her tightly in his arms. His hands moved down her back and he cupped her buttocks with rough, uncaring fingers.

She was wearing a bastardised version of the costume she used for her tightrope act, but this garment left far less to the imagination. Her backside was exposed, save for a thin ribbon of black separating the cheeks of her arse and almost covering her modesty. As he caressed her, she was painfully aware that his fingers were brushing against bare flesh. The intimate movement of his hands sent thrills of excitement shivering through her body. Touching her, his caress became more urgent. His fingers began to knead her flesh with a cruel strength that was delightfully uncomfortable.

Curtis pushed himself against her. His erection pressed hungrily at her flat stomach. She could feel its hard pulse through the stiff fabric of his jeans. When he broke their kiss, he was staring at her with a passion she found intoxicating. This was the way Chelsea wanted Curtis to look at her. This was the expression of a man who wanted to possess her.

Once again, he began to kiss her. His fingers moved away from her arse and he began to stroke the tops of her thighs. Gently, with more consideration than she thought necessary, he eased a finger inside the gusset of her costume.

Chelsea drew a short, delighted sigh. The coolness of his touch against the excited warmth of her sex was excruciating. She kissed him harder, daring to push her tongue into his mouth.

Curtis slid his hand away from her and took a step back. 'Get into the van and prepare for work.' He glanced at his watch. 'There's barely an hour before the punters arrive.'

With a heavy sigh, Chelsea began to shuffle back to her caravan. She glanced over her shoulder and saw that Curtis was studying the sign. There was a rueful grin twisting his broad, sensuous lips. 'Are you sure it's all right?' she asked nervously. After the thrill he had just given her, she didn't want to think he was unhappy with the effort she had made.

In bold, hand-painted letters, the sign read: SITUATION VACANT. Beneath that were the words: APPLY WITHIN.

Curtis shook his head. 'Still stuck in the old world, Corinne,' he murmured. 'Too much the independent to trust employment agencies and job centres.' His disparaging frown was tinged with a hint of admiration that sparkled softly in his cruel black eyes.

Chelsea swallowed, her lips quivering anxiously. She cleared her throat and said again, 'Are you sure it's all right?'

Curtis sniffed sharply, his concentration suddenly broken. 'I heard what you said,' he barked. 'Tell Corinne her sign is in place. And before she lays claim to you this evening, tell her you'll be in my van tonight.'

Chelsea nodded and hurried away as fast as her chained legs could carry her. The prospect of spending a night in Curtis's company thrilled her. They had been daytime lovers already and, while she had no complaints about the way he had treated her, Chelsea yearned to spend a night in his company. The night was special and she knew that people behaved differently during the hours of darkness. Her years with the circus and travelling fairground had taught her that much.

With his powerful, dark good looks, she suspected Curtis was the kind of man who turned into an animal during the night. She knew the transformation would be worth waiting for.

If he wanted her tonight, she dared to hope he might want her on other nights. Her heart raced faster as she tried not to think this might be the beginning of a permanent arrangement. She couldn't decide which prospect excited her more: being with Curtis, or being away from Corinne. At the back of her mind, she suspected it was the former of these two options. Nothing could compare with the prospect of spending a night with Curtis.

She was so excited that she didn't see the woman until she bumped into her. All she noticed was a short shock of blonde hair, a stark navy business suit and a pair of long, stocking-clad legs.

And then she was falling.

The combination of stilettos, uneven ground and the chain between her legs finally proved too much. Chelsea hit the ground hard and released a cry of despair as she tumbled into the sodden mud.

It was second nature to look at Curtis when she fell. She doubted her clumsiness would meet with his approval and she had to know how severe his wrath would be. When she saw his face, she frowned. He wasn't looking at her. His attention was fixed on the blonde Chelsea had bumped into and knocked over. The smile in his eyes hurt her more than his whips could ever have done. His attraction for the woman was blatantly obvious.

'I knew it would be you. Are you all right?' He was running over to the woman's side.

Chelsea glanced at her, wondering who she was, and

what she was doing here. She knew all of the fairground staff and this woman wasn't one of them. Until seven o'clock, the fairground was out of bounds to punters. She watched Curtis attempt to lift the woman from the ground and felt her heart sink. His attention was devoted to the newcomer. The expression in his eyes was filled with a concern that she should have been enjoying.

Chelsea glared unhappily at the blonde.

'I said, are you all right?' Curtis repeated. 'Georgia, are you all right?'

The blonde was frowning.

'I'm all right,' Georgia snapped. She glanced curiously at the woman who had knocked her over, then turned to glare at Curtis. 'Mr K Campion?' She asked the question with such disdain it was obvious she already knew the answer. She had been unsure about coming for this interview when she linked the name 'Campion' with a position in a fairground. It was too close to the surname 'Champion' for her liking. If it hadn't been for the initial 'K', she would have refused the employment agency's offer on general principles. There were plenty of vacancies for accounts managers in regular offices. It was only the promise of an unusually lucrative salary that had made her agree to the interview.

Curtis Champion was the last man on the face of the planet that Georgia would have considered working for. Aside from his penchant for sexual domination, his conniving power games were too intense for her. She had nothing against sexual domination, in fact she quite enjoyed it, but she preferred to be the one in charge, and she had no time for ruses or cunning tricks. She realised she had been drawn out to the fair by one of his charades and the thought angered her. Worse still, there was his sister, Corinne, to consider. Georgia struggled to suppress a shudder when she thought of the woman's name.

Acting as though he hadn't sensed how bad her mood

was, Curtis allowed an easy grin to break his lips. Even after two years, the expression was despicably familiar. 'The employment agency made the same mistakes on the invoice they sent me,' he explained glibly. 'I meant to correct them, tell them my initial is a "C", not a "K", and my name's "Champion", not "Campion", but it must have slipped my mind.' He smiled broadly at her and shook his head. 'It's really good to see you again, Georgia,' he said earnestly. 'Really good.'

Georgia backed away from the helping hand he offered and climbed up from the ground. She glared angrily at him, then turned her attention briefly to the woman who had knocked her over. Georgia was still trying to ignore the pulse of excitement she had experienced when she saw Curtis manhandling her. The memory of that spreading warmth was too close to shut out completely but she made a valiant effort.

'You haven't changed since we last met, Curtis,' Georgia commented dryly.

Curtis snatched his gaze away for a moment. Glancing at the other fallen woman, he wrenched her from the floor with one hand and waited impatiently until she had her balance. 'Go on, Chelsea,' he snapped. 'You have your instructions. Do as you've been told. And forget what I said about my van tonight. You can stay with Corinne.'

With a miserable air weighing on her shoulders, Chelsea left them alone.

Georgia scowled at Curtis. She was unhappy with the lecherous line his grin took when his gaze met hers. 'Tell me,' she began suddenly, 'was it a serious job offer, or just a ploy to get me near your shitty fairground?'

'The job offer's serious,' he said honestly. 'I need someone to manage my accounts.'

Georgia snorted rudely. 'Not that it matters. Whatever you are trying to do, it won't work. Goodbye, Curtis. I'm leaving.'

His hand was on her arm before she could properly turn away. His nearness was disturbing. She could feel the strong muscles of his fingers squeezing her arm and she resisted the urge to tremble.

'Wait,' he whispered. 'Give me a chance.'

She stared angrily into his face, trying to control the rising annoyance that was building inside her. 'You had your last chance two years ago. I'm not going to start with that foolishness a second time.'

The cruel depths of his dark eyes twinkled sullenly. His upper lip was curled into a scowl. 'Come back to my van and let's talk,' he suggested. 'Two years is a long time and even if you don't want the job, then at least we can chat about . . .'

'No!' she shouted. The exclamation startled both of them. Curtis hadn't been expecting the reaction and Georgia didn't realise she could break his spell once he had begun to charm her. 'I'm going, Curtis,' she growled. 'Do me the courtesy of releasing my arm and allowing me to leave here while one of us still has some dignity.'

His fingers slipped from her arm. The expression on his face was so pained she felt a moment's sympathy for him. Quickly, she stifled the emotion before it could take hold. From past experience, she knew that Curtis had more than one way of exerting charm. She knew it wouldn't be beyond him to exploit his obvious unhappiness.

'At least have a drink with me before you leave,' he insisted. 'We're out here in the middle of nowhere and . . .'

'No,' she broke in. 'I'm leaving.' She turned her back on him and began to storm away, anxious to put some distance between herself and the fairground owner. As soon as she had done it, she realised that turning her back was a mistake.

But by then it was too late.

8

His hands were on her shoulders, and she could feel the animal passion of his grip as he lifted her from her feet. With an effortless display of strength, he turned her around, so that she was facing him. For a moment, she wondered what he intended to do, but there was no time to follow that line of thought.

Georgia felt the ground disappear from beneath her feet, and then she was being thrown against the door of a booth. The dry timber creaked beneath the impact of her body. Her legs slipped from under her and she would have fallen if Curtis hadn't been holding her.

He pressed her to the door and pushed his face close to hers. His hands were gripping her arms with a ferocity that was brutal and painful. If she hadn't been enjoying the discomfort so much, Georgia would have cried out in protest. She stared into his commanding glare, aware that her own dark blue eyes were shining with excitement. It was a purely involuntary response and she despised herself for enjoying it so strongly. She held her breath and studied him. Past experience had taught her that Curtis was to be treated with respect when he was in this sort of mood. Memories of their previous encounters brought a dark excitement as she realised there had never been an unpleasant conclusion to such interludes. Shutting these thoughts from her mind, Georgia suppressed a shiver.

'I asked you to join me in my van, so we can reminisce about old times,' he growled. 'At least do me the courtesy of sharing a glass of wine.'

The words hinted at a string of barely controlled threats. His fingers bit painfully into the soft flesh of her arms. He was so close, Georgia could smell the subtle fragrance of his sweat. It was a clean, natural scent that rekindled memories of their time together two years earlier.

Back then she hadn't even contemplated using the word 'no'. It was the last thing she would have said to

9

Curtis, and not simply because he intimidated her. The desire to please him had always been strong. Staring into the merciless depths of his dark eyes, she could feel its familiar pull.

Her heartbeat raced and the almost forgotten thrill of arousal washed over her body. Her nipples tingled and the cleft between her legs throbbed eagerly. The symptoms of her longing were disturbing reminders of all the reasons why she wanted to stay in Curtis's company.

'A glass of wine,' she repeated. The words tumbled from her lips more easily than she would have believed. This time, she didn't punish herself with ungracious thoughts about her own weakness. Curtis was dangerously close and his nearness inspired a devastating effect. It was a triumph that she had managed to say the words without stammering.

'A glass of wine.' His black eyes studied her warily, as though he didn't completely trust the response she had given. There was a Machiavellian twist to his smile and his lips parted slightly.

Georgia closed her eyes and drew an excited breath. She sensed his kiss coming and could resist him no longer. He pushed her hard against the booth door and placed his mouth over hers.

It had been a long time since she had enjoyed a kiss so much. His hands still held her tightly and he pushed his body roughly against her. She could feel the creaking timber of the booth door bending slightly beneath their combined body weights. The swell of his erection pressed against her through his jeans. He shifted one leg between hers, rubbing the denim against her stocking-clad thighs.

Helplessly, she released a soft groan. Georgia had never wanted to see him again and now, too late, she remembered the reason why. Even if he hadn't been pinning her to the door, she knew she wouldn't have been able to move. There was something so powerful about his presence, the simple promise of a kiss would have been sufficient to make her stay where he wanted. It had always been that way in the past and she saw that little had changed.

Distantly, she realised there was more than the mere promise of a kiss between them. The shine of his eyes and the urgency of his touch told her that he was offering far more than that.

His tongue invaded her mouth with a roughness she found exhilarating. Excitement filled her body and she pressed herself towards him, unable to resist the impulse. Her earlier anger was forgotten as a wave of longing erupted in her body. His hands loosened their grip on her arms and she realised she could now move against him.

Deliberately, she lowered herself on to his leg. The hem of her short skirt rose as she tried to rub the aching pulse of her cleft against him. At the back of her mind, she knew this was the wrong thing to be doing. He was a dangerous, formidable man and she had vowed to avoid him at all costs. If the pleasure he inspired hadn't felt so good, she believed she would have heeded her own promise.

The subtle friction tickled the skin between her legs. The denim was like sandpaper against her thighs, and when it touched the crotch of her panties the fabric's coarseness was no less punishing. Rocking her pelvis slowly back and forth, Georgia felt the almost forgotten delight of an orgasm building deep inside. The shiver of excitement that she had been valiantly fighting finally trembled through her.

His hands had moved from her but he still held her against the door with the weight of his body. He stroked rough fingers against her neck as they continued to kiss, and his other hand moved purposefully to the swell of her breast.

11

Georgia drew an excited gasp of pleasure.

It didn't matter that they were standing out in the open. The fairground was still deserted and, as they kissed and caressed against the empty booth, she felt as though they were the last two people on the face of the earth. The growing shadows of the waltzers and the Ferris wheel darkened around them as he casually teased her body to a state of long-forgotten bliss. Georgia barely noticed the cool fingers of the night's chill air caressing her. Her thoughts were concentrated on the pleasure that Curtis evoked.

Memories of all the other nights they had spent like this coursed through her excited mind. It had been two years since she and Curtis had enjoyed such passion and time had played games with her recollection. He might still be the cruel barbarian whom she thoroughly despised, but he was also a capable lover.

His hands were cupping her breasts through the jacket of her suit. Instinctively, he managed to find the eager thrust of her nipples. They tingled inside her bra with an urgency that couldn't be denied. The soft caress of his hands was inspiring wave upon wave of pleasure.

'Come to my van,' he whispered, the words brushing softly against the sensitive flesh of her neck. 'We'll share that glass of wine.'

Unable to stop herself, even if she had wanted to, Georgia nodded agreement.

Curtis led her through the closed stalls and past the silent rides. His arm encircled her waist as they walked. Georgia knew she should have been trying to resist him. But his body felt so right against hers that she couldn't find the motivation to refuse. Dutifully, she fell into step beside him.

'I'm not staying,' she said firmly. She didn't know if she had said the words for his benefit or her own.

His hand squeezed reassuringly against her side. 'You've already told me that.'

'And I'm not taking your lousy job,' she went on.

'So you've said,' he agreed, leading her to the step of his van. 'You're not staying, and you're not taking my lousy job. You're just coming in my van for a civilised glass of wine, then we'll both go our separate ways again.'

Georgia nodded. 'Exactly. One glass of wine, then I leave.'

Two hours later, the second empty wine bottle clattered in the bin against the first. Georgia watched Curtis go to the fridge and retrieve a third from the shelf inside.

'No more,' she insisted. 'I really should be going now.'

He frowned. 'We've barely begun to catch up.' He held the bottle in front of him as he walked towards her. Georgia reached a hand out and stroked the neck of the green glass. Because it was below his waist, the action seemed infuriatingly intimate. Her fingers caressed the cool length of glass, touching the broader base and nearing the heat of his body.

He studied her in the sombre light of the van, his features dark in the shadows. Outside, the sounds of the funfair whispered against the windows. The merry music, raucous laughter and cheerful hectoring hinted at a different world from the one they were now inhabiting. Georgia could feel the atmosphere thickening. She was poignantly aware of her own excitement as Curtis studied her.

'Neither of us came in here to play catch up, did we?' he asked.

Georgia drew a sharp intake of breath. She could sense the intimation of his words. Despite the fact that she longed to disagree, she found herself unable. 'I have to go,' she told him.

He shook his head. 'I made the mistake of allowing you to leave two years ago. I don't intend making that mistake again.'

13

Georgia stood up. She could feel the heavy pulse of her arousal, a sensation she had always associated with Curtis. The strength of her desire was so great it was a difficult force to fight. 'As I recall,' she reminded him gently, 'you weren't around to stop me.' She found she couldn't meet the challenge of his gaze any longer. Quickly she looked away. 'I have to go,' she repeated.

He slammed the wine down on the table and took a step towards her.

Georgia wanted to back away from him. The van was one of the fairground's more spacious, but it still left little room for manoeuvring. One backward step and she was pressed against the wall. Her heart was racing like an express train.

Curtis moved closer towards her. 'I want you to stay,' he whispered.

She closed her eyes and searched for the willpower to refuse him. This was so much like the night they had first met that she felt as though she was trapped in some insane time loop.

At the time, she had been a naive young girl of eighteen. He had been a mature, worldly man of twenty-nine, and his knowledge of life and love had driven her mad with desire. He had been working a ticket booth for the circus and his slanted smile and easy charm had won her over in seconds. Within minutes she had realised she wanted him, and within the hour he had obliged.

He had taken her virginity with a gentleness that made her beg for more. He was a skilled lover, blessed with an intention to please that had made her first indulgence all the more memorable. Delightful images of that first night sped through her mind as he stared at her. Back then, after the fulfilling moment of their lovemaking, he had asked her to stay with him.

Georgia had accepted the offer without hesitation.

Now, as he repeated the words, she struggled to

14

remember a reason why she should refuse. Admittedly there had been bad times, and her reasons for leaving him still seemed more than valid, but those memories were pale in the light of more pleasant recollections. From that first night, they had spent an eternity together. Every waking moment was an adventurous exploration of one another. Their lovemaking, so tender and passionate to begin with, had grown quickly to encompass the vast boundaries of their love. After that first union, they nurtured an intimacy that was so complete it had no barriers.

She had moved into Curtis's van and together they had explored realms of pleasure that neither had imagined possible. It seemed as though no aspect of their sexuality was left unexplored. She supposed that if it hadn't been for that one night, six months afterwards, she and Curtis would still be together.

Quickly she tried to brush that memory away, but it wasn't easy. She had been trying to rid herself of the image for the past two years, without any measure of success. As the unwelcome memory recurred, she realised it did have one advantage. It reminded her she wasn't staying with him. 'No,' she said, shaking her head. 'I have to leave.'

He frowned. 'You don't want to leave. A blind man could see that much.'

She reached for her coat and snatched her bag from the chair. 'It was a mistake for me to come in here. And it was an even bigger mistake for me to share those with you.' She nodded at the empty wine bottles in the waste bin. 'Goodnight, Curtis. And goodbye.'

He pushed her against the wall. 'You haven't even considered my proposition. I'm offering a salary that's double anything you could get in the real world.'

She glared at him defiantly. 'You've offered it, and I'm refusing it. Let go of me, Curtis. I'm leaving.'

He shook his head. 'You'll leave when I say you can

15

leave.' His brow was a dark, threatening frown and he hissed his words with barely controlled malice. 'For now, I want you to stay and properly consider my job offer. You know the terms and conditions.'

Georgia could feel her anger rising. The emotion was threatening to spiral out of control. 'I've already considered it, Curtis, and I've said no. Keep pushing me and I'll tell you to shove it up your . . .'

A knock on the van door disturbed them.

Curtis kept his hands against her shoulders and shouted a sharp 'fuck off' to the visitor.

'Curt, it's Joey. I think you should come.'

'Handle it, Joey,' Curtis called back sharply. 'I'm busy.'

'Corinne's just caught a pickpocket,' the voice called. 'I thought you'd want to know.'

Cursing angrily, Curtis moved his hands from Georgia's shoulders. With a gesture of untamed rage, he slammed his fist against the table. The unopened wine bottle fell over and toppled heavily to the floor. Staring at Georgia he asked, 'Will you wait here until I get back?'

She shook her head. 'I'm leaving here as soon as I can get through that bloody door. If you insist that I stay then I'll just defy . . .'

He didn't allow her to finish. Instead, he reached for her wrist and started to pull her along with him. 'Forget it,' he growled. 'You can come with me.' Ignoring her struggles and protests, he dragged her from the caravan.

Two

Holly's itinerary was clearly set out. She would be disciplined enough to make two grand before she started having any fun this evening. After she had reached the golden total, she would do the Ferris wheel, the hall of mirrors and possibly even the circus. She didn't consider the sum an excessive amount. She had often beaten that when she was working a fairground, but she was determined to reach it before she started to indulge herself. Her resolve would have remained intact if she hadn't seen the waltzers.

The flashing lights above the ride caught her attention first. The noise of the whirring machinery was louder than the deafening rock music that pumped from the ride's speakers. She heard people screaming and laughing from their spinning seats and in an instant her plans changed.

She had to ride the waltzers first. Holly loved the waltzers.

The waltzers were fast and dangerous. In a way, they reminded her of her own lifestyle and she had to like them for that. There was also something excitingly sexual about the ride. The loss of control, the flashing lights and disorientation; it was so similar to the climactic thrill of an orgasm that she thought the ride should be X-rated.

Although the fair had been open barely a few

17

minutes, there were already a lot of people milling around. Night had fallen, cloaking the world in a shroud of darkness. She started weaving her way deliberately through the crowd, ignoring the booths and touts who cajoled every passer-by for their attention. She glanced curiously at the faces of those around her, half wondering if they were enjoying themselves as much as she was. She doubted that would be possible. The fairground had to be her favourite place in the whole world. Especially a fairground with waltzers.

Holly bumped into a fat man. ''Scuse me,' she muttered.

He turned to glare at her. Then, seeing she was a pretty young woman in a short skirt and tight blouse, he changed the expression into a smile. Holly tested an easy, apologetic grin, threw her rucksack over her shoulder and continued towards the waltzers. As soon as she had put enough distance between herself and the fat man, she began to leaf through the contents of his wallet.

She quickly counted three hundred in notes and a score of credit cards at the back of the black leather folder. She took the money and thrust it in her rucksack. Then she dropped the wallet and the credit cards into the first waste bin that she passed. Either of those items could have been seen as compromising evidence and she had more sense than to fill her rucksack with crap like that.

It didn't bother her that she had taken the man's money. In Holly's opinion, anyone who could afford to wander around a fairground with so much cash in their pocket could easily spare her a few quid. She knew without a doubt the man wouldn't go hungry tonight. Remembering his bulging waist and wobbling backside, she supposed that going hungry for a few nights might not have been such a bad thing.

Briskly, she continued towards the waltzers.

18

She caught sight of herself in a sign outside the hall of mirrors. Confidence from the night's first snatch made her feel taller than the five-foot woman who stared back from the reflection. Her diminutive size only served to accentuate her femininity. Her long legs were being displayed by the short, tight skirt she wore and her ample breasts were filling her tight blouse.

The sound of the waltzers caught her attention before she could stand in front of the mirror for too long. Unable to resist the siren call for a moment longer, she strode purposefully towards the ride.

She stopped herself from bumping into the tall woman.

There was something about her that unnerved Holly. After a lifetime spent living by her wits, she knew better than to ignore gut instinct, and stopped her hands from going to the padded pockets of the woman's long-line jacket.

Impressively built, with dark hair and a swarthy complexion, the woman had a natural confidence that made her look at home in the busy fairground. This confidence, combined with her cruel, watchful eyes and cold, omnipotent gaze, made Holly think she looked disturbingly like undercover security. The woman wore a thick black belt that seemed to take inches from her narrow waist. Attached to the belt was a bulky set of keys, hanging from a dog-leash fastener.

As she watched Holly, the tall woman toyed idly with the keys.

Holly supposed her imagination could have been overreacting but she knew better than to test her own abilities. She didn't attempt to take the woman's money. Instead, she skirted around her, trying not to feel intimidated by the glare of the woman's black eyes, and the cruel set of her lips. There was something icy about the woman's gaze that caused a shiver to run down Holly's spine.

She bumped against two people and tried to lose herself in the crowd. All the time she was looking over her shoulder, trying to put distance between herself and the tall woman. She bumped against another man, a spotty-faced youth with greasy hair and rather acrid body odour. ''Scuse me,' she muttered.

From over her shoulder, she heard him mutter the words 'clumsy bitch', but she didn't bother stopping to take issue with the remark. She was too busy looking at her profit.

Aside from the photo of a naked movie star, there were only two notes in his wallet and she cursed him for his cheapness. Glancing over her shoulder she saw he was with a peroxide blonde and pitied the woman her taste in cheap men. She idly toyed with the idea of going to the poor woman and explaining what a penny-pinching turd she was dating. Quickly, she dismissed the thought, knowing how swiftly such action would get her into trouble.

Staring at the wallet in her hand, Holly found herself thinking of the intimidating woman. She had encountered fairground security staff in the past and knew better than to trifle with them. The woman had possessed a menacing air of authority and Holly didn't want to end up on the receiving end of her wrath. Her cruel black eyes had made Holly uncomfortable and she had no intention of crossing her.

Trying vainly to shrug off her worries, she stepped on to the rough-hewn steps of the waltzers and stared fondly up at the whirling carriages as they sped past. Here, the music was so loud it sent a delicious ache through her head.

A ride operator grinned down at her. He was wearing a pale, sweat-stained T-shirt and had a leering grin. In one hand he held a half-drained bottle of lager. Instead of concentrating on the machinery he was supposed to be working, his gaze was fixed on Holly.

'You on your own?' he called down to her, taking a casual swig from the bottle. Hc wiped his lips dry on the back of his hand.

She glanced at the rippling muscles beneath the T-shirt and the large bulge at the front of his jeans. Her smile widened salaciously as she pictured the contents of the jeans being revealed to her. Dangling from a belt loop on his jeans was an effective-looking rubber truncheon.

'Is that an offer?' she called back.

He grinned a slow, easy-to-like smile, and offered her his hand.

She glanced at the truncheon hanging from his belt and then looked into his eyes. 'You seem well equipped to entertain a young lady,' she told him with a lascivious smile.

He glanced at the truncheon and then grinned back at her. 'I'm a lot more well equipped than that,' he assured her. He pushed the open fingers of his hand closer to her, encouraging her to take hold.

Without a second thought, Holly placed her hand in his and stepped up alongside him, next to the speeding carriages. She could feel her excitement building as soon as she inhaled. The aromas of hot dogs, popcorn and candyfloss were snatched from her nostrils and replaced by the smells of scorched rubber, diesel fumes, and time-worn machinery. The spinning carriages rocked the wooden platform beneath her feet.

The operator's arm encircled her waist. Holly felt his large, callused hand fall against her hip. The cool tips of his fingers brushed just below the hem of her skirt and she shivered beneath his touch. She could feel the pressure of the truncheon weighing uncomfortably against her waist, but she made no complaints. He pressed his lips close to her ear, closer than was necessary in spite of the deafening noise and music. His warm breath tickled the nape of her neck when he

21

spoke. She could detect the faint aroma of lager colouring his words. 'Fancy a ride?' he asked lewdly.

Holly laughed softly. Although his T-shirt was sweat-stained, she could detect the scent of shower gel and deodorant emanating from him. She turned to study the lecherous honesty of his smile and nodded.

He placed an unexpected kiss against her neck and squeezed her tightly for an instant. Holly was surprised by his tenderness. She allowed him to release her, then watched as he went to the operator's booth and stopped the waltzers.

As the machinery ground to a halt, Holly glanced curiously around the fairground from her higher vantage point. She could see that the crowd was bigger than when she had first arrived. People milled about, illuminated by the flashing neons, and sauntered idly from ride to ride and booth to booth, joining queues as they hugged and held one another.

Holly smiled, enjoying the crowd's good mood. Her smile only faltered when she realised she was being watched. The tall woman with the cruel eyes was staring up at her from the midst of the crowd. Her sharp gaze seemed fixed on Holly, and there was something distinctly unsettling about her predatory smile.

Holly was so rapt in the woman's attention she flinched when the operator put his arm on her waist. She quickly muttered an apology and allowed him to lead her to one of the horseshoe-shaped carriages. 'Do you want me to hold your bag?' he shouted above the roar of the music.

Holly shook her head, holding the rucksack tighter. She tried not to let him see the suspicious frown that crossed her brow. Instead, she widened her grin, placed a kiss against the razor stubble on his cheek and told him, 'I can take care of it, thanks.'

He nodded and held the safety bar up for her.

Slipping into the waltzer she pulled the bar against

her slender waist. He was still looking at her legs when she put her hand down to the hem of her skirt. Rather than demurely tugging the hem lower, to spoil his unspoilt view of her thighs, Holly pulled the hem a little higher.

His eyes widened and she saw the bulge at the front of his pants stiffen noticeably. She was wearing no knickers and had known the glimpse he was likely to get would be irresistible.

His gaze shifted from the tantalising sight she had revealed to him, to the knowing smile on her lips. Before she had the chance to catch his eye, Holly realised he was concentrating on the tops of her legs again. She reluctantly brushed the skirt back down and leant forward.

He bent down to her, realising she wanted to say something.

'You will make it last a long time for me, won't you?' Holly asked. She leant forward and rubbed the tips of her fingers against the rubber truncheon.

'Longer than you've had it before.' A shout from the operator's booth caught his attention and he glanced over his shoulder. Turning back to face Holly, he assured her, 'I'll see you after.'

'Count on it,' she told him, unable to resist the mounting urgency of her excitement. She stared longingly at the bulge in the front of his pants, watching as he unconciously brushed a finger against the straining fabric. As she sat back, she placed one finger against her lower lip and smiled knowingly at him. 'Count on it,' she repeated.

He winked broadly, then stepped away.

Holly watched him walk back to the operator's booth and grinned to herself. Studying his tight, pert buttocks she realised her eagerness for him was already growing. If her need to ride the waltzers hadn't been so great, she would have leapt from the carriage and demanded he take her somewhere discreet, where they could play.

23

Then the ride began to move. She grabbed her rucksack tightly, held on to the safety bar, and leant back against her seat. The world span past in a helter-skelter blur of flashing neon lights. Red, yellow and golden bulbs stretched into lines of colour, spiralling all around against the black canopy of the night. The rock music was a constant explosion of noise, so loud it was virtually indecipherable.

Holly could feel a grin of elation splitting her lips. It had been a long time since she had felt so good.

The world continued to spin quickly around her. Bright colours whirled past, merged together, then disappeared from sight before their beauty could be admired. This is the best night of my life, she told herself happily. The thought brought a merry laugh to her throat, but she couldn't hear it above the music.

'Had enough? Or do you want it faster?'

She glanced up from her seat and saw the operator's handsome face grinning down at her. He was standing on a step at the back of the carriage, keeping his face still as the rest of the universe span chaotically behind him. His appreciative grin was still fixed on her thighs and she smiled at his enthusiasm. It belied an urgency she could empathise with.

'I want it faster,' she told him. Her blue eyes twinkled as she said the words. 'Can you give it to me?'

His hand reached forward and cupped her breast. He placed his mouth over hers and they exchanged a high-speed kiss. The dizzying whirl of the carriage and the intimate intertwining of their tongues was an explosive combination. She could feel his fingers kneading the eager swell of her breast and the stimulation inspired a thrill as intoxicating as the ride itself.

He broke the kiss casually, obviously used to spinning around like this rather than simply standing on firm, unmoving ground. Still grinning at her, he nodded, took a backward step, and disappeared from view.

24

The waltzers span faster.

Holly shivered excitedly. She enjoyed the rest of the ride, losing herself in a world of spinning colours and lights. This is the life, she told herself.

When the waltzers eventually ground to a halt, she was breathing hard and trembling with excitement.

The operator pulled the safety bar away from her. 'Do you want to go again?'

She shook her head. 'I have another kind of ride in mind now,' she grinned.

He glanced at her curiously, his gaze shifting down to the hem of her skirt.

She lifted the hem slightly as she stepped out of the carriage, displaying herself to him with a casual arrogance. Her hand went to his chest, to steady her trembling legs and she leant her frail, feminine frame against his sturdy body. 'Do you get what I'm saying?' she asked, when he didn't respond to her invitation immediately.

He glanced warily around, as though he was fearful someone might see them talking. 'I get off for a break in about an hour,' he told her. 'Do you want to . . .'

'That's an hour too late for me. I'll be long gone by then,' Holly said. She placed her lips against his neck and kissed him. Her fingers went to the urgent swelling at the front of his jeans. 'It's now, or never.'

He made his decision without giving her the chance to change her mind. With an ear-piercing whistle, he caught the attention of a colleague. 'Boycee,' he cried. 'Pass me a bottle, and do the ride while I'm gone.'

The other man fixed him with a questioning expression, which melted into a knowing smile when he saw Holly. He nodded, hurled an unopened bottle of lager towards the couple, then went about the process of collecting money from those in the seats.

Catching the bottle effortlessly the operator called, 'Cover for me if Corinne comes looking.'

25

Holly didn't bother contemplating the comment. She allowed him to lead her from the heady excitement of the waltzers, into the surrounding darkness. They paused only once by the side of a noisy generator. He thrust the cap of his beer bottle against the metal grid on the generator's casing and peeled the lid from the lager. Holly watched him take a long draught from the bottle, then politely refused when he offered her a drink. She already felt drunk on the night's atmosphere and had no need for alcohol to help her mood.

It seemed bizarre that she could be taken so easily from the busy, bustling thrill of the fairground. Within a minute's walk, he had slipped between two booths, sauntered past a series of caravans and led her away from the crowd. The fairground's music and the roar of the people were a distant whisper in the night. She could still discern some of the noises, and the lights from the Ferris wheel cast multicoloured flashes on and about the couple. But aside from those faraway echoes, they were alone in a desert of blackness.

He kissed her, his tongue exploring the warm haven of her mouth. Holly felt his hand slide between her legs, the cool touch of his fingers simultaneously chilling and warming the intimate flesh of her inner thighs.

Her fingers worked quickly on the buttons of his fly. Brushing the rubber truncheon out of the way with the back of her hand she released his cock into the night. She stroked the length with loving fingers and his shaft pulsed beneath her touch.

'Are you going to make this ride as good as the waltzers?' she asked. After the deafening roar of the fairground, her hearing seemed disturbingly acute. Her whispered words sounded like a thunderous exclamation to her ears.

Smiling at her lurid question, he chuckled darkly. Without wasting time on a reply, his mouth enveloped hers once again.

As Holly's eyes began to adjust to the dark, she could make out the shape of a parked car. She broke their kiss and moved him over to the vehicle, guiding him on to the bonnet.

Sitting astride it, he graced her with an uncertain frown. He clearly didn't know what to expect, but there was a gleam in his eye that told her he was game for whatever she had planned. Holly ignored his consternation. She wanted him as badly as he wanted her but, as with everything else in her life, she was going to do it in her own way.

She knelt down in front of him and moved her head close to his erection. Glancing up, she watched him swallow a mouthful of lager from his bottle. His cool detachment should have been off-putting, but Holly found herself stimulated by it. Like her, he expected nothing more than a bout of satisfying, gratuitous sex with no need for tenderness, intimacy or eroticism. The very notion of such coarseness stoked the glowing embers of her arousal.

Holly placed her tongue against the pulsing flesh of his length and tasted the thin layer of sweat that coated his cock. She always enjoyed the taste of a cock in her mouth and this one was no exception.

Her fingers toyed with him, stroking and kneading his balls, then rolling the foreskin back and forth along his thick length. She concentrated her mouth on the swollen purple end of his shaft. Her lips pressed gently against the sensitive flesh as she rubbed her tongue wetly against the tip.

He moved one hand to her head and began to wind his fingers through her hair.

Holly slapped his hand away. She stared coldly up at him, a threatening light glinting in her eyes. 'Don't try and hold me against your cock,' she whispered, the warning in her voice apparent. 'I'm doing what I want and you're going to enjoy it, but don't try and force me.

27

Try that shit, and I'll be out of here, leaving you to tug yourself off. Understand?'

He nodded and moved his hand away, unoffended by her brusque tone.

Grinning reassuringly at him, Holly moved her mouth back down to his length. She stroked his balls with one hand while the other rolled up and down his shaft. Her mouth remained at the top, sucking on the swollen end. When she felt the first pulse of his climax, she made no attempt to move away. Instead, she lowered her lips all the way down his cock, allowing the head to press at the back of her throat.

His seed sprayed into her mouth with a hot rush. For an instant she was transported from the deserted field outside the fairground. She was back on the waltzers, experiencing the heady revelry of the ride as it span and enticed her to the limits of dizzying pleasure. The taste of his seed filled her mouth and she had to swallow quickly as the second pulse of his cock released more of his cream.

Her fingers continued to ride up and down his shaft, teasing every last droplet of satisfaction from him. When he was spent, she swallowed the last dribble, licked her lips, and began to suck him hard again.

'I don't think . . .' he began.

'I don't want you to think,' she broke in, speaking around his cock. Her lips delivered tiny kisses to the heated flesh until it was ramrod stiff. As soon as she was happy with his erection, she moved off the ground and tugged him gently from the bonnet.

'Now I want that ride,' she told him. 'I want you inside me and I want it bad.'

'Bend over,' he told her, the crisp edge of his voice revealing his eagerness. 'Bend over, lay across that car and I'll fuck you just the way you want it.' Without waiting for her to respond, he grabbed her shoulder with his free hand, then span her around.

28

Holly snatched a startled breath. She felt him push her face down and, before she realised it, found herself spread across the bonnet of the car. His sudden display of speed, strength and agility left her breathless and excited. Her need to experience his cock between her legs was now an insatiable craving.

The short skirt she wore, and the absence of knickers, left her sex easily within his reach. Determined to experience his length, and eager for the thrust of his penetration, she pushed the cheeks of her arse towards him. She could feel the swollen end of his cock pressing against the lips of her labia. The car's bonnet was cold beneath her chest, but she didn't think about the frigid metal. Her thoughts were concentrated on the warmth between her legs and the heat of the cock that pressed there. The car's bonnet seemed as unimportant and far away as the distant cries of the fairground.

Wriggling her backside, she braced herself for his entry. She could feel the swollen end rubbing against her inner thigh and, glancing over her shoulder, she saw him stroke his hardness in preparation for her. With his other hand, he took a last swig from his beer bottle, then hurled it carelessly into the darkness. Holly turned her head away, content to enjoy his penetration without straining to watch.

Instead of sliding his length into her, he stroked the cool end of the rubber truncheon over the warm lips of her pussy. Holly stiffened against the car's bonnet. The unexpected coolness sent a shiver through her body. She glanced back and saw he was smiling broadly. Waving the truncheon coyly at her, he winked lecherously. As Holly watched, he lowered the length of black rubber towards her sex then teased the end against her pussy lips again.

Holly gasped. She raked her nails against the car's bonnet, surprised and excited by his unexpected action. A refusal of what he was intending to do caught in the back of her throat. She wanted to stop him from penetrating her with the truncheon, but at the same time the idea of being used in such a way appealed to a dark, unexplored side of her nature.

She could feel the rounded tip being drawn against the lips of her sex in slow, sensuous circles. The firm end threatened to part her labia and bury itself deep inside her warmth. Before she realised it had happened, the threat had become a reality. The tip of the truncheon had eased itself between her pussy lips and she could feel herself being filled by the rigid length.

She released a satisfied roar into the night, beating her fists against the car's bonnet. Slowly at first, then quickening his tempo, he worked the length of rubber in and out. She could feel the wetness of her sex lubricating it, allowing the makeshift phallus to glide effortlessly into her depths.

Aware that her orgasm was imminent, she braced herself for the inevitable eruption. Her inner muscles clenched tightly in a spasmodic frenzy, and she continued to beat her fists against the bonnet of the car. Her wordless cries had tapered off into a constant, guttural growl. When the orgasm finally struck, she raised her head and screamed. The ferocity of her climax forced the truncheon from her lips in a sudden rush.

As the pulse of her climax began to recede, she heard the distant sound of his laughter ringing pleasantly in her ears. She turned to glance at him, not surprised to see he was beaming back at her. Grinning, he fastened the truncheon back on to his jeans, then stroked his hand against his stiffening length. 'Are you ready for the real thing now?'

Not trusting herself to give voice to a reply, Holly nodded up at him. A wide, satisfied smile split her lips. She reached a hand behind herself, separating the lips of her sex in preparation.

After gently guiding her hand away, he slid himself

between her legs. His thick cock filled her tight hole, pressing firmly against her inner muscles.

He tugged the blouse from the waistband of her skirt and caressed her bare flesh with his callused hands. His fingers were reaching beneath her, moving deliberately towards her breasts. Holly shifted position, allowing him to cup the heaving orbs. The tips of his fingers brushed against her nipples. She could feel the hardened nubs being teased and squeezed with gentle but determined pressure.

As he rode slowly in and out of her tight pussy, a heady whirl of pleasure took control of her body. The heat of his cock was bringing a second climax closer with each thrust.

She was only distracted from the pleasure for a moment, as she suddenly remembered the rucksack she had been carrying and tried to recall where it had been left. Her hand slid from the bonnet and she waved her fingers helplessly over the black field in a blind, frantic search. The flow of her mounting panic was halted when she brushed against woven fabric. The feeling of the rucksack's strap between her fingers reassured her that it was still close at hand. With the most important thing in her life safe, she mentally dismissed it and went on with the delightful experience of enjoying herself.

Holly pushed herself hard against his rigid length as he drove his cock deep into her. It had been a good idea to suck him first, she told herself. After enjoying one climax, he would last longer as he tried to please her this way. The taste of his seed was still in her mouth and she licked her lips, savouring the salty remnants of his come.

Her nipples tingled to his touch. The pleasure that his fingers provoked was almost unbearable. Her entire body seemed so responsive she believed he could have pushed her beyond the brink of orgasm with his caresses alone. But she wanted more than just his caresses. She wanted to feel his cock pulse inside her when he finally climaxed.

31

As he moved his hands from her breasts she didn't know whether to be relieved or delighted. The feelings had been so intense she hadn't wanted them to end. But she didn't think she could have allowed them to continue either. Another moment and she would have been caught in the maelstrom of a blissful orgasm.

Putting his hands to her hips he held her tightly. His cock continued to slide deep into her wet hole. She shivered happily with each forward thrust, the force of his entry rocking her hard against the grill of the car. The pleasure he was giving more than made up for any discomfort. As his hands worked their way below her legs, she realised he was trying to touch her more intimately while he pounded into her. Eventually he reached the sensitive flesh at the top of her thighs.

When his callused fingers brushed against the lips of her sex, she groaned. The delicate lips of her labia responded quickly to his touch, sending a shiver of pleasure coursing through her body. Her cries of ecstasy only grew louder when she felt him lifting her legs.

The sensation of being in control was quickly dissipating but, at this moment, Holly no longer cared. He held her legs and pushed her forward then pulled her back on to the rigid length of his cock. She found his strength and stamina admirable. He span her around with an almost casual ease and again she was reminded of the waltzers. The bonnet was no longer pressed against her face. Instead, she was lying with her back on it.

And still he rode into her. She glanced up and saw the dull yellow glint of the fairground's light shining on the small gold ring that pierced his ear. The heady pulse of her mounting climax beat powerfully. She could feel the blood pounding at her temples and drew ragged breaths as the moment of release finally neared.

'Faster,' she urged him, distantly aware that this was the same instruction she had given on the waltzers. 'Faster.'

He quickened his pace, pushing forward against her pliant flesh with a hectic urgency. His need to climax again was obviously as strong as her own. She could feel the tell-tale twitching of his cock deep inside her pussy as it threatened to explode. Instinctively, she clutched him tighter with her inner muscles, determined to savour his pleasure.

He pulsed hard between her legs, forcing himself deep into her as the orgasm tore through him.

Holly felt her own climax clutch her in a painful fist. She screamed as the first shock of pleasure squeezed the air from her lungs. The still night disappeared from view. She closed her eyes and was back in the fairground with flashing lights and coloured lines whirling past her. Her mind was lost in the euphoria of a powerful orgasm and she tried to revel in the moment before it was stolen by the returning shadows of the night.

He continued to push his cock forward, even though he was already spent. Holly could feel his warm seed trickling between her inner thighs. The creamy load lubricated his cock so that it slid more easily into her. The sensation of slippery wetness brought her back to the brink of orgasm. She shivered and released a contented sigh as another explosion ripped through her.

As the inner muscles of her pussy clenched tightly together, his spent cock was pushed from the lips of her sex.

Holly collapsed back against the bonnet of the car. She grinned happily and enjoyed the subsiding pulse of pleasure that shivered through her flesh.

'Enjoyable?' he asked.

She glanced up from the bonnet, watching as he fastened the buttons around his magnificent length. The rubber truncheon he had used so effectively swayed idly against his hip, still glistening dully with Holly's pussy juice. With a soft smile, she nodded her reply to him. 'Could you do one more thing for me, before we say our goodbyes?'

He shrugged. 'If I can, I guess so.'

Slipping from the bonnet of the car, she straightened her skirt and pushed her blouse into the waistband. After fastening a couple of loosened buttons, she looked as close to being respectably dressed as she had before they started making love. Pressing her body close to his, she said, 'Let me have a last ride on the waltzers.'

He grinned, barely noticing that she had bumped against him.

They walked back to the fairground holding hands, enjoying the simple intimacy of each other's nearness. It was only when she saw the austere face of the tall woman that Holly began to wonder if she had made a mistake. Unconsciously, she slowed her pace.

'Is something wrong?' he asked.

He sounded genuinely concerned and Holly felt a moment's guilt at having taken his wallet. She dismissed the emotion quickly, trying to find a way out of the corner she could see herself heading for. 'I need to go to the loo,' she said quickly. 'I'll see you on the ride when I'm done.'

He nodded quietly, accepting her lie as the absolute truth. He reached towards his back pocket and Holly knew he was going for where his wallet had been. 'Buy us a couple of hot dogs,' he began. 'Perhaps you might decide to stay a while longer.'

She nodded impatiently, aware that she was getting dangerously close to being discovered. She could see the frown of consternation on his face. Knowing that she had to say something, or rouse his suspicion, she asked, 'What's wrong?'

'My wallet's gone,' he replied, sounding more puzzled than accusatory.

She shrugged. 'Perhaps it fell out back there,' she suggested, nodding towards the field they had just left.

His frown told her that he thought this was unlikely, but he nodded anyway. 'Perhaps,' he conceded. 'I'll go get a torch and scan the field.'

She grinned at him. 'I'll go and get those hot dogs,' she said quickly. 'We can call it my way of saying thanks.'

'Let her out of your sight and you'll never see your wallet again.'

They both turned to stare at the woman.

To avoid being caught, Holly was used to watching everywhere while she worked. She had never been caught out before, but this woman seemed to have crept up on them with the stealth of a predatory animal. Holly glared angrily at her, trying not to show the fear she felt beneath the woman's cruel gaze.

'Corinne? I'm sorry I wasn't on the ride, I've lost my wallet and my friend here was just going to help me . . .'

Corinne didn't allow him to finish. 'You haven't lost your wallet, Joey,' she broke in. 'This little bitch has lifted it. You're her third mark this evening by my count.'

Holly swallowed thickly. Her heart was suddenly beating fast and for the first time she could taste fear in the back of her throat. When Corinne called the operator by his name she realised she had screwed him without knowing what he was called. It was a faraway thought but her mind seemed happier to concentrate on this rather than the invidious situation she now found herself in.

Joey was glaring at her.

Holly tested a smile on him but the expression felt greasy. Miserably she realised it would have no effect. 'Get the torch for me. I'll go back out in the field and see if I can find it,' she said suddenly.

The pair of them stared at Holly in a sullen, accusing silence.

'Who are you going to believe?' Holly demanded suddenly. 'Me, or this lying bitch?' It was a desperate show of defiance; a last hope in a rapidly declining situation. Sadly, she saw it was going to do no good.

'Your wallet's in the bag, with the rest of her takings,' Corinne told Joey.

Joey snatched the bag from Holly's hand. She struggled to keep hold of it but when he raised his fist in a half-hearted threat, she relented. As he started to examine the contents, Holly glanced around to see if there was any chance of making a break for freedom. Although the bag was important, she realised it wasn't as important as getting away from this mess.

Corinne's hand fell on her shoulder. The icy grip of Corinne's talon-like nails pressed uncomfortably into Holly's sensitive skin. She squealed unhappily and glared at her captor.

'Don't even think about running,' Corinne warned her. 'You've pissed me off already. Don't make things worse for yourself.'

Holly could tell that the woman's threat wasn't an idle one, but she still felt as if she had to try something. If she simply submitted to the woman she would lose everything that she had ever worked for, and that prospect galled her. It occurred to her that there was only one option left open.

'How dare you do this to me!' she bellowed suddenly. 'I happen to have my life's fucking savings in that bag and you get one of your gorillas to go through it while you try and break my shoulder!' She used the loudest voice she could manage, drawing the attention of curious faces from the fairground's crowd. It was her hope that Corinne wouldn't want any untoward attention from passers-by. If the woman just loosened her grip slightly, Holly believed she could make an attempt at escape. With any luck, she thought she might even be able to retrieve her rucksack from Joey.

'Keep it quiet, you little bitch, or I'll rip your fucking arm off,' Corinne growled in a menacing whisper.

'How dare you do this to me?' Holly bawled, wishing she didn't feel so intimidated by the threat in the woman's voice. This was a calculated gamble that she had used once before with some success. She was a pretty young woman and there were plenty of handsome young knights wandering around the fairground, willing to display their chivalry. 'And accusing me of theft on top of all this!' she screamed. 'This is a diabolical fucking outrage!'

'Keep a hold of that little bitch,' a man called. 'She's the one who lifted my wallet.'

Holly groaned. She watched the spotty-faced youth with the greasy hair running towards her. 'She took my fucking wallet,' he called, glaring angrily at Holly. 'I had four hundred quid in there and she robbed me of it.'

'You had two fucking fivers in there,' Holly challenged him angrily. She closed her eyes and mentally kicked herself as soon as she had said the words.

'Don't worry about it,' Corinne told her. 'I knew you were guilty all along.' She glanced at Joey. 'Is there four hundred in there?'

He grunted something Holly couldn't hear. 'Four hundred? It's closer to four thousand.'

Holly kept her eyes closed, wishing she could close her ears as well. She didn't want to see or hear the things they were saying. She simply wanted to get away from the fairground and pretend she had never been there. Without her rucksack, and its contents, life would be difficult to begin with, but she could make a new start at rebuilding her fortune.

'Give this man his four hundred,' Corinne snapped. 'And give him an extra hundred as a way of apologising for any inconvenience,' she added.

'That's fucking ridiculous,' Holly broke in. 'I told you, he only had ten pounds in his wallet when I lifted it. Can't you see the little turd's lying?'

Corinne slapped her open palm against Holly's cheek. The sound was like a whip crack and Holly felt her head

37

rock as the blow connected. She raised a protective hand to her face and stared with a different perspective at the woman. The air of cold malice she had detected initially was obviously just a veneer covering the diabolical malevolence beneath the surface.

Holly was finally beginning to realise how dangerous her situation was.

From the corner of her eye, she watched Joey count out five hundred pounds into the hand of the spotty youth. His girlfriend, the peroxide blonde who Holly had pitied, watched the situation with a scowl on her lips.

'Where did you get all that money from? You told me you were skint.'

'Shuddup,' he hissed, scowling warily at Joey, then at Corinne. 'We'll talk about it later.'

'Did you pawn my CD player?' she persisted. 'Is that where you got the money?'

'Shuddup,' he hissed in a louder, more threatening tone.

Holly ignored the pair of them and their trivial quarrel. She had more urgent things on her mind. She watched as the youth took her hard-earned money and disappeared with his girlfriend into the crowd.

'What do I do with the rest of this?' Joey asked.

Corinne glared at Holly when she spoke, but her words were directed at the ride operator. 'Take it to my van, I'll figure out what to do with it later. I have to deal with this little bitch first and make sure she never picks another pocket again.'

'What are you going to do?' Joey asked.

Holly was grateful he had supplied the question. She couldn't find the courage to ask it herself. She glanced at Corinne and saw the woman was smiling. It was an expression of the darkest intent and she found herself trembling.

'In the old days, we used to break the hands of

pickpockets, so that they couldn't do it again,' Corinne explained.

Holly could feel a butterfly of panic fluttering nervously in her chest.

Corinne continued to smile. 'But we've progressed a long way since then,' she went on. 'And our methods are no longer as archaic.' She produced a long knife from inside her jacket and held it up. The blade glinted wickedly in the bright neon lights of the fairground.

'What are you going to do with her?' Joey asked again. Holly could hear a note of concern in his words and the sound frightened her. If one of the fairground staff feared for her safety, she wondered how diabolical her fate would be.

Corinne's smile broadened. 'I'm going to take this little bitch back to my van, strip her naked, then beat her until she sees the error of her ways,' she explained. 'If that doesn't work, then I'll see how well she can pick pockets once I've cut all her fingers off.'

Three

'I don't want to go with you,' Georgia snapped angrily. She tried tugging her wrist free from Curtis's grip but his hold was like steel. 'Stop pulling me, Curtis,' she demanded.

'We don't have time for this,' he snapped, pausing for a moment anyway. 'I need to get to Corinne now. This is important.'

Georgia was surprised by how quickly night seemed to have fallen. The two hours in Curtis's van had passed like as many minutes. When she had entered, the dusk was still bright enough to look like daytime. Now it was night. A hundred yards away, the fairground was alive with lights and noise. Here, behind the funfair, the unlit world of caravans and trailers was trapped in the evening's darkest hour. It was unnerving to think she could have spent so long in his company and not notice the passage of time. Annoyed with herself, she directed her anger at Curtis.

'If you need to find Corinne,' she told him, 'then go. I have no desire to see that bitch again and I'm growing tired of your company. Just leave me, I can make my own way home.'

'You're not going home yet. Not until you've considered my job offer.'

She rolled her eyes, a gesture that was lost in the darkness. 'I've considered it and given you my answer. I'm not taking it. Now let go of me and let me . . .'

'We'll talk about this later,' he told her. 'Come with me.' With a sudden shift in his weight, Georgia felt him pull her along the uneven land between the trailers and caravans. Unhappily, she allowed him to lead the way. She could hear screams of protest coming from inside Corinne's van and sensed a confrontation brewing. Joey had led the way and when he opened the door, Curtis followed, pulling Georgia inside with him.

'Fuck off, Curtis,' Corinne growled as they entered the room. 'I'm handling this in my own way.'

Georgia recognised the woman instantly, even though it had been two years. Her raven hair was a little longer, and the creases around her eyes were a little more pronounced, but she would have recognised the sadistic light in the woman's eyes anywhere. When Corinne's gaze fell on her, Georgia noticed the woman's smile tighten cruelly.

'We're a cock's hair away from the twenty-first century,' Curtis growled. 'Stop acting like a medieval throwback.'

When Georgia saw what else was happening, she knew exactly what he meant. There was a table dominating the centre of the room. Sitting in the chair behind it was a dark-haired young woman with an expression of sheer terror straining her features. Her cheeks looked pallid and drawn, and her eyes were wide with horror. She was staring at Curtis and Georgia as though they were her salvation. Georgia hoped they didn't disappoint the girl.

Corinne towered over the brunette, holding one of the girl's hands to the table. Her weight on the girl's wrist caused the victim's fingers to splay out helplessly against the wooden top. So much pressure was being put on the young woman's fingers that her knuckles had turned white with the stress. With her other hand, Corinne held her wicked-looking knife. She brandished it carelessly over the girl's hand, stabbing the point quickly between

41

her outstretched fingers. The knife made a sickening sound as it plunged into the table's wooden surface, forewarning Georgia of how nauseating the noise would be if the knife connected with flesh. The steady thumping sound of the knife continued its relentless, staccato beat even when she spoke.

'Mediaeval?' Corinne growled. 'I'll take issue with you for that comment later on. Now, if you'll just let me finish here.' She raised her knife. The razor-sharp point caught a glint of light and glistened with evil intent. Georgia's gaze followed the arc of its descent and she was struck by the mental image of the metal penetrating the frightened girl's hand.

'No!' she shrieked. She grabbed Curtis's arm, her fingers pressing tightly through the fabric of his shirt. 'Stop her! Stop her!' The words echoed with deafening force through the van.

He smiled wickedly. 'Do you want me to?'

'Of course I bloody do,' she roared. 'Stop her.'

'Accept my job offer,' he said sharply. 'Accept my job offer, and I will.'

Georgia looked at him in bewilderment. She stared dumbly at Corinne's knife-blade winking in the light. From the corner of her eye she caught sight of the look of abject terror straining the brunette's features. There was a desperate plea in her face and the expression was directed at Georgia.

'Don't mess about, Curtis,' Georgia snapped, trying to inject some force into her words. Terror made the sentence sound limp and weak. 'Please stop her.'

'Accept my offer, but don't take too long. Corinne doesn't usually waste a lot of time taking aim.'

Georgia saw the woman's arm begin to sweep downwards. Her horror of what she might witness was so great that she had no other option. There was no time to even consider how momentous her decision was. 'I accept,' she barked quickly. 'I accept.'

Curtis stretched out his hand and stopped the knife from completing its descent. The point of the blade was mere millimetres from Holly's outstretched hand. He casually snatched the knife from Corinne and hurled it angrily to the floor. He seemed unmindful of the hatred in his sister's eyes.

'I said I was handling this,' Corinne told him, not bothering to mask the contempt in her voice. 'Just what the fuck do you think you're doing, bursting in here and ...'

'Who are you?' Curtis demanded, ignoring his sister and glaring at the young girl.

'Holly,' she muttered.

'The pickpocket?'

Holly nodded.

Curtis acknowledged her honesty with a blink. 'Let go of Holly's hand,' he told Corinne. 'You've punished her enough.'

Corinne glared at him with an expression of the darkest fury. 'I hadn't begun to punish her,' she said with an icy chill. 'You can count her fingers if you don't believe me.' In spite of the defiance in her tone, she released her grip. Holly snatched her hand from the table and began to rub feeling back into her aching fingers.

'Joey, go call the police,' Curtis snapped, still ignoring his sister. 'Georgia, get some ice for Holly's hand.'

His cool control of the situation had Georgia moving before she realised she shouldn't. He had just made her promise to take a position she had been adamant about refusing. Now he was commanding her to tend another of his sister's hapless victims, as though she had agreed to act as his slave again. Even then, when that realisation struck, she dismissed her reluctance as being petty; after all, there was Holly's wellbeing to consider. Georgia went to Corinne's fridge and removed a handful of ice cubes. She had started wrapping them in a handkerchief when she heard Corinne speak.

43

'Joey, don't call the police,' Corinne said flatly.

Joey stood and stared from Curtis to Corinne.

'Go,' snapped Curtis.

'Stay,' said Corinne.

'Who pays your wages, Joey?' Curtis prompted.

'Do you want the lot of us to go down?' Corinne asked sharply. 'You know what the police are like with us travellers. Whose word do you think they'll take? A bunch of shiftless carnies? Or some poor hard-done-by crim bitch who knows how to work their shitty fucking legal system? Think about it, Curtis. Use your brain for once and think about it.'

Curtis studied her sullenly. He frowned at Holly, then turned to Joey. 'Don't go yet.' He drew an angry breath and glared unhappily around the room. 'What do you suggest I do Corinne?' he asked tiredly.

Corinne's smile was pure evil. 'Leave her to me. I can be her judge and jury.'

'And executioner,' Georgia added sharply. She ignored the angry glare Corinne sent her, and instead concentrated on Holly's hand and the ice pack.

'What would you do with her?' Curtis asked.

'You can't be serious!' Georgia exploded, shocked that he was even entertaining the notion.

'Stay out of this,' Curtis warned her. His gaze was fixed on Corinne. 'This is between my sister and me.'

'But . . .'

'Don't make me say it twice,' Curtis growled.

Georgia fell silent and Corinne smiled. 'I see you've got your little slave back,' she murmured. 'It's nice to see her under your thumb again. Do you think you can keep her there this time?'

Curtis didn't rise to the bait of his sister's comment. 'What would you do with Holly?'

Corinne shrugged, trying to make the gesture look nonchalant and failing miserably. 'I was looking for a new member of staff,' she said, attempting a casual tone of voice. 'You had Chelsea put that sign up for me today, remember. Perhaps I could take this one on.'

Curtis studied her doubtfully, then glanced at Holly. 'Would that suit you?' he asked. 'You have two options. Either I phone the police, or you work as one of Corinne's staff. Which would you pick?'

Holly shifted her gaze from Curtis to Corinne. 'Are you serious?' she said, disbelief apparent in her voice. 'The pigs or a job? Which do you think I'd take?'

'I don't know,' Curtis said patiently. 'That's why I'm asking you.'

'The job, of course,' Holly said quickly.

Georgia closed her eyes and shook her head. She considered saying something, then remembered the warning Curtis had given her. At least, she consoled herself, she had stopped Holly from suffering the brutal punishment Corinne had originally intended. She didn't dare think what other unpleasantness might lie ahead for the young woman, but she realised there was nothing else she could do.

'Then we're all sorted out,' Curtis declared swiftly. 'Joey, you have work to do. Go and do it or I'll leave the SITUATION VACANT sign hanging and get someone useful to fill your job. Holly, welcome aboard. Georgia, come with me.' He started towards the van door and then paused. Glancing back over his shoulder he stared at his sister.

'And Corinne,' he began thoughtfully. 'Not that I don't trust you, but I'll be counting Holly's fingers every day while she works for us and if I don't reach double figures, I'll make you suffer.'

In the still air of the caravan, his words carried monumental weight.

When the van door closed behind Curtis, Holly glanced meekly at Corinne. The woman was studying Holly with a dour expression.

45

'Don't think you've gotten out of anything,' Corinne said darkly. 'I still intend to punish you, although I may have to use a little more imagination.'

Holly swallowed nervously. She glanced into the corner of the room, where her rucksack had been thrown, and wondered if there was still a way out of this. It had to be the worst night of her life. She doubted it was going to improve, but she held on to the hope of redemption like a religious devout.

'What are you going to do?' Holly asked.

Corinne smiled. 'Take your clothes off.'

Holly stared at her uneasily, wondering if she had heard the woman correctly.

'I know you intend running out of here as soon as my back is turned,' Corinne explained. 'And I do have to go out of here soon. If you're stripped naked, you won't be able to go anywhere.' Seeing Holly was still hesitating, Corinne reached to the floor where her knife had been thrown and began to toy with it idly.

Holly quickly began to unfasten the buttons of her blouse. 'Where do you have to go?' she asked, teasing the buttons from their holes. It was more than polite conversation that she was trying to make. The thought of escape was still at the forefront of her mind. If Corinne was going to be a long time, there was always hope.

'I'm going to my circus,' Corinne told her. She was watching Holly undress with an unsettling, predatory gaze. 'I'm ringmaster and my act is the big finale,' she added. 'But you'll find out all about that tomorrow, when you start working for me.'

Holly nodded unhappily. She shrugged off the blouse then stepped out of her skirt. Standing uncomfortable and naked in the centre of the caravan, she wished Corinne wasn't studying her nudity with such obvious interest.

'Put the clothes in your rucksack.'

Holly sighed, realising she was losing any hope of escape. She walked to the corner of the caravan where her rucksack lay and stuffed the blouse and skirt inside.

'Nice,' Corinne murmured. 'Very nice.'

Holly blushed furiously, suddenly aware that she had been exposing herself to Corinne's lecherous gaze. From the position she had been standing in, Holly realised the other woman would have been enjoying an unfettered view of her exposed sex. When she turned, she placed a demure arm across her chest and a hand over her pubic bush.

'I wish you'd stop looking at me like that,' she whispered.

Corinne shook her head. With two brisk paces she was standing in front of Holly. The line of her thin lips was cold and menacing. Her hand was raised and she brought a slap against Holly's cheek. It was a resounding blow that rocked her on her feet.

Holly gasped. 'You said you wouldn't hit me!' she declared. 'You promised not to hurt me.'

Corinne shook her head. 'I never said any such thing,' she pointed out. 'I simply promised to leave your fingers and thumbs intact. There's a lot I can do to you before they start falling off.' Her menacing grin widened and she added, 'I think I'll show you some of them now.'

Corinne's hand snaked up and wound itself into Holly's hair. Holly tried to flinch away, as though she expected another slap, as hard and punishing as the last. Too late she saw that the woman was merely trying to get a hold of her. By then, Holly had started moving away. The explosion of pain from her scalp was agonising.

Corinne held the tresses tightly, forcing Holly's face unnervingly close to her own. There was something more than a cruel light in Corinne's eyes and Holly could feel her disquiet building. Staring into the unfathomable depths of the woman's black eyes, Holly could sense Corinne's predatory interest.

'You'd do well to remember that I'm in charge here,' Corinne explained. 'I only expect one thing from those who work for me: absolute obedience. Anything less than that I consider to be a punishable offence.'

Holly swallowed thickly. The atmosphere in the caravan was so highly charged that breathing was a chore. She tried not to think of her own vulnerable nudity beneath the woman's cold, dark expression. However, the threats Corinne was making made it difficult to focus her thoughts on anything else. Meekly she asked, 'What do you want me to do?'

Corinne smiled. 'That's better.' She still had her fingers entwined in Holly's hair and she pushed her head against the table. The movement was performed with a slow, powerful lunge and Holly was unable to stop herself from being manipulated like a marionette. Her naked body was pressed against the cool wooden surface of the table. She could feel her backside sticking up in the air and realised how exposed she was. It was a sickening thought, made worse by the memory of Corinne's obvious interest.

'Should I show you how I punish insubordinates?' Corinne asked.

Holly wanted to shake her head. She assumed it was a rhetorical question, but she had already sensed Corinne's volatile temper and didn't want to worsen the woman's mood. Instead of responding, she simply held herself rigid with fear, trying not to think what Corinne might have in store for her.

'Stay where you are.'

The fingers in her hair released their grip, but Holly didn't dare move a muscle. Even when she felt the cool caress of Corinne's fingers against her sex, she stayed motionless, fearful of the punishment that would be dealt if she moved.

'Nice crack,' Corinne commented absently.

Holly could feel the woman's fingers teasing the lips

48

of her labia. She kept the flesh shaved, shaping her pubic bush into a neat, dark triangle. In her current position she knew this would be hidden from Corinne's view, but she also realised it meant her bare lips were on prominent display.

Words – refusals, rebuttals, pleas for forgiveness and leniency – sprang into her mind. Holly discounted all of them. She had already decided they would do no good. Corinne was determined to exact her punishment and Holly knew that begging for mercy would only make matters worse.

She stared miserably at the pock-marked surface of the table and tried to mentally distance herself from her body. She wasn't doing this just because of the pain she anticipated. Corinne's gently probing fingers were sparking an unbidden arousal that she didn't want to endure.

Corinne stroked gently up and down the wet slit of Holly's sex, teasing her lips until they were sodden with arousal. Admittedly she had been extremely horny when Joey had taken her to the field behind the fairground, but her excitement since then had waned considerably. As Corinne continued to play with her, Holly knew the spreading warmth of her arousal had only one cause. Miserably, she despised herself for succumbing to it.

'You don't like me doing this, do you?' Corinne asked.

Holly could feel her cheeks burning with furious embarrassment. 'You'll carry on whether I like it or not,' she replied stiffly.

'True,' Corinne agreed, smiling broadly. She slipped one finger into the warmth of Holly's cleft.

The sensation of being penetrated was disturbingly exciting. Holly suppressed a moan that threatened to reveal her true feelings. She considered moving away from the table, but had already seen enough of Corinne's raw, physical power not to attempt such

49

foolishness. The woman wasn't just strong, she was malicious with it.

'Hold the table legs,' Corinne snapped.

Holly did as she was told, reaching over the table and grasping the thin wooden legs. Wrapping her hands around them, she gripped tightly. She was uncomfortably aware of the woman's finger still pressed between the lips of her sex. It came as an enormous relief when Corinne finally slipped her hand away.

'Keep hold of those table legs,' Corinne said sharply. 'Let go of them, and I'll punish you worse than you can imagine.'

Holly realised the truth of that. Her vivid imagination had already conjured up a hundred scenarios and some of them were sickeningly lurid. She therefore treated the comment with a great deal of respect and tightened her grip on the table legs.

Her breasts were cooled by the flat expanse of the table top. Behind her, she could hear Corinne moving casually around the caravan. It occurred to her to glance over her shoulder to see what Corinne was up to, but a warning voice at the back of her mind stopped her.

'Do you know what I do in my circus?' Corinne asked absently.

Holly neither knew nor cared. She could have said something flippant or crass, like, 'do you scare the lions into performing?' or, 'are you one of the strongman's dumb-bells?' A good sense of self-preservation stopped her, however, from making either of these imprudent remarks.

Corinne didn't wait for a reply. 'I'm ringmaster and I have a speciality for the big finale.'

Holly still didn't trust herself to speak. Any comment she could have made would have sounded either sarcastic or derisory. She could tell that Corinne was building up to an important point, and she had already guessed it wasn't going to be pleasant. Not answering, allowing the woman to reveal her plans in her own time, gave Holly a moment longer without having to endure whatever the bitch was planning.

'You've already seen how well I handle a knife,' Corinne went on, speaking with quiet arrogance. 'I use them every night in the show. I do a big knife-throwing act in the first part of the finale. The audiences love it.'

Holly could sense there was something more. In spite of her nudity, and the caravan's coolness, she could feel a slick layer of sweat coating her brow.

'But perhaps I'm more famous for the way I use a whip.'

As she said the last word, Holly heard something slice the air with a vicious whistle. A welt of pain bit the cheek of her backside and she released a roar of surprise.

'Keep hold of that fucking table,' Corinne growled threateningly. The whip sliced the air again and a second explosion of pain exploded on her other cheek. 'Keep hold, or so help me, I'll really lay into you with this.'

Holly did exactly as she was told. She held on to the legs of the table with such force that she expected them to break free at any moment. Her body was a writhing mass of tortured extremes. She was desperate to get away from Corinne and the cruel fire of her whip, but too fearful to even contemplate moving. The tip of the whip had scored her flesh with blistering accuracy, and every muscle in her body throbbed in sympathetic understanding of the exquisite pain. Paradoxically, she could feel the pulse of her arousal beating to a faster tempo than it had before. The warmth between her legs, stimulated by Corinne's earlier caresses, was now a raging fire. She tried to ignore the heat of her arousal, but the sensation was preferable to the furious agony of her striped backside. Admittedly, extracting pleasure

51

from the pain seemed like some perverse form of submission, but Holly was prepared to make the sacrifice. She had seen the malevolent intent in Corinne's eyes and knew that a lot worse was going to come before the woman considered her work done. If she could take some enjoyment from the punishment, then she doubted it would be as horrifying as her mind had built it up to be.

'Do you think I'm good with the whip?' Corinne asked. Her fingers were caressing the red welts on Holly's backside, rekindling the burning embers of discomfort she had placed there.

Holly struggled to find the right words for a reply. 'You seem very capable,' she whispered, conscious of the erratic rise and fall of her breathing. She didn't know if the altered pitch was due to her arousal or the shock of having her bruised cheeks toyed with. Whatever the cause, she realised it made her sound weak and vulnerable. She despised the tone of her voice as much as she despised herself for submitting to the woman.

A finger pushed between her legs, sliding easily into the wetness of her sex. It was followed by a second, then a third and a fourth.

Holly gasped, shocked to have her intimate flesh explored in such a way. She considered turning around and quickly reminded herself of Corinne's warning to hold on to the table. Her fingers were already aching from holding the damn thing, but she didn't dare risk incurring any more of the woman's wrath.

She lay on the table, allowing the woman to push her hand into the tight, slippery wetness of her pussy. With the pulse of her excitement still beating fast, she couldn't properly call the intruding fingers unpleasant. Being totally honest with herself, she realised that the sensation was bringing her ever closer to orgasm and that the servility of her predicament was only helping. It

52

was a sickening thought to cope with, but in her heightened state of arousal, she was driven by the urgency to climax rather than the need to think straight.

Corinne snatched her hand away with brutal disregard for Holly's feelings. She pushed her sodden fingers in front of the young woman's face and growled, 'Lick them clean.'

For an instant, Holly considered moving her face away. She had never been particularly fond of the taste or scent of her own pussy juice. As Corinne pushed the hand into her face, Holly was forced to inhale the musky fragrance of her own arousal. Two fingers brushed against her lips and, without thinking, she tasted the smear of juice that was left there. The flavour was coupled with the salty remnants of her earlier lovemaking with Joey. The taste was a distant reminder of a moment before all this trouble had begun, and she tried not to think about how quickly her life had changed. Knowing there was only one way to shut those unsettling thoughts from her mind, she pushed her tongue against Corinne's fingers and began to lick them clean.

'Good,' Corinne murmured softly. 'Very good.'

Holly licked with more urgency, as though she was encouraged by the words of praise. An hour earlier she would have gagged on the taste of her juices, and felt even more sickened by the idea of trying to please a ruthless, domineering bitch like Corinne. Now, as she traced her tongue lovingly around the woman's hand, Holly felt her heartbeat quicken with a momentary thrill at Corinne's words.

Corinne brushed her fingers carelessly through Holly's hair. 'It seems like we're already beginning to understand one another, doesn't it?' she remarked quietly.

Holly swallowed the last droplet of her own juice, aware that Corinne had started moving away from her.

She still didn't trust herself to respond but sensed that the woman required some sort of reply. 'Yes.'

The whip sliced the air.

Holly released a scream of anguish as the tip burrowed painfully against the top of her leg. The sound of a second whip crack was lost beneath her wail. This blow knocked the breath from her body and cut the scream off like a switch.

'Yes, master,' Corinne corrected her. 'Can you say that?'

'Yes, master,' Holly said quickly.

'I'm not your fucking mistress,' Corinne explained patiently. She cracked the whip against Holly's arse with another perfectly aimed blow. 'I'm simply your superior, and the circus ringmaster. I don't think you'll have any trouble remembering how to address me from now on, will you?'

Holly didn't hesitate to respond. 'No, master,' she gasped. It seemed unreal to even contemplate, but she could feel the swell of an orgasm building and she knew that one more blow from the whip would push her beyond the brink of climax. Her heart raced and the pulse between her legs tingled with an infuriating desire to enjoy the release that the orgasm would bring. Knowing that Corinne wouldn't allow her such an indulgence willingly, Holly stared at the tabletop and tried to ignore her body's need for satisfaction.

'Now,' Corinne snapped. 'I have a show to do, but I'll be back. I'm going to trust you to stay here until I return. I'll be taking your rucksack, so you have no money and no clothes and there's no way you can escape. There's nothing in here you could use to cover yourself, and the fairground staff know better than to help you. You do realise what I'm saying, don't you? I'm telling you that you're trapped.'

Holly had already realised this. 'Yes, master,' she whispered.

'Good,' Corinne complimented her casually. 'I'll be back in two hours and I don't expect you to move while I'm gone.'

'What if I need to piss?' Holly asked pragmatically.

'You'll just have to hold it,' Corinne replied, her lack of interest apparent.

'I'll get cold,' Holly told her.

Corinne shrugged indifferently. 'If you get cold, then you'll shiver. When I get back, I want to see you laid across this table, holding the legs like you are now. If you even think about moving, I'll know, and I'll punish you properly.' She lowered her face over the table and moved it close to Holly's. Her lips were a breath away when she spoke. 'And believe me, my little pickpocket, you wouldn't want me to punish you properly.' She moved her head forward and placed a gentle, almost tender, kiss against Holly's lips. The promise of intimacy went beyond the punishment Holly had already been enjoying. This was a gesture that alluded to shared passion, but still on Corinne's terms.

Unable to stop herself, Holly shivered.

When Corinne returned two hours later, Holly was still lying on the table. The idea of moving had only occurred to her once and she had quickly brushed it from her mind. After the punishment she had received so far this evening, it seemed reasonably easy to simply lie still and avoid being disciplined. The idea of escape was still a treasured hope, but she didn't want to upset Corinne unduly tonight. The woman had already told her there was no way out of the caravan and, after having her clothes and money confiscated, Holly believed her.

For two hours, she had simply lain on the table top, holding the legs and waiting for Corinne's return.

The smell of grease paint filled the room as soon as Corinne entered. Without looking, Holly could tell the woman was smiling. 'Very good,' Corinne remarked.

55

Holly shivered against the table and said, 'I need to piss.'

The tip of the whip bit against her leg. Holly's need for the bathroom was so great she had no trouble suppressing the cry of anguish that threatened to tear from her lips. The burning pain from the whip crack was bad, but not as bad as her need for the toilet.

'Is that any way to greet your master?' Corinne asked indignantly.

Holly struggled to bite back a sob. 'I'm sorry, but I'm desperate to . . .'

A second bite of the whip brought tears to her eyes. The need to relieve herself was a constant ache, but when the third blow of the whip bit her, its importance began to lessen. Her arse cheeks were on fire and were now causing far more discomfort than the painful pressure of her swollen bladder.

'I told you what to do if you needed to piss,' Corinne reminded her. She punctuated the sentence with another deadly blow of the whip.

Holly stiffened against the table top. The arousal she had experienced earlier returned with cataclysmic force. The fiery pain and warmth of her whipped arse quickly spread to a tingle between her legs. In this position, she realised her pussy lips were dangerously exposed, but even that fear brought with it a dark excitement.

'I told you to hold it, remember?' Corinne pointed out. She snapped the whip again.

Holly bucked against the table, conscious of the mounting importance of her arousal. She wanted to let go of the table's legs and try to stop the woman, but fear held her in place. Being totally honest with herself, she realised it wasn't just fear that held her there. The whip was punishing, but the pain it administered was so intense and exquisite that she needed to experience more. Her body's heightened sexual response to the agony was something she had never encountered before.

It seemed unreal to be suffering such chastisement and enjoying it at the same time.

'I said, if you need to piss, you have to hold it,' Corinne reminded her. 'Do you remember?' She brought the whip down with a ferocity that made Holly squeal. 'I asked, do you remember?'

Holly struggled to find the breath for her reply. 'I remember,' she gasped. 'I remember.' Too late, she thought of adding the salutation, 'master'. Three punishing strikes of the whip were reminding her of her mistake before she could say the word.

Overcome by the pain of her burning backside and disturbed by her body's excited response to it, Holly began to sob miserably. Anguished tears spilt from her lower lids and burnt her cheeks. She merely flinched when the next six blows struck her. She felt too tired to respond and too scared to move. Her orgasm was dangerously close and she had no idea how Corinne might react if she dared to climax, especially without permission.

'So, you need to piss?'

Holly heard the whip being thrown to the floor and held her breath. She knew that Corinne hadn't finished with her yet and wondered if this action presaged a bout of even greater torment. It was difficult to imagine any torments greater than those she had already suffered, but Holly had faith in Corinne's malevolent abilities. She could feel the woman nearing her from behind and sensed the cool caress of her fingers before she felt her touch.

'Yes, master,' she murmured.

Corinne's fingertips brushed against the tingling lips of Holly's sex.

The gentle stimulation of her labia felt like an electric shock. Holly opened her eyes wide in an attempt to stave off her impending climax. She gripped the table legs tighter, aware that her explosion was inevitable.

The thought frightened her, not just because she didn't know how Corinne would respond to such a release. Her need to urinate was overwhelming and she was holding the flow with an intense display of willpower. In the heady throes of climax, she doubted she would be able to contain her most basic need.

Corinne teased the folds of flesh open and slipped a finger into the moist hole of Holly's wet pussy. 'You're a horny little bitch, aren't you?'

Holly hugged the table and drew a ragged breath, not trusting herself to reply. She knew such impertinence could bring severe castigation, but she was beyond caring. Her mind was a whirl of conflicting emotions. Her body ached for the release of orgasm and at the same time she dreaded the inevitable moment of delight.

Corinne pushed a second finger inside her.

Holly groaned loudly.

Rather than sliding a third finger into her pussy, Corinne teased the fingertip against the rim of Holly's arsehole. The gentle pressure against her forbidden hole was too much. The woman didn't need to penetrate her there; she didn't need to do anything else.

Her orgasm came in a screaming rush. She shrieked as the pleasure overtook her body, the sound coming from that dark place between fear and delight. The euphoric spasm broke the tentative control she had been exerting over her bladder. As the joy coursed through her, a hot spray doused her inner thighs, soaking her legs. With her face pressed against the table top she was unable to see what was going on between her legs. She knew, however, that her golden stream had to be soaking Corinne's hand. Yet still the woman kept her fingers where they were; teasing, touching and exciting the tingling lips of her pussy.

The extra intimacy only served to heighten Holly's enjoyment. The stream continued to pump from her body as the throb of her orgasm subsided. She wondered distantly if it was augmenting her pleasure – the unusual sensation of so much warmth and wetness was an experience she hadn't encountered before. It was a delightfully erotic feeling, and in the company of a less intimidating partner, she would have revelled in it.

Uncomfortable with Corinne's cool silence, Holly tried to forget the release of pleasure she had just enjoyed.

'I thought I told you to hold it,' Corinne muttered.

Holly felt cold and frightened. The casual tone of the woman's voice hinted at far more malice than her most intimidating threats. Before Holly could stop herself, she was babbling a stream of apologies and pleas for forgiveness. If she had been able to see herself from a distance, she would have despised the weak woman who lay across the table, begging for leniency from the cold, calculating bitch of a circus ringmaster. Unfortunately for Holly, she couldn't enjoy such a view.

Corinne grabbed a fistful of Holly's hair and snatched her away from the table. Holly almost fell when she felt the floor beneath her feet. After spending so long lying on the table, her legs seemed to have forgotten how to work. She stumbled awkwardly, an ungainly figure on sea legs unused to dry land. If Corinne hadn't been holding her hair so tightly, Holly knew she would have fallen.

Corinne pushed her face close to Holly's. Her moist lips moved close to the sensitive flesh of Holly's neck and she kissed the skin gently. Her lower lip trailed gently over the tiny hairs at the nape of Holly's neck. The warmth of her breath and the intimacy of her kiss were at once repulsive and arousing.

Holly tried to pull away from the woman's unwanted attention but her hair was held in a vice-like grip. With no other option, she had to stand and endure Corinne's sultry kisses.

'You need to be punished for doing that,' Corinne whispered, a cruel smile tainting her words.

Holly was too scared to speak. Corinne's grip was so tight against her head she couldn't even manage to nod. All she could do was simply stand there and allow the woman to kiss her.

'I want you to mop up your piss,' Corinne told her, whispering the words against her neck. Her warm breath sent an ice-cold shiver down Holly's spine. 'When you've done it, I'm going to start punishing you properly.'

Hadn't the woman punished her enough already? Holly could feel the humiliating wetness of her own piss still streaming down her thighs. Her arse was aflame with the burning pain inflicted by the whip. And still the woman was threatening worse to come. Even more unsettling for Holly was the fact that she believed her.

'There's a mop and some rags under the sink,' Corinne said, releasing her hair with a forceful push. 'I'll make it worse for you if you don't do a good job.'

Holly nodded and walked clumsily to the sink. She realised Corinne was beginning to undress and her stomach did a nervous somersault as images of the rest of the night tormented her. She tried to brush the mental pictures away but they continued to live within her mind's eye. Every torrid moment was brought to life in vivid detail, and she began to shake with fear and trepidation.

Her disquiet was stopped only by the glimpse of something from the corner of her eye. Fear and nervousness disappeared as she realised she wasn't mistaken. Sitting in the corner, where she had left it earlier, was the rucksack containing her clothes and money. She wondered if it had been there as she lay frightened but unguarded on the table. The thought that it might have been there all along was so galling she was loathe to even contemplate it.

Unfastening her blouse, Corinne saw Holly's gaze and began to laugh. 'What do you know?' she chuckled. 'I must have forgotten to take that with me.'

Holly tried to shut the woman's words out, but even with her hands over her ears she could still hear every syllable.

'Can you believe it?' Corinne laughed nastily. 'You spent two hours in here with your clothes and your stolen money and you didn't take the opportunity to use them.'

Holly glared furiously at her. She could suddenly see a way out of the situation and although it would be a bloody fight, she suddenly found she didn't care. The chance to repay a fraction of the hurt that Corinne had given would make it all worthwhile.

As though she had sensed the threat from Holly's stance, Corinne stopped laughing and snatched her whip from the floor. 'Try it,' she whispered, 'and I'll teach you the meaning of the word sorry in ways you never dreamt.'

Holly could tell the woman meant what she said, but that didn't make her anger abate. 'You'd better keep hold of that whip,' she whispered softly. 'And you'd better make sure I never get a chance to wield it.'

Corinne's smile was tight and wicked. 'Don't worry about that,' she replied. 'You'll never get the upper hand where I'm concerned. I'd already decided to keep a close eye on you. I know that with your sort, the more I crack the whip, the harder you'll work for me.' Corinne tugged her blouse from the waistband of her jeans and shrugged the top from her shoulders. Standing only in her bra and jeans, she took a step towards Holly, holding the whip high. 'Now, get on with the cleaning, and start praying that I don't decide to hurt you more because you threatened me.'

Miserably, Holly obeyed the woman.

Four

Sunlight streamed through the caravan's windows rousing Georgia from a restless night's sleep. She glanced to the other side of the bed and saw Holly's sleeping face pressed miserably into the other pillow. A wave of empathy rushed from her and she repressed the almost irresistible urge to tousle the girl's hair.

'What have you let yourself in for?' Georgia murmured. She hadn't intended to speak the words aloud and when she did, she couldn't decide if she was directing the question at Holly or herself.

Unwilling to disturb the sleeping woman, she stepped from the bed, wrapped a robe around herself, and made for the kitchen. It had been an eventful night and, even though she was still tired, Georgia was glad it had finally ended. She only wished the new day would prove better than the day before, but even with her natural optimism, she thought this was extremely unlikely. Admittedly, the day would have to be pretty bad to be any worse, but Georgia's hopes were not high.

Curtis had spent the final hours of the previous evening congratulating Georgia on her wise decision to accept his offer. Still shocked by the thought of what Corinne might have done if they hadn't stopped her, Georgia had barely heard a word. She accepted several glasses of the wine he had been pouring, then went through half a bottle of the brandy he kept for special occasions.

When he had finally shown her to her caravan, she had fallen into bed and dropped into a drunken sleep, trying not to think of the way the evening had progressed. An hour later, she had been woken by someone shouting her name and banging on the caravan door. She had stumbled out of bed to find Corinne and Holly standing there. Corinne was wearing a robe wrapped around her slender frame. Holly was stark naked.

Seeing the pair of them, Georgia was reminded that she was back in the fairground. She had dressed like this herself in the past, thinking nothing of walking barefoot between the caravans on the most inclement nights. She had never dared to parade herself naked like Holly, but she doubted the young woman had been given any option.

Even in her semi-drunken stupor, Georgia had been able to see that Holly was no longer the confident young woman she had glimpsed earlier in the evening. Her shivering body was marked with the tell-tale red lines of a severe whipping. Georgia felt her heart go out to the young woman. She could also feel her hatred of Corinne return with vehemence. However, she struggled to keep that emotion to herself. Experience had taught her not to let Corinne see such antipathy.

'She can sleep with you,' Corinne had declared, pushing Holly up the step and into Georgia's caravan. 'You were so concerned about her before, you can take care of her now. Just remember: I want you to keep an eye on her. If she escapes, I'll hold you responsible.'

Shocked, still groggy from the night's drinking, and unwilling to incur Corinne's wrath, Georgia had stepped to one side and allowed Holly to join her. She didn't particularly want the responsibility of having the pickpocket in her van, but she was loathe to send Holly back into Corinne's custody. Remembering the way the evening had begun, she swallowed unhappily and cast a nervous glance at Holly's fingers, just to see if Corinne had dared carry out her original threat. When she saw that all the digits were still there, she released a small sigh of relief.

'You're a cruel bitch,' she told Corinne, unable to stop herself from voicing the thought.

Corinne smiled as though she had been complimented. 'How sweet of you to remember that,' she replied. 'You'd better keep it in mind. If she's missing in the morning, I'll be punishing you tomorrow night.'

Georgia sneered derisively at the threat. 'I don't know what Curtis would have to say about that.'

Corinne dared to laugh in her face. 'You can't hide behind my brother for ever,' she said evenly. 'I've punished people before and he's known nothing about it.'

Georgia could feel her lips curling into a sneer of contempt. 'I doubt you could manage it with me,' she told Corinne defiantly.

Corinne shook her head, her confident smile glinting infuriatingly in the darkness. The neckline of her robe pulled open when she threw her shoulders back arrogantly. The firm swell of her ample breasts jutted proudly forward. Georgia wished she didn't find the sight so exciting.

'I've already done that once,' Corinne said coolly. 'And neither you nor Curtis knew about it. I think I could manage it again.'

Georgia stared at her uncertainly, not sure if she had heard her properly through the drunken haze of her sleepiness. Before she had a chance to ask Corinne for an explanation, the woman had disappeared into the night.

Georgia glared angrily into the curtain of shadows that enveloped the woman, then slammed the caravan door closed. She guided the naked Holly into bed, then lay down next to her, hoping sleep would take her

64

quickly in its embrace. Corinne's parting words kept recurring to her and she tossed and turned as her mind toyed with the meaning behind them. Her thoughts kept returning to a single incident, but it was an unhappy memory and she wasn't willing to torture herself with the recollection. Admittedly, it was more than just an incident; it was the reason why she had left Curtis, but still she shied away from the prospect of mentally reliving it.

Sleep had allowed her a few hour's grace from the unhappy trip down memory lane but now, as she left Holly alone in the bedroom, every detail of that night long ago returned. Georgia's mind seemed determined to replay that fateful night in its entirety. As she made herself a coffee and sat sullenly at the kitchen table, she found herself reliving the whole event. Closing her eyes over the steaming mug, she was transported back in time.

The relationship between Curtis and herself started off passionately, and progressed in the same vein. After discovering the delights of loving sex, they moved their relationship on to a more inquisitive plane. Curtis had a penchant for experimenting and, because he made her feel so happy, Georgia had been willing to indulge him.

Her feelings towards his games were cautious at first. Repeatedly she found herself screaming with delight at the end of each new experience, but still she treated each variation with a degree of caution. As bad luck would have it, the one night when her fears were justified was the one night when she couldn't do anything about it.

They were alone and naked in the glorious haven of Curtis's caravan. Georgia was stretched beneath him as he placed tender kisses all over her body.

'I want to tie you up,' Curtis whispered.

Georgia shivered, trying not to give in to the excitement of his words without a word of caution. 'No,

Curtis. That's never appealed to me, I don't want to try that.'

He laughed darkly. 'You're a lying little bitch,' he chastised good-naturedly. 'Look at the way your nipple is standing hard as you think about it. You want me to tie you up and your nipple is proving it. If it could speak, it would be begging me.'

Georgia giggled at the thought of a talking nipple, but the sounds of mirth were quickly lost beneath the groans of excitement Curtis inspired. His tongue was flicking gently against the sensitive bud of her flesh. The thrill his mouth evoked was still debilitating, even after all the excitement they had shared.

'Do you really want to?' she asked, the words coming through faltering breath.

He grinned and nodded. 'I want us to do a lot of things. There's one thing I'd love to do with you but I'm not sure yet and . . .' he paused, shaking his head as though he were trying to rid himself of an idea. 'We can discuss that some other night,' he said enigmatically.

'What?' Georgia frowned.

He shook his head and placed a silencing finger against her ripe, succulent lips. 'We'll discuss it another night.'

'This isn't your fantasy about having me and another woman, is it?' she asked churlishly. 'I've told you already, I'm not doing that and . . .'

He silenced her words with a kiss. Their tongues explored one another as their naked bodies entwined in a loving embrace.

'I've promised you that I'll respect your limitations,' he reminded her. 'Are you going to spend the rest of the night trying to talk, or are you going to let me tie you up?'

Georgia frowned, but let the matter go. She was already feeling excited at the prospect of being bound by him and she didn't want to spoil the mood by arguing.

'OK,' she agreed, with a tender smile teasing her lips. 'I trust you, and I know you're an honourable man.' She kissed him passionately, then moved away so he could see the excited shine of her eyes. 'What do you want me to do?'

His lecherous grin was infuriatingly exciting. With a sudden, powerful lunge he pushed her back against the bed, holding her hands above her head.

Georgia released a soft gasp of surprise.

'The first thing I want you to do is try to forget I'm an honourable man.'

She smiled, excited by the idea of a role-playing game. With cool efficiency he tied her to the bed, using the clothes they had discarded earlier in the evening. She was already naked and, when he had finished, her spread-eagled body was secured to the bed. The feeling of vulnerability was disturbingly arousing and Georgia found herself grinning up at him.

'What now?' She could see his long cock was already hard and, if her wrists hadn't been tied, she would have reached out and stroked his rigid flesh.

'Now we make it more exciting,' he informed her clinically. He reached to the side of the bed and retrieved one of the stockings she had been wearing. Without asking if she objected, he began to wind it around her face, covering her eyes with the sheer fabric.

'Wait,' she told him. 'I can't see what you're doing.'

'That's the whole point,' he replied, securing the stocking with a knot at the side of her cheek. His mouth fell on to hers and he kissed her as she lay bound and blindfold.

It hadn't been the entire truth when she said she couldn't see anything. The hosiery was very sheer and not the true black she preferred to wear. The bedroom was almost visible to her, but it came through a sepia mist that clouded every object she tried looking at. She was trying to take comfort from this, enjoying the fragment of control she was managing to exert from her position on the bed. Then Curtis switched the lights off.

Georgia's world was plunged into a universe of blackness. She knew that no matter how long she lay there, her eyes wouldn't adjust to the darkness through the blindfold of the stocking. A rueful smile broke her lips and she cursed his foresight. It came as no surprise when he turned the CD player on beside her. The loud volume of an Italian opera concealed all the sounds he was likely to make. She felt as though she had been plunged into a void where the only sensations she was allowed to enjoy were tactile.

The whole situation was far more exciting than she would have believed and Georgia relaxed against the mattress, allowing him to do whatever he wanted.

His tongue explored the cleft between her legs, and she shivered excitedly. Curtis lapped lovingly at her sex, quickly teasing her arousal to a dull ache. The way he moved his mouth and shifted his head was done with particular care. Shrouded in darkness and unable to hear his exact movements, she could almost have forgotten it was Curtis who was making love to her. It felt as though she had been privileged enough to discover a ghost lover; a kindly spirit who simply made one small part of his body tangible just for her pleasure.

Curtis's mouth sucked at her breasts, teasing the erect nipples to a plateau she couldn't tire of reaching. He caressed her skin with cool hands, exciting the responsive flesh of her thighs with languid strokes. If she had been able to see and hear him, Georgia knew that the caresses would have felt pleasant, but unspectacular. In the darkness, they were so thrilling she felt drunk with joy.

The first climax struck her like a slap.

His tongue delved deep into her pussy as he drank at her juice. The urgent need of his mouth against the lips of her sex was a powerful aphrodisiac in itself. With the skill of his cunnilingus, Georgia knew she didn't stand a chance.

She lay back on the bed, struggling half-heartedly against her restraints. Happily she succumbed to the waves of delight as they washed over her. He continued to lick her, pushing her to the point of orgasm again and again. She didn't know whether he was unmindful of her protests for him to stop, or simply unable to hear her beneath the roar of the arias from *Madame Butterfly*. Whatever the cause, the effect was the same. Georgia had to lie there as Curtis forced her to endure climax after climax.

At that moment, she was prepared to declare the evening a success.

When she felt his cock nuzzling against her mouth, she accepted him eagerly. The taste of his excitement filled her and she sucked greedily on him, wishing she had more of a chance to move on the bed. Her longing to taste his come was an overwhelming passion and it was only the awkward position that stopped her from turning this desire into a reality.

She thought she heard him curse just before he snatched his cock away, and there could have been the distant sound of someone knocking at the caravan door, but Georgia couldn't be certain. The volume of the CD player was so great she couldn't hear her own words when she called out to ask if something was wrong. Before panic started to wind its cold fingers around her chest, she tried to rationalise her fears. This could be a part of his game, she assured herself. He obviously wanted to do more than just tie her up and fuck her. She guessed that he was trying to add an element of excitement to the scenario.

Feeling her heart beating nervously inside her chest, she had to admit that if that was his plan, he was succeeding quite well. The moment seemed to last for ever, amplified by the darkness and the all-encompassing sound of the music. As the seconds stretched into minutes, she began to feel her arousal slip, as fear took hold.

When the finger touched against the hard bud of her nipple, Georgia almost flinched away from it. Her curse was lost in the shriek of a soprano's warbling crescendo, but she had forgiven Curtis before the word was properly spoken.

Her nipple was squeezed between a forefinger and thumb.

The hand moved away from her breast and went between her legs. She felt the gentle pressure of the fingertip against her wetness and then realised she was being penetrated. Her gasp of pleasure turned into a groan of absolute joy as the finger rode slowly in and out of her. A second finger brushed purposefully against her clitoris and she struggled to stave off a scream of elation.

The lips of her pussy were suddenly being spread wide open and she groaned when a tongue began to flick against her exposed flesh. The thrill of cunnilingus under these circumstances was far more intense than she would have anticipated. Not knowing what Curtis intended to do, and not being able to second-guess him, added an unexpected stimulation to the fun. She was quietly congratulating him on suggesting such a diversion, when her disquiet returned.

It was only a small unsettling thought, brought on by a pause between tracks on the CD. For an instant, she could hear the sounds of her lover's breath and she felt certain it wasn't Curtis.

The thought was like an ice-cold fist gripping her stomach. She tried to rub the blindfold from her head but Curtis had secured it properly. She tugged against the restraints at her ankles and wrists but there was no give in the bindings. A light coating of sweat covered her body as nervousness took hold.

The CD started to play again, the strains of a full orchestra and an amorous tenor filling the room with a noise she couldn't hope to compete against. Regardless of how futile it was, Georgia shouted words of protest, begging her unknown lover to stop.

The tongue between her legs was deft, and stroked languidly against the silken lips of her sex. The fingers that teased her were blessed with an innate skill, knowing exactly where to touch and how much pressure to apply.

But Georgia felt certain it wasn't Curtis and she wanted the whole episode to end. Trying to ignore the pleasure she was experiencing, she screamed his name again and again, wishing her body wasn't shivering with the delights of an impending climax. Without that give-away tremble, she felt sure Curtis would have stopped things. Even though the lights were out and she had no knowledge of who was with her, she felt certain Curtis was somewhere close by. Remembering his earlier suggestion of sharing their love with another person, she wondered if this was his way of fulfilling that fantasy without waiting for her permission.

She knew it would have been the act of a despicable man, and under ordinary circumstances she wouldn't have equated such actions with the honourable Curtis, whom she had come to love. However, it was dark, she was bound and helpless, and her protestations were being ignored. Under these conditions her imagination was capable of ascribing all sorts of base behaviour to him.

With the blindfold cloaking her eyes in the darkened room, she could mentally picture him watching the scene. She could see an image of him with his cock in his hand, wanking off as her mysterious lover teased her unwilling body to orgasm.

The mouth moved to her breasts, sending tiny explosions coursing through the tingling rocks of her

71

nipples. She groaned excitedly and cursed with anger in the same breath.

When the lips pressed against her mouth, she knew for certain it wasn't Curtis who was making love to her. She would have recognised his familiar kiss in the dark and this was most definitely not him. Worse still, she realised, her most sickening fear seemed to have come true. Although she couldn't be certain, Georgia felt sure she was being kissed by a woman. The faint aroma of perfume and the subtle taste of lipstick accompanied the kiss.

Her need to get away from the bed returned and she struggled against the bonds with renewed urgency. She could feel her wrists straining against the bindings with an urgent passion, but it was a futile attempt at release.

The stranger continued to kiss her, the lips pressing against her own with an eagerness that bordered on brutality. She could feel her lips being bruised by the urgent need of the unknown lover and she wished she could find the resolve to fight back. But her treacherous body had its own desires.

Giving in to the lecherous needs of her libido's demands, she simply lay there, praying that she had mistaken her lover's sex. It had to be a man, she told herself. Curtis knew how repulsed she was by the idea of making love to a woman. If he had set her up with another partner for the evening, Georgia felt sure he would make it a man.

The lover's mouth moved from hers and Georgia was granted a moment's rest. She felt the tongue return to her pussy lips and her body exploded with rapture as the tongue traced against the velvety wetness of her sodden hole. Continuing to lick, the mysterious stranger climbed on to the bed. Georgia felt the pressure of a leg near her face and realised she was about to find out for certain if her lover was male or female. She had experienced enough sex with Curtis to know when she was being placed in a sixty-nine position. When the

72

second leg rested against her other side, she realised she had gauged the situation correctly.

It was an unsettling moment and she drew a nervous breath, not daring to make a sound even though the chaotic noise of the opera still deafened her. She lay rigid beneath her lover, fearful of what would be pressed against her face.

The scent of a woman's sex juice bristled in her nostrils.

Georgia opened her mouth to protest and felt a pair of sodden pussy lips pressing against her. She gagged and spluttered against them for a moment then, before she could stop herself, she darted her tongue against the wetness.

Her lover's tremor of delight was so strong, Georgia felt it shake the bed.

She wanted to be repulsed by the taste of the woman's sex. She wanted to feel sickened by the sensation of the pussy lips against her tongue. Instead, she found the intimacy disturbingly exciting. Wishing she had the willpower not to, Georgia pushed her tongue deep into the woman's cleft, relishing the erotic scent and flavour.

Her own orgasm coursed through her virtually unnoticed. The thrill of climactic pleasure was lost on her as she tasted and explored the woman above her. She drank greedily at the pussy honey, lapping the fluid up as though she were drinking an elixir. As her tongue worked against the woman's flesh, she was filled with an infuriating desire to please her mystery lover.

The pussy lips were then moved from her face and Georgia felt the bed rocking beneath her as the woman shifted position. She felt the unfamiliar form of a naked female figure pressing against her, and then a mouth was enveloping hers. She could detect the scent of her own pussy juice on the woman's lips and her excitement intensified. Pressing her mouth close to Georgia's ear, the woman asked, 'Do you know what I want to do?'

The loud music made it impossible for her to hear anything but the words. There was no accent or tone of voice she could try to recognise. All she could hear was the simple question. She strained to hear what else the woman had to say, cursing Madame Butterfly for singing so loudly at that moment.

Afterwards, she realised she hadn't needed to strain her ears. Her mystery lover wanted her to hear the words and would have turned the music off if the need had arisen. Speaking clearly and distinctly, the woman said, 'I want to piss in your mouth.'

Georgia had detected something familiar about the woman's voice then, but the horror evoked by her words was far more compelling. She screamed a refusal, straining against her binding and trying to get away from the bed. This was her third attempt at escape, and she had already realised how futile the struggle was, but it didn't stop her from twisting her ankles and wrists in a desperate bid for freedom.

Her lover shifted back to the position she had been in before. Her mouth was teasing the wet lips of Georgia's sex as she pushed her pussy against Georgia's face.

Waves of pleasure washed over her, but Georgia tried furiously to ignore them. She tried shifting her head away from the threat of the woman's sex, certain that she was going to do as she had promised. The woman's pussy lips lowered closer to Georgia's face. Georgia could still sense the musky fragrance of her arousal but now it was mingled with a darker perfume. She was trying not to think what the aroma reminded her of when the warm spray of the woman's piss spattered against her face.

Struggling and straining to escape, she rocked her head from side to side.

The golden shower soaked her cheeks and hair, the scent of the spray a cloying odour that bubbled up Georgia's nose. She gagged and coughed and, on

74

opening her mouth, felt the warm, amber fluid spilling against her lips.

At the same time, the woman plunged her tongue into Georgia's pussy.

The wealth of pleasure was so great that Georgia screamed as the orgasm tore through her. Every muscle in her body stood taut as she pulled against the restraints on her arms and legs. The strength of her climax was more powerful than anything she had experienced so far. That thought brought with it a wave of revulsion stronger than the one inspired by the woman's passionate waterfall. The stream seemed to go on for ever. Georgia could feel her head, neck and shoulders being doused in the warm yellow flow.

By the time it had subsided to a trickle, Georgia had stopped fighting against the restraints. She simply lay where she was, meekly accepting the punishment the woman had chosen to bestow on her. She didn't even think to move when she felt her wrists being untied from the bed. She lay rigid, allowing the woman to kiss her farewell before leaving the caravan.

When the caravan door closed, Georgia finally dared to move from the bed. She unfastened the restraints from her ankles, went to the bathroom and showered. Half an hour later she still didn't feel clean enough, but thought it was the closest she was ever going to get. A distant part of her mind seemed surprised to note that Curtis wasn't there, but she assumed he was still with his unknown lady friend. She guessed he had taken the woman back to her own residence and was still busy fucking her. She imagined that memories of the way he had humiliated her were enhancing his excitement. It was a chilling thought, creating enough impetus to make her pack her bags. She left the caravan before he returned.

Sitting with her morning coffee two years later, Georgia could still remember the humiliation that encounter had

75

brought. The pain it evoked was far sharper than the dull thud of her hangover. Sipping her drink, she realised that, until yesterday, she hadn't seen or spoken to Curtis since. Before she could dwell on this point, she snapped her thoughts back to the unhappy cause of her trip down memory lane. Corinne had said something about getting at Curtis and her. Weariness and alcohol made it difficult to remember exactly what the woman had said, but Georgia felt certain it had something to do with that fateful night long ago.

She wondered if Corinne knew the identity of the woman who had treated her to the golden shower. She had never given the matter any great thought in the past, and had simply assumed it was one of the many fairground groupies who threw themselves at Curtis. Now, she found herself wondering if Corinne had sent the woman, and questioning the idea that Curtis had been watching it all. She began to wonder if he even knew of the incident.

'Is the kettle still warm?'

Georgia glanced up from her coffee, jolted from her unpleasant memories. Holly stood in the doorway of the caravan, tiredly rubbing a hand through her sleep-tousled hair. Georgia, trying to ignore the woman's nudity, nodded and moved to the kettle.

'Coffee?'

Holly nodded. 'Black, strong and with a hefty shot of arsenic.'

Georgia grunted sour laughter as she filled two cups. 'If we had arsenic, I'd have used it all up by now. Do you want to grab the spare robe from the bathroom?'

Holly disappeared for a moment, then returned, fastening the white towelling gown around her waist. 'You look like you had a rough night,' Holly ventured.

Georgia shrugged, passing a cup to Holly and joining her at the small table. 'I've had better.'

Holly attempted to make a sympathetic sound, but

Georgia could understand her lack of compassion. The glimpse of Holly's nudity had shown fading red welts and vanishing bite marks. Georgia realised that whatever the brunette had been forced to endure last night must have been far more upsetting than her own unpleasant reminiscences.

'Why didn't you choose the police as an option?' she asked suddenly.

Holly shrugged and shook her head. 'The police are never an option,' she replied. 'Besides, they're still looking for me in connection with a few other transgressions I've made in the past.'

Georgia grinned, amused by Holly's glib reference to her criminal record. 'Wouldn't jail have been preferable to Corinne?'

'I've tried jail and I didn't particularly care for it.' She grinned sourly and added, 'Not that I particularly care for Corinne.'

Georgia exercised a sympathetic smile and sipped at her coffee. 'What are you going to do now?'

Holly shrugged. 'Until this crap is over, I suppose I'm going to do whatever Corinne tells me.' She glanced at Georgia and asked, 'You?'

Georgia considered the question for a moment. 'If I get to do some shopping today, I'll get some arsenic for these coffees.' She was surprised to hear her own laughter joining Holly's, and as the sound of their mirth filled the caravan she realised she had made a friend. It felt like the first good thing to happen to her in the last twenty-four hours. She was thankful that something had started to go right. Thoughts of Curtis, Corinne, and the woman's knowledge of the night two years ago, were far from her mind.

A knock on the door roused Georgia from the morning's lazy reverie. She noticed Holly flinch at the sound and realised the brunette was dreading Corinne's appearance. A wave of sympathy touched her and she

77

patted the woman's hand reassuringly. When the knock was repeated, louder and with less patience, Georgia slid from her chair and opened the door.

Standing outside was Curtis, accompanied by Chelsea. Watching the submissive woman drape herself over him in an obvious show of affection, Georgia guessed that the couple had spent the night together. She tried to convince herself that she didn't care, but it was early, she was tired and the charade didn't work. The depth of her own feelings surfaced when she caught herself smiling while Curtis shouted insults at Chelsea.

'Fuck off away from me and take that "situation vacant" sign down,' he growled.

Georgia grinned when she saw the hurt look on Chelsea's face, then chastised herself for being so malicious. Curtis seemed oblivious to Georgia's enjoyment of the scene. He stared past Georgia and fixed his gaze on Holly. Speaking with peculiar emphasis, he said, 'That position has now been filled.'

Holly shivered and wrapped the robe tightly around her chest. Georgia suspected that Curtis knew the sort of treatment his sister would be administering. That thought brought a cold shiver to her heart, and she tried to hold on to it as a protective amulet against his charms.

Two hours later, wandering around the empty fairground with him, she wished she still had that protective amulet. At least with her mind filled with unpleasant thoughts, she could have felt immune to his charismatic appeal.

'I keep accurate records for each ride, stall and ticket booth,' Curtis explained, gesturing idly at the silent booths and rides. 'That way I can keep on top of what's working and what I'm carrying as ballast.'

Georgia sighed. 'Do you really intend keeping me to the promise I made last night?'

He grinned easily. 'Would you stay anyway?'

'Of course not!' she declared.

He shrugged and carried on walking. 'Then the answer is yes, I intend keeping you to your word.' He was moving away from her and Georgia quickened her pace to keep up with him. She supposed she should have admired his candour, but she wasn't in the mood. She was already trying not to appreciate the sight of his tight, pert buttocks encased in faded jeans. His presence was having a disturbing effect and she didn't feel comfortable with it.

Stopping that thought, she realised she was wrong. It wasn't that she felt uncomfortable with his presence; she felt far too comfortable with it. As they walked alongside one another beneath the forgotten relics of the fairground's rides, she longed to have him put his arm around her waist. Memories of the time when he had done that instinctively were still strong enough to excite her and she fought against her need for his attention.

'The problem is, I haven't had a chance to look at the balance sheets for a few months,' Curtis went on. His cold, explanatory tone reminded her she was there for one reason and one reason only. It had nothing to do with any feelings he might have harboured for her. He simply wanted someone to help him manage his finances. The thought that he still cared for her seemed more ludicrous than ever in the cold light of day. Seeing him with Chelsea should have told her that he no longer had a need for her. If he did harbour any feelings, Georgia knew they were purely sexual. While that didn't bother her, she berated herself for thinking that he may have had more spiritual intentions.

'The balance sheets I've seen don't seem to add up right,' Curtis told her. 'I want you to do the figures for me so I can decide the best way forward.'

'That's a month's work,' she replied flatly. 'A week if all your paperwork is in good order. Will I be free to leave once it's completed?'

He glanced curiously at her. 'It's an ongoing job,' he said easily. 'You could stay as long as you wanted.'

She snorted unhappily. 'I've already passed that milestone. I'd decided I didn't want to be here about two hours before you extracted my promise to stay.'

They were standing in front of the hall of mirrors. She turned her back to him, but because of the ornate display outside the attraction, she could see his reflection. As ever, he looked inordinately resplendent. It was annoying that he could look so handsome and desirable without seeming to make the slightest effort. His jeans were faded but clean, as was the plain white shirt he had tucked into them. His short hair fell into a naturally tousled look that suited his lean, youthful face. Aside from the lack of razor stubble on his chin, he had put no discernible effort into his appearance.

Staring into the mirrored front of the attraction, she watched him turn to her.

'Why are you fighting me so hard?'

She glared at his reflection, wondering how he had the nerve to ask such a question. 'Do you really need to ask?' She laughed scornfully.

His arms moved to her shoulders and he span her around so that she was facing him. His cruel black eyes studied her quizzically and for a moment she was touched by the depth of expression she saw in his face. Again, she felt a tremor of doubt, wondering if she had been wrong to blame him for that night two years ago.

The sight of his lips close to hers brushed the unpleasant memory from her mind. She could see he was thinking of kissing her and, because his nearness inspired such excitement, she was prepared to allow that.

'You're right,' he agreed suddenly. There was a starkness to his voice that she hadn't anticipated. 'I don't need to ask you anything. You're here on my terms and you know damn well that my employees do exactly as I say.'

80

Georgia released a nervous cough, surprised by his sudden mood swing. 'What the hell does that mean?' she demanded. He was tugging her towards the hall of mirrors, his mouth set in a determined line. She tried resisting but his strength was far greater than she could fight against. 'I asked, what the hell does that mean?' she repeated angrily.

He stopped and fixed her with a cold, unnerving smile. 'You're about to find out. And by the time I've finished, you'll probably wish you hadn't asked.'

Georgia tried pulling away from him but he held her in an iron grip. He pushed the door to the hall of mirrors open, and dragged her inside. Georgia tried to raise a scream of protest but he had clasped a hand over her mouth before she could make the sound.

'Don't try the pathetic screaming on me,' he growled. The menace in his voice chilled her. His cold gaze fixed on hers and she could see the reflection of her wild staring eyes caught in his. She supposed this was how a rabbit would see its own reflection when caught in the grip of a fox or other large predator. The blood pumped through her veins with a rapid pulse. Yet, despite her fear and nervousness, Georgia realised she wanted him. It was annoying to be so intimidated and excited in the same moment, but she couldn't stop the emotions. She envied his physical strength and wished that her own matched his. Her body urgently needed him, and she was willing to submit, but she wished it could be the other way round. The chance to take the position of power was a prospect she found intensely arousing.

The throbbing between her legs was as urgent as the furious pace of her heartbeat. She had to wilfully stop herself from pressing her body against his as he glared menacingly at her. The need to touch and hold him were powerful urges that she couldn't resist.

'You won't start screaming?' he asked, still holding his hand against her lips. He moved his fingers away slowly when she began to shake her head.

'Only if you want me to,' she whispered.

He grinned and ushered her forward into the hall of mirrors.

'What are we doing in here?' Georgia asked.

It was a light, spacious hall. The mirrors looked as though they had been polished after the night's fun had ended. Each glass surface glistened brilliantly beneath the glow of a series of neon tubes. She caught sight of her reflection a thousand times, stretching for miles in one direction, coming towards her and walking away. The whole experience was unnervingly disorienting.

The pale grey suit she had chosen for the day complemented the officious look of her short blonde hair. The jacket was pulled in tightly at the waist, showing off her slenderness, while the short skirt revealed her long, bare legs. She had intended to wear a pair of stockings with the ensemble, but had been unable to find any in her suitcase. She suspected that Holly had taken them but she hadn't wanted to accuse her new friend of theft, even though Georgia knew it was the most likely explanation.

In spite of the fact that they were bare, her long, muscular legs looked very good in the thousand reflections. She caught herself grinning narcissistically at herself and then mentally chastised her vanity. Remembering she had asked a question, and hadn't heard a reply, Georgia repeated her words. 'What are we doing in here?'

The sight of a thousand images of Curtis smiling lasciviously back at her was answer enough. His callused hands were on her shoulders, holding her from behind. With the all-round imagery of the mirrors, she could see a different aspect of their bodies whenever she turned her head. She watched his fingers move down her back, then encircle her waist. As she stared into the mirror, she saw his hands cup her breasts through the flimsy fabric of her suit's jacket.

'Strange things, mirrors, aren't they?' he asked.

Georgia nodded easy agreement, barely hearing his words. The touch of his fingers against the sensitive swell of her breasts was inspirational. It was too great a distraction for her to concentrate on mere words. Her nipples ached for his touch but his fingertips were tracing circles around them. She knew he was allowing the nipples to build up to a peak of desire before he deigned to grace them with any attention. But Georgia made no move to hurry him. It had been two long years since she had enjoyed his lovemaking and she wanted to savour every memorable moment.

'What does a mirror show you, Georgia?'

His words blew warm breath against her neck. She shivered, aware that her inner muscles were pulsing in eager anticipation. Curtis was standing behind her, holding his body close to hers, and she could feel the urgent swell of his arousal. His erection was straining against the fabric of his pants and she found the gentle pressure against her back fantastically erotic.

'What do you see when you look in a mirror?' he whispered again. 'Do you see yourself?'

Closing her eyes she moved her hands to her skirt and teased the hem with splayed fingers. She remembered having similar conversations with him years ago. He was a philosopher at heart and she could spot the beginning of a debate when she heard one. But he had already inflamed her arousal, and if he wanted to talk about ideology or misplaced perceptions, he would have to pick another time.

'A mirror simply reflects my image, not my true self,' she told him softly. 'Look in the mirror and tell me what you see, Curtis,' she went on. 'Tell me honestly, what do you see?' She opened her eyes to watch his face in the mirror. His gaze was caught by the way she had raised her skirt and his eyes were focused on the gusset of her panties. With his attention caught, she teased one

83

carefully manicured fingernail against the fabric and pulled it to one side. The lips of her sex were clearly exposed and she heard his excited swallow.

'What do you see, Curtis?' she repeated, breathing the words in a husky whisper. 'Do you see a woman who wants you? Or do you just see her reflection? Do you see the reflection of light against a polished surface? Or do you see a woman desperate for you to fuck her?'

He didn't bother wasting words on a reply. He turned her around and placed a kiss on her mouth. Because the walls were made of mirrors, Georgia felt herself turning, but she seemed to stay in the same position. Curtis was in front of her now, but as he moved to kiss her neck and nuzzle her breasts, she realised she was staring at the same view she had seen before. A thousand Georgias each allowed Curtis to unfasten her jacket and tease open the buttons of her blouse. She gasped with pleasure when he released her breasts from her bra. The perfectly formed orbs were reflected to infinity in the mirrors and she was inflamed by the sight of so much naked flesh. Her passion increased when he placed his lips to her skin and began to deliver a series of gentle kisses. He had only opened enough of her jacket to allow his mouth access to the eager flesh of her breasts. With a display of animal passion, she tugged the garment from her shoulders and hurled it to the floor. Still filled with the urge to be naked before him, she began to tear the blouse from her body. As soon as she was rid of it, she pushed her skirt down her hips.

He made a soft noise of appreciation once she stepped out of her panties. She was completely naked, save for the pale grey stilettos she was wearing. Georgia kept these on to bring her height close to Curtis's towering six foot. The bright light of the hall was often unkind to visitors, but Georgia's pale complexion seemed to glow beneath the neon. Her areolae were the rose-red colour of deep arousal, tipped with dark pink nipples that

84

yearned for his touch. Her flat stomach led down to a neatly trimmed thatch of blonde curls so pale they were barely discernible.

He sucked each breast in turn, warming her with the fire of an arousal she had almost forgotten. She ached to possess him and wished he would strip so she could feast on the glorious vision of his naked body.

Even as his tongue began to slide against the glistening flesh of her sex, bringing explosions of elation with each subtle kiss, she still wanted him to undress. Determined not to rush things, she stood with her hands at the back of her head, allowing him to kneel before her and lick her pussy.

It occurred to her that he had probably made love to Chelsea in here. The thought didn't upset her as she had imagined it might – in fact the idea warmed her as much as his tongue did. Perhaps he and Chelsea had made love in the hall of mirrors, but Georgia doubted it would have been like this. She couldn't picture Curtis kneeling in front of the submissive Chelsea. After seeing the way he had bullied and threatened her on that first day, it seemed obvious their relationship wasn't based on mutual pleasure. Instinctively, she knew that he reserved this type of sex for her and her alone. They were making love as equals and that realisation brought with it a warmth as passionate as her desire for him. She doubted he had made love to anyone else in this way and that made her feel special.

Determined to take a dominant position, even if it was only for a moment, Georgia raised one foot and placed the heel of her stiletto against his shoulder. Curtis made a soft sound of disapproval beneath her, but his tongue continued to excite miracles in the haven between her legs. She threw her head back and smiled up at the bright light above. The feeling of power and domination that the position gave amplified her pleasure a million times. The heady euphoria of an orgasm felt closer already.

His tongue entered her hole, his lips brushing against the tingling folds of her sex. Using his fingers, he held her thighs and strained his neck so he could delve deeper inside.

Georgia shivered. Behind her head, her hands felt useless, so she moved them to the tips of her breasts. She considered holding his head tightly against her; she could picture her fingers curling into his dark hair and pulling the short locks hard as she forced him to go down on her. It was a warming image, but she didn't dare to attempt it in reality. Past experience had taught her that Curtis could only be pushed so far. Crossing her arms over her chest, she began to tease her nipples between thumb and forefinger. She rolled the hardened nubs back and forth as he continued to work his tongue against her cleft. The sensation of euphoria that grew inside was stronger than anything she could recall. Georgia sucked breath greedily as waves of pleasure stole over her. She could feel the climax building and, before she had a chance to contemplate it, the eruption took over.

A satisfied groan spilt from her lips.

She squeezed hard on her nipples, as though she were forcing the pleasure from her body. The power of the orgasm was so strong she could feel her knees beginning to give. She leant against one mirrored surface in an attempt to steady herself. Her breath was falling from her lungs in broken gasps and she stared at Curtis with wild-eyed rapture.

As the moment of bliss had stolen over her, he had slipped from his clothes. His shirt lay on the floor and his jeans and boots were buried beneath it. He stood before her, naked and erect. She took a moment to admire his slender frame before the need for his cock overwhelmed her. Her fingers reached out to touch the stiff length. When the fingertips connected with his pulsing flesh, she felt an electric charge burn her skin.

Before she could stroke him properly, his arms were around her. He pushed her back against the cool surface of the mirror, and raised her left leg high in the air. His strength was formidable, especially when combined with his need for her. Holding her tightly, he pressed the tip of his cock against the tingling wetness of her sex.

Georgia growled with desire. She wanted to lower herself on to him but because he was holding her leg, she couldn't move. His shaft rested at the entrance to her sex for an eternity, rubbing softly against the heated lips of her pussy. She rocked her pelvis back and forth against him, trying to guide the bulging dome to where it was so desperately needed.

He grinned wickedly, as though he could sense her urgent need and was enjoying her mounting frustration. She cursed the expression and cursed the excitement it evoked in her. 'Fuck me,' she urged him. 'Fuck me.'

His grin broadened. 'Beg me.'

She drew a stilted breath and stared defiantly at him. 'You'll be rolling your cock against my cunt lips for a long time before I start begging,' she replied. 'I want you, Curtis. But I'm not going to beg for you.'

As he studied her face she knew that defiance was shining in her eyes.

'If anyone else said that to me, I'd take it as a challenge,' he told her. 'But you . . .' He left the sentence unfinished. Pressing his mouth against hers, he pushed her hard against the surface of the mirror and thrust his rigid cock against her pliant lips.

Georgia gasped as the tip pushed easily into her hole. She could feel every inch of his length as it slowly penetrated her. His cock was long and thick, and she was enthralled by the sensation of having him fill her. As he continued to push forward, she could hear herself from a distance, gratefully snatching gulps of air.

Their ecstatic cries joined in unison as he plunged ever deeper into the tight wetness of her sex.

Georgia felt his hand fall to her right leg and before she could stop him, he was lifting her from the floor. He held her by the thighs, impaling her on his cock as he rocked his pelvis to and fro. His shaft slid easily in and out of her sodden pussy and she could feel a shrieking climax building again. She wrapped her arms around his neck, showering kisses on his face as his length rode between her legs.

His groin rubbed against the sensitive nub of her clitoris, sending daggers of pleasure coursing through her. Curtis was holding her tightly in his strong, muscular arms. As his bare chest rocked against the tips of her breasts, Georgia felt an exhilarating friction. The length of his rigid cock ploughed into her again and again as he ground against the pulsing ball of her clit. With each forward thrust, Georgia was being pushed towards the brink of another orgasm.

When the climax finally struck, she screamed. In the narrow confines of the hall the sound was deafening, and she half expected the mirrors to shatter with the ear-piercing shriek. It didn't matter that her face was so close to his. She realised that he too was screaming as his cock pumped forcefully into her. The euphoria of a shared climax was a pleasure she had forgotten and she wondered how the memory of something so exquisite could have slipped her mind.

Curtis released her legs slowly, allowing her to regain her footing before letting her unwrap her arms. She continued to hold him for a while, showering kisses on his face with words of thanks and appreciation. When his spent cock slipped from between her legs, she smiled gratefully down at it then kissed him passionately. Her fingers teased the flaccid flesh and she saw that he was already pulsing and preparing to grow hard for a second time. It was an exciting prospect and she could feel her carnal appetite hungering for him. She curled her fingers around his stiffening length, wondering if she could tease him fully erect again.

'Maybe later,' he whispered, kissing her and moving her hand.

Georgia frowned but nodded reluctant agreement. A movement from the corner of her eye caught her attention and she glanced uncertainly to see if she had seen correctly. She wasn't particularly surprised that someone had been watching their lovemaking. They hadn't been very quiet, and she realised the hall of mirrors was a relatively public place, even if that only applied to the fairground staff at this time of day.

Curtis watched her study the corners of the hall, a quizzical smile on his lips. 'What did you see?' he asked.

Georgia shook her head and smiled reassuringly at him. She began to pick her clothes up from the floor and step carefully back into them. 'Nothing, I guess,' she lied easily. She knew how volatile his temper could be and saw no reason to inflame it. Besides, she told herself, she couldn't be a hundred per cent sure that it was Corinne who had been watching them. And even if it was, she doubted Corinne could hold a grudge against her for having a relationship with Curtis.

Five

Holly glanced at the keys hanging from Corinne's belt and wondered just how important they were to the woman. She had noticed them hanging there before. They were attached by a shiny, silver dog-leash fastener and, not for the first time, Holly watched Corinne toy absent-mindedly with the various lengths of metal. She was too self-confident for it to be a nervous habit; the woman seemed to have absolute control over everything. Holly guessed she kept touching them to reassure herself of their presence. If that was the case, and Holly strongly believed it was, she realised the keys were incredibly important. She made a mental note to try to find out which locks they fitted before attempting to steal them.

Holly sat beside Chelsea in the front row of the circus, staring silently into the ring. The stage was covered with the remnants of last night's sawdust, its soft, tired perfume brushing gently against her nostrils. She watched a horse canter around the ring, quickening its pace whenever Corinne cracked her whip. The whip crack echoed magnificently in the empty hall, making Holly flinch each time she heard it. She didn't know if she was feeling particularly jumpy that morning, or if the previous evening had made her acutely sensitive to the sound. Whatever the reason, Holly flinched repeatedly, even though she could see the whip's tip sparking dust clouds in the sawdust behind the horse.

The horse, a magnificent piebald stallion, reared on to its back legs and continued to canter around the circus ring. Holly caught her breath as she watched the sight, imagining the audience's reaction to this spectacle. Reluctantly, in spite of her loathing for the woman, Holly had to concede that Corinne was bloody good with the animal.

'No!' Chelsea made the sound at the back of her throat.

Holly glanced at her guard and saw the expression of wild-eyed panic shining in her face. Holly frowned unhappily, wondering what was so wrong as to make the woman behave like this. Chelsea was standing in her seat and shouting the word 'no' louder than before. If she hadn't been feeling so weary after the previous night's activities, Holly would have seen this moment as the ideal time to make her getaway. Chelsea was climbing over the barrier between her seat and the circus ring. She waved her arms above her head and shouted for Corinne to stop. Puzzled, Holly watched and then took a tentative step in pursuit of Chelsea.

Holly had been enjoying watching Corinne go through her morning rehearsal. The woman wielded a bull whip with a skill that Holly had never seen before; she could imagine Corinne taking a cigarette from between someone's lips as part of her act. This morning, she had simply been bursting balloons with the whip, but her consistent accuracy left Holly with no doubt about how good the woman was. After her practice with the whip, Corinne had pinned half a dozen balloons to the knife-thrower's wheel, which she used in her finale. The outline of a person was drawn on the seven-foot wooden wheel and, as Holly watched, one of Corinne's helpers began to revolve the wheel. The drawing of a person turned round and round as Corinne tested the weight of her blades.

Holly had swallowed, unnerved by the thought of this woman using such dangerous implements.

Corinne hurled all six blades at the spinning wheel in rapid succession. Holly flinched as each balloon exploded then disappeared. When the work-hand brought the wheel to an abrupt stop, Holly saw that each blade was buried in the pock-marked surface of the wood, well away from the drawing of the body. Her reluctant admiration for the woman had begun to grow then.

It increased even more when she saw Corinne was purposefully ignoring Chelsea. Her attention was devoted to her work with the animal and Holly had to admire the woman's single-mindedness.

'Stop!' Chelsea shrieked.

Too late, Holly saw what she was protesting about. A work-hand was approaching the circus ring, on a direct collision course with the cantering horse. The pile of boxes he carried spoilt his view of what was going on and Holly could see the accident happening in her mind's eye. Aside from the pile of boxes, she also realised he was carrying a rucksack and, although she didn't want to believe it at first, she felt certain it was hers. If she hadn't been so nervous about the impending collision, her heart would have started to race with the hope of freedom.

Chelsea reached Corinne and placed a hand on her shoulder. She pointed at the oblivious work-hand lumbering towards the horse's path, and muttered something Holly couldn't hear.

Too late, Holly saw Corinne stiffen as the work-hand fell beneath the hooves of the cantering stallion. The horse released a nervous whinny and rolled over, while the work-hand fell to the floor with a groan of despair. His collection of boxes tumbled on to the sawdust. Holly watched as her rucksack rolled along with them. It remained fastened but it was still a lot closer to

Corinne than it was to her. Warily, Holly took a step towards it.

Corinne was running over to the horse's side before it had found its legs properly. She hugged it briefly, gave a cursory inspection of its fetlocks and then hugged it again. Once she was certain that the beast was unharmed, she turned a dour expression on the helper. He still lay on the floor and was trying to get up. Holly noticed a dusty hoof print on the back of his black T-shirt and tried not to imagine how much the injury might hurt. She took another step towards her rucksack.

'You arsehole, Ken,' Corinne declared. She was still holding her bull whip and, in a gesture of absolute fury, snapped the tip against the sawdust near the man's face. 'What kind of fucking arsehole are you?' she screeched.

Holly held her breath, sympathising with Ken. She supposed he should have been thankful Corinne was holding her bull whip and not the throwing blades. If the woman had been holding those, Holly doubted she would have refrained from using them. Holding her breath, Holly took another tentative step closer to her rucksack. It now looked as though the bag was halfway between her and Corinne.

Ken glanced up fearfully at the ringmaster. He pushed his hands beneath his chest and started to ease himself slowly from the ground. Corinne stopped him with a blow from the whip. The tip bit the back of his hand and his arm collapsed underneath him. He rolled against the sawdust and stared up at the bowed canopy of the big top. Corinne walked briskly over to him and stood astride him.

'Be fucking thankful that my horse is unharmed,' she hissed menacingly. The words were supposed to be a whispered threat, but Holly heard them echo around the circus ring. 'If Lightning had suffered so much as a scratch, I would have had you fucking gelded.'

Judging by the malice in her voice, Holly didn't think

93

this was an idle threat. She moved closer to her rucksack, unable to draw her gaze from the terrified expression in Ken's eyes. She wondered if she had looked like that throughout the previous evening, then tried to block the memory from her mind. Getting the rucksack and then making her escape from the circus were her main priorities. She could dwell on the misery of the previous evening when she was far away from this place.

As though she were reading Holly's thoughts, Corinne glanced up at her and smiled. It was a cruel, foreboding expression, and Holly realised it didn't reach the merciless black depths of the woman's eyes. Her gaze shifted from Holly to the rucksack and her smile tightened.

'Planning to cut and run?' Corinne asked sweetly.

Holly tried to stammer a reply but she couldn't find the words.

Corinne nodded, as though this silence was enough of a reply. 'Touch that bag, and I'll hurt you.'

It was a simple threat but the earnest tone of her voice left Holly in no doubt that the woman was sincere. She swallowed, nodded and took a reluctant step away from the rucksack.

Corinne turned her attention back to the work-hand. 'Get off your lazy fucking back, take Lightning back to his stall, and report back here for punishment after tonight's show.'

'I was only . . .' Ken began.

The sound of the bull whip striking the sawdust-strewn floor echoed through the ring. It cut the work-hand's sentence in two and left a chilling silence in its wake. 'I won't repeat the order,' Corinne murmured.

He was on his feet in an instant, an apologetic smile creasing his lips.

Corinne turned her back, ignoring him. She glared at Chelsea, then graced Holly with the same expression.

94

'Where did you steal those clothes from?' she demanded.

Holly glanced down at the jeans and T-shirt she was wearing. 'Georgia gave them to me,' she replied honestly. 'You didn't expect me to come here naked, did you?'

She could see that the remark had been a mistake as soon as she made it. Corinne started bearing down on her, anger emanating from every forceful step. Holly took a nervous step backwards but she knew it would do no good to try to distance herself from the woman.

'Of course I expected you to come here naked,' Corinne declared. 'That's why I've had your rucksack brought here. I'm going to give you the opportunity to earn it back.' She fixed Holly with a threatening look and said, 'Undress now.'

Holly stared at her, not sure if she trusted the woman but unwilling to openly defy her. The prospect of getting her rucksack back was too great an opportunity to pass up, but she didn't think it likely Corinne would allow this. It occurred to her that, if she ever played cards with the woman, Corinne would use a marked deck. Hesitantly, she reached for the button at her waistband, then stopped herself.

'I feel stupid doing this,' she said.

Corinne was dangerously close. Holly could sense the fragrance of her sweat as the woman stepped closer. 'Would you rather feel stupid, or hurt?'

Quickly, Holly unfastened the jeans and stepped out of them. She was wearing a pair of hold-up stockings she had borrowed without Georgia's knowledge and decided to leave them on. After tugging the T-shirt over her head, she stood wearing only the stockings and a pair of high-heels. As usual, she had deigned not to wear any panties and Georgia hadn't possessed a bra that fitted. Glancing down at herself, she saw that her nipples were standing hard on the perfect round orbs of her breasts. The pale pink of her areolae had darkened to a lush rose hue, a colour Holly associated with her own arousal.

Determined that Corinne shouldn't think she was completely cowed, Holly threw her shoulders back and tried to maintain a defiant posture. It was a difficult act to perform in such a public place. Even though the circus seats were all empty, she still felt as though she were being watched by a thousand pairs of eyes. Her rational mind told her there were only three people in the circus ring – Ken had already led the horse outside, so she was alone with Corinne and Chelsea – but that didn't stop her from feeling distinctly uncomfortable. The openness, her own nudity and Corinne's eager smile left her feeling exceedingly vulnerable.

To reassure herself, she cast a glance at her rucksack. The sight of the familiar bag warmed her. She wished she could have clung to that warm feeling, but Corinne was studying her naked body with a predatory smile and Holly felt all thoughts of comfort disappear.

'You're a true pickpocket, aren't you?' Corinne muttered. She took a step closer to Holly and rubbed a hand against her bare breast.

Holly shivered and tried to fight the erotic stimulation. A thrill of pleasure trembled through her body. 'I don't understand,' Holly said, the words husky with an arousal she hadn't wanted.

Corinne frowned. 'I mean, you're a genuine pickpocket. Not one of these snatch-and-run merchants, but a true pickpocket.' She teased Holly's hard nipple between her thumb and forefinger as she spoke.

Holly shrugged, trying fervently to remain indifferent to the exciting touch against her breast. 'I guess so,' she replied.

Corinne slapped her hard across the face. The slap came as a startling contrast to the pleasure she had been experiencing. Her cheek stung as though it had been bitten, and she felt dizzy with the force of the blow. It was a struggle to stop herself from falling.

Corinne's features were contorted into a threatening grimace. 'The next time you answer without calling me master, I'll use the bull whip on your tits.'

Holly drew a nervous breath that was somewhere between anger and fear. 'Master,' she said quickly. 'Master, master.'

'Good,' Corinne said, pleased with the response. She placed her hand against Holly's other breast and began to tease the sensitive flesh with the tips of her fingers. The stimulation sent tingles of electricity shivering through Holly's body.

'I want to see how good a pickpocket you are,' Corinne explained carefully. 'I want you to try and steal something from either Chelsea or myself, without us noticing. If I think you're good enough, you may get your rucksack back.'

Holly was suspicious. 'Why would you give it back to me, master?' She added the word 'master' only as an afterthought, when she saw the darkening frown of Corinne's anger.

The woman smiled and continued to caress her. 'If I think you're good enough, I could use you in the circus. Pickpockets can make quite entertaining acts. I've had a few in the circus before and while they don't draw big crowds, they keep the punters happy.'

'You'd want me to work for you? On a kosher basis?' Holly couldn't hide the surprise from her voice. She realised she had forgotten to address the woman as master, but that didn't seem to matter this time. Corinne appeared to be enjoying herself too much to care. Her tongue was lowered to Holly's nipple and traced wet, passionate circles around the rose-coloured areola.

Holly stifled a sigh.

'I think you could enjoy working for me,' Corinne

told her. She moved her lips close to Holly's, her dark eyes studying Holly's pale ones. Without warning, she pressed her mouth against Holly's and kissed her. As their lips explored one another, Corinne's fingers went to Holly's breasts and continued teasing the flesh. Her other hand went lower and Holly was startled to feel an exploratory finger probing through the dark curls of her pubic thatch. Shocked by the woman's intrusive behaviour, she wanted to gasp and move away. Fearful of the repercussions that such a rejection would cause, Holly allowed the woman's finger to continue its journey.

When Corinne finally moved her mouth away, Holly asked, 'Would I have to do all these shows naked, master?' Said aloud, it sounded like a stupid question, but Holly was fiercely aroused. The sullen pulse that beat in her breasts, and between her legs, was clouding her thoughts.

Corinne looked thoughtful. Her suspicious frown was enough for Holly to know the woman couldn't decide if she was joking or trying to antagonise her. 'You're naked so you can't pocket any of the trophies you snatch today,' Corinne explained. 'If you joined the show, we'd obviously organise a costume for you.'

Holly nodded, satisfied by Corinne's reply. Surreptitiously she stroked her fingers along Corinne's keys. She was tempted to lift them there and then, while the woman was least expecting it, but the dangers of such a move rang alarm bells in her mind and she resisted the urge for the moment. Her fingers teased the cool metal of the fastener, showing her how easy it would be to take the set without Corinne noticing. Gently releasing the keys, she turned to face Chelsea. As she moved, she bumped against Corinne's waist with her right hand.

Chelsea, like Corinne, was wearing a light jacket and a short skirt. Holly guessed there was something in the inside pocket of the jacket and as she took a step past her, she deftly snatched the contents.

98

'Did you feel that, Chelsea?' Corinne asked sharply. Chelsea frowned and shook her head.

Corinne's hand snaked out and caught Holly's wrist. She held the hand high in the air and twisted it round. Holly gasped, and the sudden flare of pain forced a cry from her lips. She dropped Chelsea's purse to the ground, where it landed in a cloud of sawdust.

'That,' Corinne said flatly. 'Did you feel that being lifted?'

Holly made a disgusted sound and snatched her wrist from Corinne's fingers. 'She felt that as much as you felt the loss of this,' she growled triumphantly. With her left hand, she held up the cigarette lighter she had pulled from Corinne's pocket. 'Do I get my rucksack back now, master?'

Corinne smiled tightly. She graced Holly's body with a lewd smile and shook her head. Her grin broadened as her face turned from side to side. 'You're very good,' she allowed. 'Very good indeed. I didn't see you take anything from Chelsea; I just guessed you had with you going so close. I never felt a thing when you took my lighter.' She continued to shake her head, an admiring smile gracing her lips as she studied the naked woman in front of her. 'You really do have a gift.'

Holly brushed the praise away with a casual shake of her head. 'So can I have my bag back?'

'There's a couple of other things I'd like you to do first,' Corinne said. 'You can pick Chelsea's purse up for a start.'

Holly frowned, not trusting the tone of voice Corinne had used. She could sense that the woman had something unpleasant in store but she dreaded to think what it might be. Her heart began to beat faster as nervousness took its hold. Lowering herself gracefully to the floor, she reached for the purse that Corinne had made her drop. From the corner of her eye she saw the foot coming towards her but it moved too quickly and kicked her over before she could attempt to move away.

'Whoops!' Corinne said with no emotion or concern.

'You . . .' Holly stopped herself from uttering the curse that was about to spill from her lips.

'Accidents will happen,' Corinne grinned. She stepped over Holly, beaming wickedly down at her.

From her position on the floor, Holly could see up the woman's short skirt. Corinne's exposed sex was just above her head, an enticing sight held in the shadows of her clothes. She dragged her gaze away from the vision, trying to focus on the woman's face.

'But while you're down there,' Corinne murmured, 'there's one other thing you can do for me.'

Holly's lower lip trembled, and her heartbeat was pounding furiously in her chest. Despite her nudity, and the cool air of the circus ring, she could feel small beads of sweat glistening on her brow. She swallowed and stared nervously up at Corinne. The gentle sway of Corinne's skirt kept shifting the perspective of Holly's view. One moment she could see Corinne, towering over her and grinning broadly. The next, she was treated to the tantalising sight of the cleft between the woman's legs. Beneath the neatly trimmed thatch of dark pubic hair, Corinne's pink pussy lips glistened. As a light breeze wafted the skirt to and fro, the scene continued to switch from one to the other. Reluctantly, Holly could feel her gaze being drawn to the forbidden view of the woman's sex. She realised what was expected of her and wanted to cringe away. 'No,' she said firmly, shaking her head from side to side. 'No fucking way.' She knew she had forgotten to use the word 'master' but in that moment she didn't care. She felt certain there was nothing Corinne could do or say that would entice her to perform that particular act.

Corinne laughed softly, as though she hadn't heard Holly's outright defiance. 'You're a quick learner,' she encouraged. 'You've already learnt what sort of person I am. I think you know what you have to do if you want to get your rucksack back.'

Holly glanced at the rucksack, her face breaking into an expression of slack-jawed hope as she stared desperately towards it.

'Do as I tell you,' Corinne went on, 'then you can have your bag. Once you've got that, you can either leave, or we can talk about you working in the circus.'

Holly stared into the dark folds beneath Corinne's skirt. Unconsciously, she licked her lips, vaguely aware of a parched dryness in her throat and mouth. Holly tried not to notice the lecherous twinkle in Corinne's eye as the woman watched her.

The offer was a tempting one and she couldn't think of any practical reason to refuse. She had never had this kind of sex with another woman before. Although the idea didn't really appeal to her, she thought the rewards would make any unpleasantness worthwhile. Struggling to convince herself that it was the right thing to do, Holly cast an unhappy gaze at the wet lips of Corinne's sex. Kissing the woman's mouth had been one thing but this implied a much deeper intimacy that she was wholly uncomfortable with. A nervous shiver travelled quickly down her spine.

'So, come on,' Corinne urged. She seemed to have sensed Holly's hesitation. Teasing the hem of her skirt upwards she said, 'Do as you've been told and eat my pussy.'

Holly's shivers turned into a tremor of unease. She moved to her knees and pushed her face close to the exposed heat of Corinne's sex. The musky fragrance of the woman's excitement was only a subtle perfume but Holly found it filled her nostrils and made her rapid pulse beat ever faster.

Again, she licked her lips nervously, not sure if she should be performing this act. Her mouth was inches from the exposed pussy and she could see it glistening beneath a film of wetness. She didn't know how long Corinne had been excited and she tried not to think

101

about it. Casting a wary glance upwards, she caught sight of the woman's merciless black eyes staring down at her.

In the same instant, Corinne pushed forward.

Holly felt the dark thatch of pubic curls brush against her nose, and then the lips of the woman's sex were touching her mouth. It felt as though she were being kissed by Corinne's labia. Rather than the nausea she had expected, Holly felt her pulse race with unexpected passion. The wet lips of Corinne's pussy covered her mouth and her nose. For a moment, Holly was deprived of air. She could feel the folds of delicate flesh pressing against her mouth and jaw. The wetness of that dark kiss filled her with an arousal she hadn't been expecting. Not sure if she was doing the right thing, Holly pressed her tongue into the velvety wetness of Corinne's hole.

Corinne sighed happily. She rode her hips backward and forward over Holly's face, gasping louder and louder as the pleasure swept over her. 'That's it,' she said, pleasure obvious in her sultry tone. 'You carry on tongue-fucking me, just like that.'

Excited by the woman's words, Holly continued to work her tongue against Corinne's sex. She was amazed by the sweet taste of the woman's pussy honey. The woman's clitoris was pulsing against her lower lip while the soft flesh of her labia created an electric frisson against Holly's mouth.

As though she was responding sympathetically to the woman's enjoyment, Holly could feel her own arousal mounting. As she plunged her tongue in and out of Corinne's tight, wet hole, she eased a hand between her legs and started to tease the heated flesh of her own sex. Her inner lips were sodden with excitement and she slid a finger easily inside herself. She teased the nub of her clitoris, squeezing the aching ball between her knuckles. Within moments of touching herself, Holly could feel the orgasm welling. She drew a pussy-scented breath

102

through her nostrils, still licking Corinne's wet hole as she fingered herself. Her eyes were wide open, not wanting to miss a moment of the torrid encounter.

A second pair of hands, Chelsea's she guessed, had started to toy with her breasts. Holly made a soft sound of appreciation as the fingers teased the hard buds of her nipples. Her areolae were flushed a dark red with arousal. Chelsea tweaked and tugged the sensitive nubs, further inflaming the wet fire between Holly's legs. It no longer mattered that they were in the centre of the circus ring, performing openly for anyone who cared to watch. All that mattered was the divine thrill of doing exactly as Corinne demanded.

As she kissed Corinne's cleft, Holly could feel Chelsea delivering loving kisses to the cool flesh at the nape of her neck. The woman's fingers still toyed with her breasts, tormenting the nipples and igniting starbursts of pleasure in the aching flesh.

Holly screamed as the delights of a climax washed over her. She buried her tongue deep into Corinne, extracting a scream of joy from the woman. At the same time, she rubbed her fingertips against the burning pulse of her own pussy, pushing herself beyond the brink with a forceful rush. Her growl of elation was so intense it sounded pained when she heard it echo throughout the big top.

'Bitch!'

She heard the word muttered from high above and realised she had done something to incur Corinne's wrath. Through the subsiding waves of pleasure that her climax had drawn, Holly began to feel the familiar knot of fear tighten in her stomach. It was a sensation that she now knew was inextricably linked to any sign of disapproval Corinne might show. She wondered briefly when she had first begun to react like this. It could have been a product of the previous evening, but this was the first time she could consciously recall the feeling.

Knowing there was no time to waste on such introspection, Holly stared expectantly up at the woman.

Corinne glared angrily down at her. 'You were supposed to be pleasing me,' she said in a moderate voice that suggested her anger wasn't as great as Holly had feared. 'You weren't supposed to be wanking yourself off.' Her voice raised with mild disgust as she spat the last three words out.

Holly opened her mouth to say something in her own defence, then stopped. She realised Chelsea was still fondling her breasts and, with a cruel jerk of her shoulders, she shrugged the woman's intimate embrace away. 'I didn't mean to . . .' she began.

Corinne stopped her words with the palm of her hand. It wasn't a hard blow but Holly had already learnt not to try to talk beyond that first slap. Corinne could make the subsequent ones hurt a lot worse. The woman pushed her fingers into Holly's hair and grabbed a fistful of the dark locks. Dragging her to her feet, she pulled Holly towards the knife-thrower's wheel. Holly managed to keep pace with her, coming close to tumbling a couple of times. One of her high heels fell off as Corinne dragged her along. To stop herself from tumbling, she kicked the other from her foot.

'This should keep your nasty little fingers away from your pussy,' Corinne growled angrily. She threw Holly against the wooden wheel and glared menacingly at her.

Holly struggled to find the right words for an apology but none would come. She glanced over her shoulder at the wheel and tried to equate it with Corinne's current mood.

'Climb on,' Corinne growled.

Holly frowned, not sure what the command meant. Realisation only began to dawn when she saw the small footrests beneath the ankle straps. She glanced at the outline of a human figure that was drawn on the wheel then noticed the straps around the wrists. Shaking her head, she glanced back at Corinne, about to say the word 'no'. The expression of resolute menace in the woman's eyes made Holly change her mind. Unhappily, she placed her feet on the footrests.

'Fasten her to it,' Corinne snapped.

Chelsea jumped into action as soon as the words were spoken. She tied the straps tightly around Holly's ankles. As she bent down to do this, her face brushed unnervingly close to the exposed cleft between Holly's legs. The strength of her orgasm had left her pussy feeling tender and hypersensitive towards the slightest pressure. The casual brush of Chelsea's hair against the throbbing pulse of her flesh was enough to make her cringe. The feeling of pleasurable pain was too intense for her to cope with and she tried to shun the excruciating sensation from her mind. It was difficult to ignore the pulse of pleasure, a problem made worse when Chelsea stood on the footrest with her to reach for the wrist straps. The wheel was designed so that its occupant could be held with their hands above their head. As Chelsea reached up to fasten Holly's wrists in the straps, the swell of her breasts pushed rudely into Holly's face.

Writhing from side to side, Holly tried to move her face away but it seemed like each time she turned, Chelsea shifted position. If the woman hadn't been wearing a T-shirt, Holly knew she would have had no option but to suck one of her nipples. The thought brought a wave of excitement that she tried to deny. Her pussy was still filled with a desperate tingle that she wanted to ignore but, instead of losing that urge, Holly could feel the sensation mounting to a dull, demanding ache. She needed to feel the satisfaction of a climax again to release the growing sexual pressure that was building inside.

When Chelsea finally stepped down, Holly realised

she had no way of satisfying that urge on her own. Her hands were bound securely above her head, her diminutive size making the stance distinctly uncomfortable. Her legs were stretched wide apart to a position that was just as harsh. She had closed her eyes when Chelsea pushed her breasts against her, and when she opened them she saw that Corinne was once again holding her whip. Holly's eyes widened and she tried unsuccessfully to suppress a shiver.

'I could score any part of your body with this,' Corinne remarked casually. To clarify her statement, she snapped the whip casually, cutting the air above Holly's head.

Holly tried to shrink from the noise. Sweat coated her nervous body and she stared at Corinne with wide-eyed terror.

'I could hit your leg,' Corinne explained, flicking the tip sharply against Holly's inner thigh.

She released a squeal and pulled her ankle ineffectually against the restraint.

Corinne was smiling broadly. 'I could hit your tit, if I wanted,' she went on. To prove her point, she snapped the whip against Holly's right breast.

The tip struck smartly against her exposed nipple, and a shard of explosive pain erupted in her breast. It took a massive effort of willpower to stop herself from screaming. The blistering pain was an infuriating fire that seared the flesh. Holly sucked in lungfuls of air in an attempt to regain her composure. If the pain hadn't brought her so much pleasure, she would have been screaming.

There was something surreal about the combination of pleasure and pain. If she hadn't been restrained, Holly knew she would have been bent double, holding her injured breast and glaring furiously at Corinne. Instead, she tensed every muscle in her body and felt the thrill of a climactic rush building within her. The flare

106

of discomfort in her throbbing nipple was severe but it brought with it a dark delight she had never dreamt of.

'And there are other places I could aim for,' Corinne continued, seemingly oblivious to Holly's mounting euphoria. Her gaze was fixed on the thatch of dark curls between Holly's legs. Her cruel smile thinned and her eyes narrowed to slits as she took aim.

Holly drew a startled breath as she realised what was about to happen. She struggled to find the courage for the word 'no', but her dry lips and tight throat made the refusal impossible.

She shrank back from the crack of the whip, feeling more pain with her imagination than her body. The tip snatched at the dark curls above her sex, tugging a couple of pubic hairs rudely from their follicles.

Holly shrieked and strained helplessly against the straps at her arms and legs. The orgasm hit her like a knockout punch. Every muscle quivered with excitement as the pulse of her pleasure became a rapid trill. She trembled against the wooden wheel, her convulsions increasing as the magnitude of her orgasm increased. A scream of pure rapture fell from her lips and she pushed her head back to release it.

'Perhaps now you'll do as I ask, rather than what pleases you,' Corinne observed.

Breathless, Holly nodded. She watched Corinne throw the bull whip to the floor and walk close to the wheel. With a familiar hand, she started to revolve the contraption and Holly watched the world turn upside down. It was only a short journey. Corinne stopped the wheel's revolution when Holly's feet were directly above her head. In this position, Holly realised, her mouth was at exactly the same height as Corinne's pussy. As though she were proving this point, Corinne raised the hem of her skirt and pushed herself forward.

Holly pressed her mouth against the now familiar swell of Corinne's sex. She didn't like to admit that she

107

was gleaning pleasure from this intimacy. If anyone had asked, she would have assured them that she was only doing this to get her rucksack back. This reassurance kept going through her mind. As she drew her tongue against the slick wet slit, she tried fervently to believe it.

'Yes!' Corinne growled happily. She placed a hand on each of Holly's ankles and held her tightly. While Holly lapped greedily at the heated flesh between Corinne's legs, Corinne lowered her lips to the delicate folds of the pickpocket's sex. Her tongue hovered hesitantly over the glistening flesh, then she pushed her tongue inside.

The feel of the whip crack against her breast had been painful but it had also provided some pleasure. Now she was experiencing the opposite effect. Her pussy ached for Corinne's touch but, as the woman pressed her mouth against the tingling flesh, Holly felt an explosion of pleasure so strong it wasn't truly enjoyable. Another orgasm washed over her but the satisfaction was bitter. Unused to such extreme enjoyment, the feeling was too exquisite for her to properly relish.

With her lips against Corinne's sex, she was terrified to moan as the discomfort tore through her. Not daring to incur the woman's wrath again, Holly licked harder.

Corinne growled soft words of approval, riding her hips backward and forward against Holly's face. Her measured pace was slow and deliberate, pushing the lips of her sex on to Holly's tongue, then slowly pulling them away.

A movement in the shadows above made Holly glance up. She saw Chelsea sliding her body between Corinne and herself and idly wondered what to expect next. The presence of two women, both so obviously aroused, was a greater aphrodisiac than Holly could have imagined. She closed her eyes, wilfully trying to shut out the excess of pleasure.

'Suck my tits!' Corinne roared.

Holly flinched, as though the command had been

directed at her. She wondered how she could possibly be expected to obey from this position, then realised the instruction had been aimed at Chelsea. From her unreal perspective on the two women, she watched Corinne pull her top open and push one bare breast into Chelsea's face.

The dark-haired submissive sucked on the proffered nipple, using her lips and tongue with obvious enjoyment. Holly could feel her own excitement quickly mounting as she studied the pair. The heady scent of Corinne's pussy juice was sweetening every breath she took and the taste of her arousal was a constant flavour in Holly's mouth. Chelsea's body was rubbing carelessly against Holly's breasts as she worked her lips on Corinne, and the combination of intimacies pushed her ever closer to a shivering climax.

Corinne groaned loudly, rocking her hips with a far more urgent pace.

Holly struggled to find the sweet hole of her sex whenever the pussy was offered to her. She could tell the woman's orgasm was close and, incredulously, Holly found herself longing to push Corinne beyond the brink. It seemed bizarre that she should want to please such a nasty, manipulative bitch, especially one who had inflicted so much pain on her, but Holly didn't waste time on self-analysis.

Corinne flicked her tongue haphazardly against Holly's wetness. Then, as her imminent climax neared, she simply pressed her head against the pickpocket's inner thigh and moaned softly. 'I could enjoy dominating you,' Corinne whispered. 'I could enjoy doing this every day.'

Holly could barely hear the woman's words but she sensed the sincerity underlying them. Her heart pounded furiously, nervousness adding to the perplexing set of emotions she had enjoyed so far. It was all right to indulge herself with someone like Corinne occasionally, but the idea of making it a permanent thing would be an act of gross stupidity. She swallowed down the cloying trickle of pussy juice that coated her lips, then licked harder. As long as her tongue was working against Corinne's labia, she knew she wouldn't be able to say anything. That meant there was no danger of upsetting the woman, angering her, or accepting the offer she had just made.

Wishing she didn't feel excited at the prospect of being continually dominated, Holly closed her eyes and worked the tip of her tongue against the raging pearl of Corinne's clitoris. The woman screamed excitedly, the cry echoing throughout the big top. The shrill sound was so severe it frightened a pair of trapped birds into flight high above their heads. She hadn't quite reached orgasm but Holly knew the woman was close.

Speaking between tightly clenched teeth, Corinne said, 'The last time I had this much fun was nearly two years ago.' A sigh trembled from her lips and Holly didn't know if her kisses had provoked this noise or the moment's recollection. 'That time,' Corinne went on, 'I gave an unsuspecting young woman a golden shower. Do you think I could do that to you?'

Holly swallowed thickly, nervousness getting the better of her. She had never heard the words 'golden shower' before but it didn't take a great deal of imagination to work out exactly what they meant. She shook her head, wide-eyed with panic, trying to refuse the woman's suggestion. Moving her lips from the haven of Corinne's sex, she began to say no. She knew it was wrong to deny the woman. She knew it was particularly dangerous in this position – but she didn't care. The thought of having the woman piss on her face was frightening. Her fear was so great that for a moment she forgot about the rucksack she was working to reclaim.

Corinne moved herself closer to Holly's face, allowing

110

her no hope of escape. 'Don't worry,' she assured Holly. 'Lick me well and I won't do that to you.'

Holly closed her eyes and licked. She didn't trust the woman and felt sure Corinne would be quite capable of treating her to the golden shower she had suggested, regardless of how well Holly pleased her. But it was her only hope. Remembering the rucksack, and knowing it was her passport away from this insane circus, she did as she was asked. She pushed her tongue deep inside Corinne's tight, wet pussy, teasing the inner walls. Her lips moved lovingly against the pouting flesh of Corinne's labia and she used them to caress the pulsing nub of her clitoris as her tongue delved deeper.

Corinne screamed triumphantly. She clenched hard against Holly's ankles as the orgasm swept over her, the tips of her fingers burying deep into the flesh, then pushed her mouth against Holly's pussy and licked greedily at the exposed cleft of her sex.

For a moment, Holly thought the woman had made good with her threat of a golden shower. She felt the spray douse her lips and nose and pulled her head back hard against the wooden wheel she was tied to. With her eyes open, she saw that Corinne wasn't pissing as she had first thought. The spray she had felt was merely the brief ejaculation which accompanied the woman's orgasm. That thought brought such a wave of relief that Holly actually smiled as she licked the pussy honey from her lips.

Corinne was grinning down at her, an expression that remained even when she turned the wheel and moved Holly back to an upright position. Chelsea was pushed to one side as Corinne climbed on to the footrests and began to unfasten Holly's wrists. The cool pressure of the woman's keys pushed uncomfortably against Holly's flat stomach but it was only a mild discomfort and Holly barely even thought about it. Thoughts of lifting the keys couldn't have been further from her mind.

After the two women had kissed softly, Corinne stepped down and told Chelsea to unfasten the ankle straps. 'We could do that all the time if you chose to stay with me,' Corinne said quietly.

Holly stepped from the wheel and tried to judge if this was a genuine offer. She still felt uncomfortable with the idea of making love to a woman, and needed a moment to try to rationalise the turn of events to herself. She held her smile and glanced over at the rucksack.

'It's yours,' Corinne said honestly. 'You've just worked hard for it, so you can take it, but,' she paused, placing a hand on Holly's bare arm. 'Think about my offer,' she insisted. 'I think you and I could have a lot of fun together.'

Holly eased herself from Corinne's hand and grabbed her rucksack from the floor. She felt sure Corinne would have a lot of fun if she stayed but she didn't know how long her own enjoyment of such servility would last. It had been an unusual and liberating experience but she felt sure the pleasure would quickly lose its appeal.

She considered saying this much, then decided against it. Corinne was a good lover but Holly had already learnt that the woman was given to dramatic mood swings. She exercised a tentative smile and lifted her rucksack from the floor. 'I'll think about it,' she conceded gently.

Corinne nodded.

Gauging the weight of her rucksack, Holly realised it was a lot lighter than she had anticipated. 'This is empty,' she said quietly.

Corinne smiled and nodded again. 'Of course,' she said simply, as though Holly should have known this.

Holly could feel her anger mounting and she struggled to control it. 'You promised me that if I did as you asked, I could have my things back. I've just done as you asked, you sick, twisted bitch – now where the fuck are my things?' Her voice had risen to an angry bark by the time she got to the end of her sentence. She realised she was standing inches from Corinne. In spite of her nudity, her posture was as intimidating and threatening as she could make it.

The woman who had just pleasured her was grinning with an infuriating expression on her lips. 'If you think back,' Corinne said softly. 'I said that if you did as I asked, you could have your rucksack back. I never promised anything more than that.' Her voice was soft and light, and a sweet smile twisted her lips as she spoke. With a sudden change in her mood, she began to glare angrily at Holly. Her hand shot out and grabbed a fistful of long dark hair. She tugged hard, bringing the pickpocket down on her knees before she carried on speaking.

'But since you want clear explanations about everything, Holly, I'll put this into words that even you can understand.'

Holly shrieked at her to let go. She aimed useless punches at the hand that held her but none of it did any good. The woman had complete control.

'If you want your things back,' Corinne said with barely controlled menace, 'you're going to have to work for them.' She smiled wickedly. 'If you take me up on my offer, then perhaps you might find out what a sick, twisted bitch I really am, because –' she licked her lips and her grin slipped away as she stared solemnly at Holly '– up to now, you've only seen my nice side.'

Holly glared at her furiously, wishing she could find the courage to tell Corinne to fuck off.

Corinne smiled and released her grip on Holly's hair. 'You don't need to give me your answer now,' she assured Holly in a deceptively kind tone. 'I'll call round to your caravan later and discuss it with you in depth.' Her broad smile glinted wickedly, adding unspoken meaning to her words. 'I'm sure we'll both look forward to that.'

113

Holly shook her head slowly from side to side, wishing she could find a way of venting her rage. It occurred to her that if she ever got the chance to dominate Corinne, the woman would really be in trouble. She stopped that train of thought before it could develop. She already knew there was no way she would ever get to brandish the whip.

Six

Georgia tried to keep her mind on the accounts but it wasn't easy. Her body still tingled from having made love to Curtis. An hour after orgasm, as she had showered the sweet smell of their sex from her body, Georgia had still been enjoying the after-tremors of her climax. There had been a strong temptation to rub herself off as she used the soap between her legs. The bar felt slippery yet hard against the wet folds of her pussy lips. Her clitoris had ached for more pressure and her nipples had throbbed gently with the desire for complete satisfaction. She had touched them with one damp palm, allowing the flowing spray of warm water to pulse against her tingling flesh. With a gargantuan effort of self-control, Georgia had denied herself that pleasure. She had finished washing and stepped quickly from the shower before dressing.

Now, working through the books, she wished she had found time for the moment's self-indulgence. The pulse between her legs still ached with the need for release. An untouched salad sat on one corner of the cluttered table she was using. Georgia stared at the fresh pieces of lettuce and celery she had prepared for herself without any measure of enthusiasm. After this morning's interlude with Curtis, she could think of only one appetite that needed satisfying and it had little to do with food. As she flicked blindly through the pages of accounting journals and expense records, Georgia tried to focus her thoughts away from the lurid channel they wanted to follow. Unconsciously, she stole a hand between her legs as she pored over the journals.

It wasn't a difficult task to be working on, she reminded herself. Perhaps, if the work had been a little more challenging, she might have been able to lose her thoughts in the various twists and nuances of the ledgers. As it was, the books were so straightforward they were quite tedious.

Curtis had asked her for a profit and loss statement for the fairground. She remembered him saying the intention was to use the information to streamline business. New rides and attractions would be purchased to replace the least profitable ones. The poorer sources of revenue could then be removed from the fair. It was a simple piece of accountancy for a woman with Georgia's experience. The meticulously maintained journals had left her with little to do except add totals. Aside from one notable exception, everything in the books seemed to balance. With nothing to properly occupy her mind, and the memory of Curtis still warming her body, she stroked her fingers idly against her inner thighs.

It wasn't her intention to masturbate.

She sat behind a table piled high with books, trying wilfully to concentrate on the neatly maintained lines and columns of numbers. If she had thought about it, Georgia would have realised that she was facing the main door of the caravan. Anyone opening that door would be greeted by the view beneath the table. A moment's thought would have stopped her fingers from moving upwards and she would have snapped her mind back to the ledgers.

Her thoughts instead drifted back to the bliss she had experienced and her fingers travelled higher. She eased the gusset of her panties to one side and idly teased the hot flesh of her pussy lips with a languid fingertip.

If there had been a moment when she could have stopped herself, Georgia knew it had now passed. She moved a second hand between her legs and held the panties to one side. With the other, she pressed a finger against the yielding flesh of her eager hole. Explosions of pleasure erupted between her legs.

The heady thrill of arousal came to her so quickly that she wondered why it had been so long since she had last indulged herself in this way. But it wasn't a matter she gave a great deal of thought to. As the tip of her finger traced quickening circles against the pulsing ball of her clit, Georgia concentrated her efforts on the more pressing concern. She drew a lazy finger against the wet, tingling lips of her sex, gasping as the touch of her own hand warmed the flesh.

She briefly contemplated locking the door, or moving position, then discounted the idea. Her need for orgasm was urgent and she didn't want to spoil her current mood of hedonistic self-indulgence. Holding the panties to one side with her little finger, she used the index and forefingers of one hand to spread the lips of her labia wide apart. The index finger of her other hand brushed gently against the wet flesh. Shivers of pure pleasure coursed through her. As the fingertip drew wetly against her sex, she teased the pulsing inner lips of her hole. Her pussy ached for penetration and she could feel her emotions spiralling towards a climactic crescendo as her hand rubbed harder.

It wasn't often that she fantasised while masturbating. For the past two years, on those rare occasions when she had treated herself to such solitary pleasure, her thoughts had been devoted to the enjoyment of the moment. But today was different. Her mind returned to the joy she had experienced with Curtis. The memory of his body pressing against hers was as thrilling as the finger she now used on her pussy. Remembering the way his hands had caressed and stroked her body, she felt the threat of orgasm steal closer.

Unable to resist the temptation a moment longer, she eased the tip of her finger into her own dark wetness. Gasping softly, she rubbed the eager flesh harder. In her mind's eye she wasn't simply wanking herself off. The memory of Curtis and his divine cock was being replayed in an obscene private picture show.

Her hands began to shake as she tried to tease herself closer to the point of climax. The solitary finger she had eased into her tight folds didn't seem sufficient to satisfy. Curtis had a lean build to his body but his length was considerable and her own slender finger could never hope to imitate it.

She pressed a second finger alongside the first and slid it deep into her velvety depths. With a small groan Georgia realised she was struggling to mimic the inimitable. Even a third finger, pushed deep inside her wet channel, didn't help. As she attempted to spread her lips wide and force the three digits ever deeper, she decided that her hands were inadequate for the task.

Her thoughts were momentarily distracted by the length of celery from her lunch. She barely hesitated once the idea had struck her. She snatched it from the plate and licked the clean crisp end. The distinctive fragrance of the vegetable filled her nostrils as she inhaled. She glanced at the smooth flesh of the celery then pushed the base between her legs.

The wide end of the celery pressed uncomfortably against the lips of her pussy and for a moment she considered not using it. The hesitation was very brief – her need for satisfaction was too great. Although she was uncomfortable with the idea of fucking a vegetable, her desire for orgasm overrode such prudish notions. Still holding her panties to one side, she pushed the length of pale green celery into her aching depths.

The satisfied moan Georgia released echoed against the thin walls of the caravan. Her inner thighs shivered uncontrollably, causing her hand to shake as it pushed the length deep inside. The width of the celery delivered an extra thrill that her fingers had lacked. Feeling the walls of her pussy being treated to such a fulfilling, tactile penetration, she knew orgasm was imminent. She eased the cool, green length in and out of herself with a quickening pace, occasionally tracing her fingertip against the heated pulse of her clit.

The pleasure of orgasm was a mere moment away and she luxuriated in the thrill of anticipation. Her hand moved back and forth with slow, yet determined movements, and she rocked back in her chair so that she could force the celery ever deeper. As it plunged even further into the confines of her dark wetness, the first tremors of an orgasm began to course through her. Tiny electric shocks of pleasure began in her pussy, quickly enveloping her entire body. Georgia shuddered as the shocks became a climactic torrent. Unable to stop herself, she released an ecstatic cry of joy.

At the same moment, the caravan door opened. Chelsea stood there, a questioning smile on her lips. The expression was quickly replaced by a knowing, lascivious grin. Her gaze was fixed beneath the table and Georgia knew the woman was staring at the makeshift dildo penetrating her sex. She watched Chelsea raise her eyes and realised the woman was staring directly at her face.

If it had been anyone else, she supposed she would have been embarrassed. She wouldn't have welcomed Curtis catching her like this, but with Chelsea, it didn't seem to matter. She had already realised how Curtis used the woman. From her first moments at the fairground, she had learnt that Chelsea was a toy, shared by him and his sister.

These thoughts, and her urgent need for another climax, forced her to a quick decision. She glared defiantly into Chelsea's face and said, 'Step inside and close the door.'

119

The woman responded without hesitation.

Still wrapped in the blissful waves of her first climax, and desperate for the release of a second, Georgia continued to ride the celery between her pussy lips. She stared warily at Chelsea as the woman came into the caravan and closed the door behind herself. She stepped to Georgia's side and knelt beside her. Her ripe lips were open in a sensuous pout and, as she moved her face closer, Georgia realised she was about to be kissed.

She knew the idea would have tightened a nauseating knot in her stomach this morning. Her one and only experience with a female lover had been unwelcome and unpleasant. For the past two years, she had thought it was because she had no attraction to the same sex.

Staring into the meek expression in Chelsea's pale cerulean eyes, Georgia could suddenly see how wrong this thought had been. Still frigging herself, she pushed her mouth towards Chelsea's and kissed her.

The climax pushed ever closer, threatening to whisk her away to the brink of ecstasy at any moment. As their tongues met and explored one another, her arousal heightened. It didn't seem possible that she could feel so excited and still not climax, yet her body seemed to hold her in this infuriating limbo. She rubbed the rigid length faster, desperate to feel the second climactic rush her body needed so badly.

Chelsea placed a cool hand on her leg.

The thrill of the woman's touch added a new, exciting element to her body's responses and Georgia opened her eyes wide with excitement. She broke their kiss and stared at Chelsea with renewed passion. Her hand hesitated for a moment as they studied one another. At the same time, Georgia realised Chelsea was edging her fingers up the bare flesh of her inner thigh.

'May I?' Chelsea asked softly. Her hand had reached Georgia's and the intimation of what she wanted to do was unquestionably clear.

120

Georgia didn't hesitate to reply. Her excitement had reached a point that transcended rational thought. Her previously held opinions no longer mattered. While she knew she should either be revolted or repulsed by another woman's nearness during this moment, Georgia couldn't find enthusiasm for either emotion. Her one overriding thought was for her own gratification. If Chelsea could help her to attain that goal, then Georgia was quite willing to let her.

She nodded and shifted around in the chair.

Before, Chelsea had been kneeling beside her. Now the woman was kneeling between her legs. Simply having the woman in this servile position inflamed Georgia's passion and she could feel the moment of orgasm creeping dangerously close.

As Chelsea touched the base of the celery, Georgia drew a deep breath. She felt the woman's fingers move to her panties and realised they were being removed. Still using the makeshift phallus inside herself, Georgia lifted her backside from the chair so the panties could be pulled off. She watched Chelsea slide them down her legs, conscious of how close the woman's face was to her exposed sex.

Once she had removed the panties, Chelsea moved her face unnervingly close to Georgia's pussy and placed her fingers around the celery. She glanced hesitantly up as she took the vegetable from Georgia's hand and whispered, 'Let me do this. You play with your tits.'

It wasn't until Chelsea mentioned her breasts that Georgia realised how much she had been neglecting them. The ache in her nipples seemed to flare as Chelsea spoke the words, and Georgia snatched her fingers towards them in an attempt to soothe their furious pulse. She quickly released the buttons of her blouse and pushed her hands against the swell of her aching breasts. The nipples stood taut against the lacy fabric of her bra and they thrilled to the delicate caress of her fingertips as she traced their outline.

121

Her inner muscles tightened around the celery and she could feel the impending climax move unbearably close.

Between her legs, she could feel the silken tendrils of Chelsea's hair brushing against her thighs. She was pushing the celery slowly in and out of Georgia's tight hole and her fingers teased the sensitive flesh, circling the makeshift dildo as it filled her. From the way her head was moving, Georgia knew the woman intended to use her tongue and the idea made her tremors grow ever more urgent.

All thoughts of revulsion were so far from her mind it was difficult to imagine they had ever been there. She pushed herself forward, allowing the celery to penetrate deeper. Her hips moved closer to the warm breath spilling from Chelsea's lips and she felt the delightful pressure of a warm, wet tongue against her sex. The sensation was incredible. She felt Chelsea's tongue flick twice against the furious pulse of her clit and her entire body stiffened. A euphoric rush of elation filled her and a scream was wrenched from her lungs as the climax erupted.

Chelsea moved her head closer. The celery slid swiftly from Georgia's pussy and was replaced by Chelsea's tongue.

Georgia drew deep breaths, not sure if her body could cope with any more pleasure just yet. She considered saying something to stop the woman, then paused. Relaxing in her chair, she decided she could tolerate Chelsea's tongue a little longer. She tugged the clasp of her front-fastening bra open and released her breasts. The orbs still tingled with excitement, and as she touched the sensitive areolae a dizzying wave shook her body.

Chelsea was holding the lips of Georgia's pussy open, using her tongue to trace wetly against the labia, occasionally teasing the tip into her eager depths. When she brushed her nose against the thundering pulse of Georgia's clitoris, it evoked waves of dark pleasure.

This orgasm was nowhere near as strong as the last but Georgia found it just as satisfying. It occurred to her that she should have taken a female lover years ago. Curtis had suggested they try to introduce that sort of dimension to their lovemaking when they had first met. She had dismissed the whole idea as being torrid and unnatural back then, and her unease with the whole idea had hardened after the incident when she was tied to his bed. After that night, the thought of having a female lover had sent shivers of revulsion coursing through her whenever she had contemplated it. Now she could see nothing wrong with the idea – it seemed more repulsive to let the memory of one unpleasant incident spoil her enjoyment.

Waves of joy shook Georgia's body as she rolled the tips of her nipples between thumbs and forefingers. She was grinning through fiercely clenched teeth, and it took a determined effort to sit still as Chelsea licked at her pussy. The need to ride herself back and forth, as the tremors shivered through her, was almost impossible to ignore.

Chelsea moved her head from the haven between Georgia's legs. The two women smiled hesitantly at one another and Georgia found her gaze drawn to the creamy pussy juice that covered the woman's mouth. The urge to taste the fruit of her own climax was powerful and before she could stop herself, she was reaching out, then pulling Chelsea towards her.

Before, their kiss had been exciting because it was so unusual. Now it was made more exciting because it seemed so commonplace. She had kissed her own juices from Curtis's face in the past. That moment of post-coital pleasure had always thrilled her, and with Chelsea it was no exception. The fact that she was tasting her own pussy honey on another woman's lips only added an extra dimension to the intimacy.

She could have endured the kiss longer, and would

have, if she hadn't felt Chelsea's finger stealing towards her breast.

'Enough,' Georgia said, not unkindly. She smiled reassuringly into Chelsea's hesitant frown and kissed her. 'Enough for now,' she amended.

Chelsea grinned and moved slowly away.

Georgia pushed the hem of her skirt down, fastened the buttons of her blouse, and blushed a crimson red. 'I'm sorry you had to catch me like that,' she said, glancing at the table top when she started to speak. She looked up and risked a nervous glance at Chelsea's pale blue eyes. 'I'm sorry. But I'm not sorry,' she said firmly.

'I'm not sorry at all,' Chelsea told her. She took a seat close to Georgia and said, 'Curtis asked me to check on you after I'd finished in the circus. He said I had to make sure you had everything you needed.'

'I think you managed that better than he would have expected,' Georgia laughed.

'He meant accounts and ledgers and things like that,' Chelsea said seriously. 'He seems determined to get the fairground's finances in some sort of order.'

Georgia nodded. 'He already keeps things in faultless order. I just wish I could say the same thing about Corinne. I wish I could get all of her books in here.'

Chelsea frowned. She stared at a pile of ledgers on one corner of Georgia's desk and leafed idly through them. 'These are all of Corinne's accounts,' she said earnestly. With an unmistakable air of pride, she added, 'I should know.'

'All of them?' Georgia couldn't keep the shocked tone from her voice. 'You have to be kidding me.'

Chelsea shook her head. 'Among other things, Corinne has me keep her records in order at the end of each night. I note down all the incoming money and all of the outgoing expenses. I doubt it's as good a job as you would do but I know better than to do it wrong. Corinne has a vicious temper and she insists I keep the books without making mistakes. I've worked hard on all of those books and I know what each of them is. What you have there is all of Corinne's accounts.'

Georgia sat back heavily, trying to rationalise the information with what she had already learnt about the fairground's finances. 'If that's true,' she said quietly, 'then the travelling circus is about to come to a standstill.'

'I don't understand,' Chelsea said.

Georgia shook her head, hardly aware she was speaking out loud. It was difficult to believe she was staring at all of the circus's financial records. There had been indications in some of the ledgers that the fairground was supporting it, but Chelsea's revelation added an entirely new dimension to Georgia's thoughts. 'Curtis wants to get rid of the deadwood,' she explained quickly. 'He's trying to streamline the fairground's business by getting rid of non-profitable ...' She stopped abruptly, aware that she had already said too much.

'Go on,' Chelsea urged.

Georgia shook her head. 'I should really be telling this to Curtis first, don't you think?'

Chelsea shrugged, obviously intrigued but unwilling to press the point.

'You won't tell anyone what I've said, will you?' Georgia asked quickly.

'Of course not,' Chelsea replied. She sounded indignant but Georgia realised the woman's gaze wasn't meeting hers.

Pushing her hand across the desk and touching Chelsea's, Georgia squeezed her wrist. 'I appreciate that,' she said, trying to impart trust and confidence into her words. A smile broke her lips and, in a lighter tone, she added, 'I've appreciated your entire visit this lunchtime.'

Chelsea looked up, meekly daring to meet Georgia's

gaze. Her pale blue eyes shone with the memory of their earlier excitement, and her ripe lips were parted in a warm smile that silently spoke of the intimacy they had shared. 'Your secret's safe with me,' she said, squeezing Georgia's hand in return. 'I won't tell Curtis what you've just told me. I won't tell anyone until you say it's OK.'

Georgia sat back in her chair, reassured by Chelsea's words. 'Thanks,' she said quietly. 'I can imagine the shit would really hit the fan if Corinne found out about this before Curtis wanted her to.' The thought sent a cold shiver running down her spine.

Chelsea was still shaking her head. 'I wouldn't go and tell Corinne,' she said earnestly, as though she resented the very suggestion. 'She loves that circus and I know she'd do anything to protect it.' Glancing at the clock behind Georgia's head, she frowned and stood up quickly. 'Oh God! I'm late,' she exclaimed. 'You'll have to excuse me but I should be somewhere else.'

Georgia glanced over her shoulder at the clock. When she turned back to face Chelsea, she saw the woman was already halfway out of the caravan door. 'Late? Late for what?'

The caravan door slammed shut, cutting off any reply that might have been forthcoming. Alone, Georgia wondered if she had just made a very grave mistake. She didn't like to entertain suspicions but it was difficult to stop herself. Chelsea had seemed in a sudden rush to leave. While Georgia wanted to believe she would keep quiet about the circus's finances, she hadn't felt wholly confident with her promise.

Cursing herself for being so stupid as to speak without thinking, Georgia stepped away from her desk and straightened her clothes. She had no option except to follow Chelsea and see where she was going. There was no way she could stop Chelsea from repeating what she had said, but Georgia felt sure that if she were there, she could minimise the damage.

Closing the caravan door behind herself, she prayed that she was misjudging Chelsea.

She caught a glimpse of the woman hurrying between a row of caravans and had to sprint to catch sight of her again. Chelsea stood before a large, dusty van and raised her hand to knock against the door. Georgia couldn't decide if she had seen this van before. They all looked so similar there was little to tell them apart. Admittedly, some had ornate etchings on the windows. There were big vans, small ones, subtly decorated ones and unkempt crap heaps. But to her uninterested eye, they were all simply caravans. She supposed there was something vaguely familiar about this one but she honestly couldn't recall what it was. The only thing that looked particularly distinctive about it was the set of closed blinds that covered its windows.

Wary that Chelsea might see her watching, Georgia stepped discreetly between two vans to hide, making sure she still had a good view of the caravan. She swallowed nervously as she watched Chelsea knock a second time, aware that her heart was beating nervously. She saw the caravan door open and tried to decide whose arm she was looking at. Shadows held the rest of the figure from her view. Before she could adjust her eyes and decide what was happening, Chelsea was squeezing through the narrow gap afforded to her.

The door closed.

'Shit!' Georgia said sourly. Unhappily, she took a tentative step towards the caravan.

Chelsea knocked on the door four times. There was no reply from inside and she stood in silence for a full minute before daring to knock again.

'You're late,' a muffled voice called from inside. There was the sound of a key turning awkwardly in the stiff lock and then the door was pushed slightly open. 'Hurry up,' he said brusquely.

Not daring to disobey, Chelsea squeezed through the narrow gap that had been opened for her and pushed past the man. The caravan's interior was shrouded in darkness. Venetian blinds at the windows blocked out the bright rays of crisp golden sunlight. She heard his key rattle in the lock as soon as the door was slammed shut, and a part of her mind wondered if he had actually locked it. It didn't sound as though the tumblers had caught and she considered saying something, then stopped herself. She was already late and she didn't want to compound that crime by questioning his ability to lock doors. Besides, she reminded herself, no one was going to interrupt them. Everyone at the fairground knew better than to enter this caravan unannounced.

'You wouldn't have been this late for Corinne,' he growled. 'You should know better.'

'I'm sorry,' Chelsea whispered. She had started to shiver, anticipating the punishing slap he invariably administered. She was pleasantly surprised to feel his hands touch her cheeks and hold her face. With infinite care, he placed a kiss against her lips.

'Don't do it again.' He reached behind her and flicked the light switch on. The room seemed less intimidating with the shadows banished. It wasn't just the pale decor of the walls, or the pretty pastel hues of the bed linen. Chelsea realised that he wasn't as daunting without the shroud of darkness. Without the light, his cold crisp voice and demanding tone sent a shiver through her heart. Now she was able to see him, Chelsea thought he didn't look threatening at all. He looked sensational.

Dressed in sheer denier white stockings his legs looked shapely and truly feminine. The matching V-cut suspender belt accentuated his flat stomach. He was wearing a silver-white basque stretched snugly across his broad chest. The garment had been tailor-made so there was no unsightly sagging around the chest.

Chelsea couldn't stop herself from smiling excitedly at

128

his outfit. She dared to risk a glance into his eyes, still wary that his mood could change. She assumed that in these clothes his entire disposition was different, but she had never dared to test that assumption. Time spent under Corinne's punishing tuition had already taught her not to act on such groundless feelings. Nevertheless, excitement added enough courage to her mood that she could continue to study him openly.

He was wearing a thinly applied veneer of make-up. His eyes were darkened by mascara and his broad, sensuous lips were highlighted by a subtle layer of pink. She remembered that those lips had just been kissing hers and she felt a tremor of arousal.

He wasn't wearing panties and she guessed there was a good reason for that. The huge length that sprouted from between his legs was too large to be contained inside any of the panties Chelsea had ever seen. His foreskin had rolled back and the purple dome shone wetly in the bright light of the caravan. His balls were a tight sac and she sensed he was close to his own climax already.

On a handful of rare occasions in the past she had watched him dress in these clothes. His arousal had always begun when he slid the first stocking over the shaved skin of one leg. His flaccid member had twitched between his legs to begin with. As the erotic friction of silk against skin moved up his calf, over his knee and on to the sensitive flesh of his thigh, his arousal always increased. By the time he had the first stocking straight, Chelsea knew he was rock-hard. His erection invariably stayed as he dressed and he was able to maintain it until the moment of his climax, regardless of how long that took.

She reached a tentative hand forward and brushed her fingers against his cock.

He groaned softly. His hands reached out, pulling her into his warm embrace.

Chelsea could feel herself being pressed against the stiff length of his eager cock. Close to his chest, she placed soft kisses on the smooth expanse of flesh available to her. She teased her fingers under the low-cut basque and freed his nipple. It was a small nub, pressed flat against his chest, the same dark pink as his areola. When she brushed her tongue against the tip, she heard him moan softly. Because her head was pressed against his chest, the sound seemed to reverberate. She could feel his body quake with excitement and she knew she had used just the right amount of pressure.

Rather than remaining immobile beneath her kisses, he began to undress her. Chelsea felt her blouse being tugged from her shoulders and the bra she wore was deftly unfastened. His hands moved down to her skirt and she shifted position so he could tug the button free and open the zipper. She stepped out of the skirt to reveal her nakedness and pressed her cool bare flesh against him. The heat of his cock warmed her flat stomach and she felt the familiar euphoric thrill of arousal.

He lifted her head and kissed her again. His urgent tongue slid between her lips, exploring her mouth. She could feel the tips of her nipples harden as they rubbed against the stiff fabric of his basque.

When he stepped away from her, Chelsea couldn't resist the impulse to touch herself. The tingling in her breasts was like a low-grade fever and her fingers ached to caress the desperate nubs. Crossing her arms over her chest, she traced careful circles against the areolae. She teased the flesh until she could no longer stand the intolerably sensuous pleasure. Unable to resist the temptation any longer, she brushed a fingernail against the thrusting tip of each breast. The soft, rounded orbs seemed to burn with the sensation of pure pleasure that her fingers brought. Distantly, she realised her deep arousal wouldn't just be satisfied with the subtle stimulation of her breasts.

'Stop showing off,' he said, lying down on the bed. His gaze was admiring her body and she couldn't miss the rueful appraisal glinting in the dark depths of his eyes. 'Come over here and join me,' he commanded.

Chelsea knew better than to hesitate. Reluctantly, she released the nipples from her fingers and climbed on to the bed beside him.

There was an erotic duality about his appearance that she found totally irresistible. Dressed in stockings and a basque, his body was exciting and feminine. The swell of his hips and the shapeliness of his legs looked as good as any woman's. Even his face had a pretty femininity, she thought absently. It wasn't a trait that she had ever noticed before, but as he lay beneath her in the lingerie she had to admit that he looked surprisingly good as a woman.

At the same time, the rigid length of his stiff cock didn't look out of place. Chelsea knew it should have looked odd, but the truth was that it didn't. His long solid shaft seemed somehow right between the shapely thighs. The bulbous purple dome of his cock's head looked divine twitching against his smooth flat stomach. It wasn't how every man should look, she thought carefully. But it was exactly how this man needed to look. This made him appear complete.

Unable to stop herself, she moved her hand towards his length and lowered her head. The heated flesh of his rigid length pulsed beneath the pads of her fingers. As she stroked her hand slowly down the erection she felt the trembling of his mounting excitement. Chelsea grinned and licked her lips suggestively. Moving her face slowly down, she rubbed her lower lip against the underside of his fraenum.

His legs stiffened and he cursed, words of praise mingling with the occasional obscenity. 'That's fucking marvellous,' he growled thickly.

Chelsea glanced up at him as she flicked the tip of her

tongue over the swollen head of his length. The salty taste of his cock was an invigorating flavour and she lapped gently at the head. Her fingers continued to stroke up and down as she rolled her tongue wetly against his pulsing flesh. Before she realised she was doing it, she had taken his entire cock in her mouth. Her lips were pressed tightly against his throbbing member and she was sliding her mouth from the glistening tip to the thatch of short, curly hairs around his balls.

His groans of ecstasy rattled the windows beneath the venetian blinds. He wound his fingers into her hair and held her head gently as she worked on his cock. Between long, drawn-out sighs of pleasure, he told her how good it felt.

Elated by his words of praise, Chelsea sucked harder.

'Turn around while you do that,' he snapped. 'I want to taste your juicy cunt.'

Chelsea moved her lips from his length and smiled at him. She held his cock at the base and twisted the skin in a loose circle as she changed position. When her legs were on either side of his face, she lowered her sex to his mouth, then pushed her mouth back over his cock.

His tongue was a blessing against the desperate pulse of her pussy. As the tip touched the eager swell of her clit, Chelsea realised just how neglected that part of her body really was. He licked softly at the folds of skin, wetting her labia and drinking her arousal. Daringly, he teased his tongue against the rim of her anus and she almost shrieked with pleasure.

As the excitement mounted, she worked her mouth hard on his erection. Her fingers teased the tight sac of his balls and she realised he was very close to coming. The idea of swallowing his seed appealed to her but she knew that he wanted more from her before that moment arrived. When the intrusion of his tongue suddenly ceased she realised he was trying to say something. She raised her sex from his face and glanced over her shoulder at him.

'You're going to suck me dry doing that,' he said, a mock reprimand apparent in his words.

Chelsea recognised the humorous tone he was using and responded with the same light air. 'If I'm going to suck it dry, perhaps I should wet it some more before I carry on.' She didn't wait for his instruction or approval. Instead, she tugged herself forward on the bed and placed the wet lips of her pussy over the tip of his rigid cock. Because she wasn't facing him, she couldn't see whether he approved of her impulsiveness. It was a gamble she had never taken before and her heart beat fast at the thought of her own audacity. Only when she felt his hands circle her body, and cup the swell of her breasts, did she realise that he approved of what she had done.

Chelsea's fire of arousal turned into an inferno. She allowed the purple dome to tease her sex for a moment longer before indulging herself with his penetration. Holding the base of his cock with one hand, and guiding the tip between her lips with the other, she slowly lowered herself on to him.

They cried out in unison. Their combined voices echoed through the caravan and she didn't doubt the sound would have carried across the fairground. At that moment, with his length filling her and his hands caressing her naked back, Chelsea didn't care.

The convulsive shocks of the orgasm tore through her. She could feel his fingers digging into her hypersensitive flesh while her pussy muscles tightened on his shaft. As his length spread the lips of her pussy wide open, she felt a fulfilment that was so extreme it was almost painful. Frantically, she rode her hips backward and forward along his cock. She dared to move forward a little, allowing him to slide from the depths he had penetrated, then plunged herself back on top of him.

This time, their screams were louder.

The strength of her previous orgasm seemed infinitesimal compared to the wealth of joy that this one gave her. Her heart beat so fast she felt certain it would explode in her chest. She could feel her cheeks burning and knew her face would be coloured with the deep red blush of pure ecstasy. From deep inside her pussy she could feel his cock twitching determinedly. She paused for a moment, fearing he had already climaxed. Her fingers were still caressing his balls and the sac felt exceptionally tight.

Moving quickly, she pulled herself from his cock and placed her mouth where her pussy had been. The mingled flavour of her juice and his excitement was intense and overpowering. Her arousal was great and she struggled to ignore the feeling, determined to please the man beneath her.

He growled with pleasure as she wrapped her lips around his cock. She could feel his entire body stiffen as he struggled to hold back his climax. His resolve was furious and, as she licked her own pussy juice from his length, she realised this was like a battle of wills. He was fighting to stave off his orgasm and she was working furiously to force it from him.

With a muttered curse, he relaxed on the bed.

Chelsea felt him spurt furiously into her mouth. The taste of her own pussy honey was lost in the sudden, salty flood of his ejaculation. Without swallowing, she continued to suck the seed from his body. Her nostrils seemed to fill with the scent of his climax and she felt dizzy with the feeling of shared intimacy. His cock continued to pulse into her mouth and she felt trickles of the thick cream spilling from between her lips. As soon as she had felt the last twitch of his member against her lower lip, she moved her mouth from him and turned around. With her lips tightly pursed she moved her face close to his.

He stared up at her warily, seeming unsure of what to expect.

And then Chelsea was kissing him. She pushed her tongue into his mouth, forcing as much of the creamy load between his lips as he would allow. At the back of her mind she half expected him to stop her. She feared that he might be revolted or repulsed by this unprecedented action but the moment's passion urged her to be daring. Repeatedly pushing her tongue into his mouth, she forced him to taste the sweet-salty flavour of his cream.

At first he appeared to be struggling beneath her. Then she felt his tongue enter her mouth and with a subtle movement of his throat she knew he was swallowing. The realisation sent a shiver tingling through her pussy muscles.

When their kiss broke, she moved her lips away from his and stared at him expectantly. The reprimand she had anticipated didn't follow. Instead she found he was smiling up at her, his eyes shining brilliantly with excitement. Thick rivulets of his creamy come were spilling from his lips. She reached out a hand and wiped her finger carelessly against his chin. Scooping up a smear of his load, she raised it to his lips and allowed him to lick the finger clean.

His broad smile widened and Chelsea realised how happy she had just made him. It was a warming thought and the pulse between her legs began to beat to a faster rhythm.

'I don't fucking believe you!'

Chelsea glanced up, startled by the woman's voice. All thoughts of arousal were suddenly swept from her mind. She remembered thinking earlier that the caravan door wasn't locked and now she realised she been right. In all honesty, she hadn't believed any of the fairground staff would dare to walk into this caravan unannounced but she had forgotten about this woman. This woman hadn't been with the fairground long enough to know all of the unwritten rules.

135

'Georgia,' Chelsea began quickly. She stopped when she realised the woman wasn't staring at her. Her angry glare, and look of revulsion, were devoted to the man Chelsea had just sucked dry. Chelsea turned to stare at him, watching him wipe a rough hand against the spilt seed that moistened his lips. A panicked expression lit his eyes and she could see he was searching for an excuse to qualify his behaviour. Unhappily she turned to look at Georgia, aware that the woman's fury was mounting.

'I don't fucking believe you, Curtis!' Georgia exclaimed. Seemingly unable to think of another thing to say, she turned her back on the pair of them and stormed out of the caravan, slamming the door closed behind her.

Seven

'Where's the mad bitch?' Holly demanded. 'Where the fuck is she?'

The stall-holder graced her with a curious expression, cupping his hand behind his ear. With the circus finished for the night the fairground had come to life again. The waltzers span noisily behind her and each ride and attraction seemed to fill the dark night sky with its own cry of deafening glee. Against the backdrop of a pitch-black night, the sparkling lights shone with a multicoloured glow that was almost magical. In her foul mood, Holly saw none of this. Not even the waltzers with their siren call could tempt her from her current course of action.

'Where is she?' Holly screamed, determined to make herself heard over the roar. She had been drinking since lunchtime and the alcohol had inspired her confidence beyond all measure.

The stall-holder shook his head and shrugged. 'Dunno who you mean,' he growled. Glancing at the line of punters waiting ahead of Holly, he added, 'Now sod off. I'm busy.'

Holly pushed to the front of the queue and pressed her face close to his. She didn't doubt he could smell the whisky on her breath but in her present mood, she didn't care. 'I want to know where I'll find the mad bitch.' She spoke through gritted teeth, anger forcing each word out as though it were being spat. 'Where is Corinne? Where will I find her?'

He shook his head. 'You shouldn't call her names like that. Corinne could get pretty upset if she found out. And you don't want to upset Corinne.'

'I doubt she could hurt me any worse than she already has,' Holly retorted. 'Where is she?'

'She's in the top. Now sod off.'

Holly thanked him tersely and walked away. She stormed angrily through the crowd, trying to ignore the faces that passed. Twenty-four hours ago she would have been looking at each one, trying to gauge how easy it would be to relieve them of their money. But since then a lifetime had passed. Tonight, she didn't dare look at a single one of them in case that wayward impulse returned. Even with her alcohol-soaked confidence, she knew better than to risk incurring Corinne's wrath again.

It was infuriating to think that she was so intimidated, and she hoped to get over that feeling by confronting the woman in the big top. Her hatred for Corinne welled inside her with the blackest malice. As she strode towards the unmistakable black silhouette of the big top, she glanced into the face of a passing man.

He was tall, dark-haired and seemingly besotted with the stunning blonde on his arm. He wasn't even looking at Holly when she bumped into him.

' 'Scuse me,' Holly muttered.

He grunted something by way of reply but she wasn't listening. The comforting weight of a fat wallet was filling her palm. She flicked the leather folder open and stared at the wad of crisp banknotes inside. Years of practice had honed her abilities to estimate, and she guessed she was looking at the best part of three hundred pounds. It wasn't a fortune, but it could prove to be a start, she told herself. A change of clothes, a warm meal and a night in some three-star hotel. If she went downmarket for the meal, she could upgrade the hotel by a star.

As this thought passed through her mind, she smiled to herself.

And then she changed her mind.

'Hey! Hey! You! Mister!' She called after the man, waving at his back to get his attention. She glanced at the name on one of the credit cards and shouted it aloud. 'Captain Wilde. Wait!'

He turned and fixed her with a puzzled expression.

'You dropped your wallet,' Holly explained, folding it shut and handing it to him. 'I saw it fall out of your pocket just now. Here, be more careful with it next time.'

He frowned unhappily, not reaching for it at first. His hands went to the empty jacket pocket from where she had lifted it. When he discovered the wallet was missing he smiled with disbelief and took the offered wallet from her. 'Thank you,' he gasped. His fingers were leafing through the money and Holly saw he was trying to pull a wad of notes out. 'Here,' he said, pushing a sheaf of notes towards her.

Shaking her head, Holly waved away the gesture. 'I was just doing what any decent person would have done,' she assured him.

'I want you to have it,' he insisted, raising his voice to make himself heard above the roar of the fairground. 'You could have kept it all for yourself but you didn't. I want to give you a reward.'

Holly took a step back from him. What was wrong with this fucking idiot, she wondered. He couldn't keep his money safe in his pocket and now it was in his hand he still wanted to give it away. 'Virtue is its own reward,' she babbled quickly. It was a sentence she had read scribbled in the back of a hotel Gideon once. 'You keep that, and keep a tight hold on it.' Ruefully, she added, 'I lost some money here last night. I know how distressing it can be.'

He looked puzzled, and then hurt, as he stared at the offered notes in his hand. The stunning blonde placed a reassuring hand on his arm and he smiled uneasily at her.

Dismissing them, Holly turned away and ran towards the circus. Another moment and she realised she would have taken his money simply to appease him. It occurred to her that to do such a thing would have been as bad as stealing. In a way, it would have been worse because he believed she was some sort of do-gooder.

She made a deliberate point of not colliding with anyone else as she ran to the circus. Weaving her way through the fairground's crowd, her hatred for Corinne intensified. The bitch had done more than hurt and humiliate her, she realised. Because of Corinne, Holly saw that she was now being troubled by a conscience.

She had to argue her way past the ticket booth at the big top's main doorway but the attendant recognised her from the previous night and eventually allowed her to enter. Still passionate with whisky-fired fury, Holly wouldn't have allowed him to bar the way for long. She was determined to make a stand against Corinne.

Inside the tent, she tried to ignore the smell of sawdust and excitement. She was poignantly aware that the pleasant fragrance was likely to spoil her bad mood. A sound in the centre of the ring caught her attention and she held her breath as she realised she had finally caught up with Corinne. Now that the moment of confrontation had arrived, she felt her heart sink. Not only did she feel at a loss for what to say, she also felt certain that her task was hopeless. That feeling intensified when she heard the hateful crack of the whip and a familiar groan of agony.

With her heart pounding in her ears, she wished she had brought the whisky bottle with her. She walked quietly along the back bank of benches, aware that Corinne was lost in her own tyrannical world of punishment. Settling herself on one of the uncomfortable seats, she watched the ringmaster discipline her staff.

Corinne was still wearing the long red tails of her ringmaster's costume, but her top hat had gone. The mane of her luxurious raven locks spilled over her shoulders, down to the small of her back.

Holly guessed this wasn't the only alteration she had made to her costume. Each time Corinne moved her arm backwards to crack the whip, the swell of a naked breast was revealed. She suspected that Corinne was completely naked beneath the tail-coat, a suspicion that grew when she saw Chelsea kneeling between Corinne's legs. The glimmer of wetness on her cheeks and lips was enough to tell Holly exactly what she had been doing.

Holly tried to ignore the murmur of excitement that shivered between her legs. She had come to the big top to demand her things back from Corinne. She wasn't going to spoil it all by getting turned on. Wilfully stopping herself from becoming aroused, she tried to view the scene with distant impartiality.

Kneeling in the sawdust on the circus floor were two naked men. They had their backs to Corinne and the burnished red cheeks of their arses were being held up for her use.

Holly watched the whip strike one of the men and heard his cry of despair echo around the big top. She recognised him as Ken, the work-hand who had been foolish enough to get trampled by Corinne's horse that morning. Part of her recognition came from his long blond hair, but she also guessed it was him because of the ugly hoof-print bruise on his back. Distantly, she realised this was the punishment Corinne had insisted he report for.

'I use this whip so that arseholes like you remember who's in charge. As long as I'm holding it, I know I'll have your unquestioning obedience.' She drew it back

141

and cracked the tip against Ken's bare backside. 'Now, what don't I tolerate?' Corinne bawled fiercely above his roar of pain.

'Fools,' Ken gasped, his words coming through tortured gasps. 'You don't tolerate fools.'

She snapped the whip against his arse again. His anguished cry reverberated like a cannon shot. 'You're learning well,' Corinne smiled. She turned her attention on the other man. As she moved, Holly saw the swell of her breast again. Her nipples were standing erect and she wondered if Corinne's arousal was caused by the woman between her legs, or the whipping she had just delivered. She supposed it could have been a combination of the two, but she suspected it was principally the domination that had aroused her.

She noticed that Corinne wasn't completely naked beneath the tail-coat. Accentuating her flat stomach was the broad band of the black leather belt she always wore. Holly could see the familiar sight of the woman's key's dangling from their dog-leash fastener. She remembered her initial thoughts about those keys and wondered just how important they were to the woman. For her to be wearing them now, in this moment of personal pleasuring, she supposed they had to have some great significance. It was a curious thought and she would have devoted more time to it if her attention hadn't been caught by the sight of Corinne's other victim.

Holly recognised him as Joey, the muscular operator from the waltzers. She wondered what his crime had been and then realised that she was probably the cause of it. Corinne ruled her employees with the heartless malice of a dictator. It didn't take a great stretch of Holly's imagination to realise Joey had committed the crime of fraternising with a pickpocket. Like every other misdemeanour in Corinne's empire, it was a punishable offence.

'What don't I tolerate?' Corinne asked, flicking the whip cruelly against his exposed backside.

'Fools,' Joey gasped breathlessly. 'Fools.'

'And why am I punishing you?' Corinne went on. She snapped the whip against him. The crack echoed like a gunshot.

Joey drew a breath of tortured ecstasy before replying. 'Because I'm a fool,' he told her, the words shaking as they fell from his lips.

'Good,' Corinne smiled. 'Now you've both realised what arseholes you are, I can begin to punish you.'

Holly swallowed and moved forward in her seat. Hadn't the woman just been punishing them? she asked herself. If the whipping she had just administered wasn't the chastisement, what did she intend to do to the poor bastards?

'A slap on the arse isn't enough for the likes of you two,' Corinne told them both. 'Before the reddening has gone down I know you'll both be up to your old tricks and acting like fools again.'

Holly shifted further forward. Her heart was racing inside her chest.

Corinne stood with her legs astride, allowing Chelsea to lick her as she spoke. A bitter smile twisted her lips. She had one hand held down and Holly thought she might be caressing Chelsea's head as the woman lapped at her pussy. When Corinne shifted position slightly, Holly saw that she had been wrong. Rather than caressing the woman who was pleasuring her, Corinne was stroking the length of keys that dangled from her belt. She held them tightly as she began to bark her words at the two work-hands. 'Fools like you two will remain fools until you've been taught otherwise. The only way to teach you is by humiliation. Stand up.' To emphasise this command, she cracked her whip into the sawdust floor.

Holly flinched from the noise, as though the whip had

struck her. She watched Joey and Ken raise themselves from the kneeling position and turn to face Corinne. They were both strapping men, Holly noticed, and she saw they were both excited by the punishment they had received. Each one sported a proud erection, Joey's slightly longer than Ken's.

Corinne was staring at their lengths with a cruel glint in her eye. 'I haven't humiliated either of you yet, have I?'

The pair shook their heads in silence. Joey whispered the words, 'No, master,' and Ken repeated them as though they were an incantation.

'Kneel down, Ken,' Corinne instructed crisply. 'Kneel down, facing Joey.'

Ken was staring at her with wide-eyed fear. Holly recognised the expression from her experiences over the past day. She watched him stare helplessly at Corinne and, when he had seen the lack of compassion in the woman's stern features, he did as he was told.

'Good,' Corinne cooed indulgently. She was grinning broadly and Holly could see the tips of her nipples standing harder than ever. She glanced at Ken and a horrifying thought stole over her. His face was on eye-level with Joey's cock and for one wild moment, she thought he looked like he was about to blow the other man. Surely, she told herself, not even the malicious and vindictive Corinne would force one man to do that to another.

As though she was giving the instruction to confirm Holly's worst fears, Corinne said flatly, 'Suck him, Ken.'

Joey and Ken stared unhappily at her.

Holly pushed further forward in her seat, unable to believe what she was about to witness. She felt certain that Ken would refuse, or Joey would move away and state firmly that he wouldn't allow it. Her rational mind assured her that neither of these men would permit themselves to be subjected to such humiliation.

And in her heart, she knew that neither of them would dare to disobey Corinne.

Hesitantly, Ken moved his head close to the stiff length of Joey's cock. Holly remembered the excitement she had felt when she moved her own lips close to that throbbing length of flesh. She doubted Ken was feeling the same thrill, but she noticed that his own erection remained hard and twitching.

'Suck him now,' Corinne growled. The cool hint of a threat tainted her voice. She was glaring fiercely at Ken, not bothering to conceal her obvious contempt. 'I'm losing patience.' As if to prove this point, she cracked her whip hard against the ground behind him, sending clouds of sawdust into the air.

As Holly watched, Ken slowly edged forward. His cheeks were burning a furious red with embarrassment and dark humiliation. She noticed that Joey looked extremely uncomfortable. Admittedly his erection was still hard, and pointed directly at Ken's face, but he was glancing awkwardly in every direction other than at the man before him.

With his cheeks glowing crimson, Ken opened his lips and took Joey's cock into his mouth.

Holly drew a short breath. She couldn't stop the sound from escaping, even when she snatched a hand over her mouth. Tension in the air had made the big top silent, and she wasn't surprised to see all four of the ring's performers stare at her.

'What the fuck are you doing here?' Corinne demanded coldly. She took a moment to push Chelsea's face back to the sodden cleft of her pussy, her eyes never leaving Holly.

Beneath the fearsome gaze, Holly could feel the last of her will evaporating. She had been determined to confront Corinne and demand her possessions back. Throughout yesterday evening, and this morning, she had been subjected to the woman's perverse brand of discipline. Her arse ached from the severe beatings she had received and the lips of her pussy still tingled with mixed feelings of pleasure and pain. The humiliation of it all had finally proved too much and Holly was determined to have it out with the woman. But now, staring into the cruel depths of Corinne's black eyes, Holly couldn't think of what she had intended to say.

'I asked why you're here,' Corinne repeated tersely. 'I expect an answer.'

Holly swallowed the nervous lump in her throat. 'I wan . . . want my things back,' she stammered.

Corinne cupped one hand to her ear, then shook her head unhappily. Snapping her fingers, she summoned Holly to join them in the ring.

Hating herself for responding so quickly, Holly climbed from her chair and made her way over and between the rows of benches. She was conscious of four pairs of eyes burning into her as she made her way down the steps to Corinne's side.

'What did you say?' Corinne repeated. The anger in her voice was clear.

'I want my things back,' Holly repeated. Her words sounded meek but she was pleased that the stammer was no longer there.

Corinne made a harsh, dismissive sound. 'You haven't earnt them yet.'

Minutes earlier, Holly would have disputed this sentiment passionately. Now, trapped beneath the glare of Corinne's barely tempered rage, all her arguments had vanished. The fire that her drinking had inspired was now well and truly doused. She stared helplessly at the woman, wishing she could remember that passion. 'Please,' she whispered. 'I've done as you asked. I just . . .'

'Go away,' Corinne told her stiffly. 'Go away, and come back when you can speak in a clear, audible voice. In case it slipped your attention, I happen to be a little busy right now.'

Holly shook her head, determined not to be dismissed in such a way. Tears of self-loathing welled on her lower lids and she squeezed her eyes tightly shut, unwilling to cry in front of the woman. 'I'll do whatever you ask,' she hissed. 'Just give me my things back and let me go.'

Corinne shook her head, barely listening. 'You'll do whatever I say anyway,' she reminded her. 'Now fuck off, and expect to be punished for this intrusion tomorrow.' She turned her attention back to the two men in front of her.

Holly shook her head, determined that the meeting wouldn't end like this. 'I'll spend the night with you,' she insisted. 'I'll spend the night with you and I'll do exactly as you say. I just want you to give me my things back and let me go.' As she spoke, the words came out in a garbled hurry.

Corinne paused and turned to consider her. 'Very well,' she conceded. 'Go back to my van and wait for me. I'll sort you out tonight, as soon as I've finished with these two . . .'

'No!'

Chelsea's sudden exclamation startled them all. Ken and Joey stared at the woman with matching expressions of surprise. Holly glared questioningly at her and Corinne glowered back at her.

Speaking quickly, Chelsea told Corinne, 'You promised me I could spend the night in your caravan. You gave me your word. You said I could stay with you tonight.'

Corinne shrugged. 'So I lied. Carry on licking my pussy, Chelsea, or I'll punish you before I go back to my van.'

Surprising them all, Chelsea didn't instinctively move her face back to the warmth of Corinne's wet sex. She remained on her knees but glared defiantly up at the woman. 'I need somewhere to stay for the night. Please, Corinne,' she begged. 'You have to let me.'

147

Corinne ran splayed fingers through her hair. The mounting fury in her expression would have been obvious from the big top's worst seats. She glared from Chelsea to Holly and then turned her angry gaze on the two men. 'You two worthless tosspots have to be the luckiest bastards alive,' she told them. Ignoring their questioning frowns, she glared down at Chelsea. 'You want to spend the night in my caravan?'

'I have nowhere else to go,' Chelsea told her.

Corinne sniffed rudely. 'What about Curtis?'

Chelsea stared unhappily at the floor. 'He doesn't want me tonight.'

Corinne nodded. 'He's back playing home-maker with that pathetic bitch?'

'No!' Chelsea shook her head quickly. 'They're not talking to one another at the moment, but neither of them wanted me with them. That's why I need somewhere to stay tonight.'

Holly noticed that Corinne seemed to extract a great deal of pleasure from this news. She seemed happy that all wasn't well between her brother and his lover. Her malicious interest in the subject made that much apparent. Holly didn't know whether to pity her or despise her even more. If she had been given time to contemplate the options, she felt sure she would have selected the latter. Unhappily, she realised Corinne was staring at her.

'Chelsea wants to spend the night with me and so do you, right?' Corinne demanded.

'I'll do whatever you ask,' Holly assured her in a flat tone. 'I just want you to give me my possessions back and let me get away from here.'

Corinne shook her head and ran her fingers through her hair again. 'I have a rule that stops me from spending the night with more than one submissive,' she explained. Her gaze was fixed on Holly and from the tone of her voice, it was clear that she was saying

148

this for her benefit. Watching Chelsea nod earnestly, Holly guessed that the woman had already learnt this much.

'As you will already have realised, I have a tendency for thoroughness when it comes to dealing with my inferiors. Some people may call this tyranny but I consider myself to be just. However, I'm always wary of the dangers of an insurrection. I know I won't have a problem controlling the situation on a one-to-one basis. But I realise that, if there's more than one submissive, they might succumb to the temptation of rebellion, and that might prove too much for me.'

Holly frowned, trying to hide the disparaging sneer that broached her lips. It was easy enough to understand what Corinne was saying. She felt confident of being able to control one person but with two, she feared they might make her try a taste of her own medicine. She supposed the woman was being quite prudent. Holly knew that if she ever got the chance to wield the whip over Corinne the woman would have to perfect the art of begging before she would relent.

'So, let's get this over and done with quickly,' Corinne went on. 'The pair of you can compete for a place in my van tonight.' Her cruel smile tightened and she turned to face Ken and Joey. After summoning Ken to stand up, she said knowingly, 'Don't think that you two have avoided punishment. The night isn't over yet.'

Before either of them could ask her exactly what she meant, Corinne had turned her back on them. She glared fiercely at Holly, a disparaging frown creasing her brow. 'Undress,' she snapped briskly.

Holly rolled her eyes. She felt as though she were suffering from the worst case of déjà vu ever known. Each time she had seen Corinne in the last two days, the woman had demanded she undress. The regularity of the situation would have been monotonous if it wasn't so unsettlingly exciting. As Holly unfastened the buttons at the front of her jeans, she glared moodily at the woman, trying to exert a last show of defiance.

Corinne ignored her, and turned her attention to Chelsea. 'Take your clothes off and tell me why you're so eager to spend the night in my van,' she demanded sharply.

Chelsea was undressing before the woman had finished her sentence. 'I have nowhere else to stay tonight,' she said quietly. Her obvious reluctance to say anything more was blatant. Even Holly, still sobering up and distracted by the threat of having Corinne chastise her, could tell that Chelsea was trying to hide something. She was quite surprised when Corinne let the woman's meek response go unchallenged. Her reaction seemed so uncharacteristic that Holly found herself staring curiously at the dominating woman as she stepped out of her jeans.

'When you're naked, you'll kneel in front of those two,' Corinne snapped. She directed her voice somewhere between Holly and Chelsea, addressing them both simultaneously. 'Chelsea, you can have Joey. Holly, you'll have Ken. It's a simple task really. I want you both to blow these two. Whichever of you two girls makes your man come first will spend the night in my caravan.'

Holly drew a sharp breath. She had just pulled her T-shirt off to reveal her nude body. Now she pulled the garment over her breasts, suddenly feeling demure and frightened by the prospect of such sluttishness.

Corinne saw her shocked expression and smiled. 'If you want to forfeit your chance, just say the word.'

Holly glared miserably at the woman. Her loathing for Corinne had never been stronger. Not only did she inspire feelings of terror and infuriating, unwelcome pleasure, but now it seemed that Corinne was even blessed with the ability to read her mind. Aware of how much depended on spending the night with the hateful bitch, Holly threw her T-shirt to the floor and stood defiantly naked in front of them.

Her cheeks burnt bright red as she realised the two men were staring excitedly at her bare flesh. She could feel the tips of her nipples hardening beneath their gaze and, without looking, she knew her areolae had reddened to match the crimson tones of her cheeks. She met each of their gazes with a shameless expression. It was only when she met Corinne's eyes that she felt the need to look away. The merciless depths of the woman's dark eyes were so intimidating that Holly didn't dare to risk making a silent challenge. She sensed there was enough danger in her current predicament already.

'I trust you'll try hard for me, Holly,' Corinne whispered. 'I'm looking forward to having you in my caravan tonight.'

It took all of Holly's willpower to suppress a shiver of revulsion from coursing down her spine. She dared to meet the intimidating threat of the woman's eyes, and found herself nodding. 'But you will give me the chance to earn the rest of my possessions back, won't you?' she asked.

Corinne's lips were stretched into a tight smile. 'We can talk about that afterwards. Now kneel down in front of Ken, just like I told you.'

Obediently, Holly took two paces, stood in front of the man, then knelt down. Her face was on the same level as his long, hard cock, and she tried not to think of the indignity she was about to subject herself to. Yesterday evening, she hadn't been troubled by any such feelings when she sucked Joey, but that had been different. Yesterday evening, she had been acting of her own volition, indulging an appetite that had needed to be satiated. Tonight she was acting on the command of another woman. The act she was about to perform was to be an exercise in control. She wasn't doing it for her own pleasure, or for the man whose cock she was expected to suck. She was doing it because Corinne had told her to and she was too scared to disobey.

From the corner of her eye, she watched Chelsea take her place in front of Joey. Like Holly, Chelsea made no move to push her mouth close to the eager rod of her man's erection. She remained calm and immobile, her eyes focused on an unseen image somewhere beyond the man's flat, muscular stomach.

'Are we all ready?' Corinne asked sharply.

Chelsea nodded, and Holly followed suit.

Corinne smiled. 'You may start to please your men when I next crack my whip,' she explained. 'Prepare yourselves . . .'

At first Holly thought the whip crack was so loud she could feel it. It was only when the silver shards of pain began to sting like nettles in her backside that she realised she had actually felt it. A horrified gasp of breath snatched the air from her lungs and she turned to glare angrily at Corinne. She was about to make a protest, say something about her behaviour not being fair, when she realised that Chelsea had started sucking.

She glanced at the woman and saw her lips were all the way around Joey's cock. She was sucking hard and, judging by the sounds the man was making, Holly doubted he would stave off his orgasm for long.

Muttering the word 'bitch', under her breath, Holly moved her mouth around Ken's length. All thoughts of unwanted promiscuity were gone from her mind. She didn't bother herself with the notion of how degrading this act was. Nor did she consider the stinging pain in her buttock where Corinne's whip had struck so sharply. Her attention was devoted to sucking the orgasm from Ken's body.

She heard the whip crack a second time.

It was automatic to flinch, even though she knew the tip hadn't struck her. She heard Chelsea make a small gasp of pain and saw the woman falter forward from her kneeling position. Staring sideways, not letting Ken's stiff length leave her lips for a second, Holly watched as Corinne started to circle the four of them.

A broad, wicked smile was splitting the ringmaster's lips. As she idly drew the whip back with one hand, her other hand went to the keys on her belt. She gently toyed with the bunch as she walked in a circle around the four of them. The malevolent light in her eyes danced wickedly as she watched.

Holly tried not to think about the woman, concentrating her thoughts on Ken's cock. She could feel the bulbous purple dome pressing at the back of her throat and she sucked harder. Rolling her tongue against his solid, rigid flesh, she began to move her mouth backward and forward.

His hands fell to her head and she suppressed the urge to get him to move them. When she had been in control yesterday evening, that had been her prerogative. But now things were different. She wasn't in control; Corinne was. If holding her head was something Ken wanted to do, then Holly was perfectly happy to let him do it. His fingers curled in her long dark locks and she felt him exerting a little pressure on the follicles as he pulled gently.

Still moving her mouth backward and forward along his shaft, Holly realised he was fucking her face. There was something base and humiliating about the thought and it made her feel uncomfortable, but at the same time she felt a dark arousal twitch between her legs. Perhaps she was being humiliated, she told herself, but she had already come to realise that submission wasn't always devoid of pleasure.

The whip cracked again.

Joey groaned softly and Holly stared at him in alarm. She wondered if Chelsea had managed to suck him to a climax, then realised his cry was the sound of pain rather than joy. He was rubbing one hand against his chastised backside and trying hard not to glare at Corinne.

Her infuriating smile almost begged him to glower at her, but he obviously knew better than to grace her with such an expression. Staring forward, he ignored Corinne, his hand rubbing at the stinging bite mark her whip had left in its wake.

Holly took advantage of his distraction and moved her mouth slightly away from Ken's length. She rolled her tongue against the pulsing flesh of his erection, desperately willing him to come. Using the fingers of one hand, she teased the tight sac of his balls, exerting the gentlest pressure she felt capable of.

Ken groaned softly and she was encouraged by his moans. The sound was suddenly snatched away and replaced by a shocked cry. His hips bucked sharply forward and she felt him tug hard on her hair. Instinctively, Holly realised that Corinne had caught him with her whip. She tried not to let the pain affect his nearness to climax, rolling her broad wet lips against the swollen end of his shaft. Her tongue flicked eagerly at the delicate fraenum and she felt his cock twitch purposefully against her mouth.

Beside her, she heard Joey groan.

'You're both doing well, aren't you?' Corinne observed. 'It's so nice to see you rising to the competitive urge.' She snapped the whip twice.

Holly only felt one of the blows. She heard Chelsea gasp as she took the brunt of the other. Before the pain took hold, she felt a moment's sympathy for the submissive brunette by her side. The thought quickly evaporated when the spreading fire of the whip bite made itself known. A burning weal of exquisite pain erupted between her buttocks. The agony was so close to the puckered rim of her anus that she wondered if Corinne had deliberately caught her there. She was a good enough shot with the whip, and Holly doubted that such a target would present her with any moral dilemmas.

The spreading fire brought with it a euphoric sensation. The pulse between her legs was becoming more and more ardent, and she felt surprised by her body's treacherous response to the torture it was enduring.

With a furious effort, she ignored her own arousal. The importance of winning this stupid competition came back to her and she pushed her mouth back on to Ken's length. The idea of spending a night with Corinne was a frightening prospect but she knew it was the only chance she would have to get away from the fairground.

Joey groaned again and, for one awful moment, Holly thought he was in the throes of orgasm. She could see herself spending a miserable night in Georgia's caravan, the hope of escaping the fairground having been snatched from her once again.

The whip whistled sharply close to her ear. She was beyond flinching from the sound now, but her body still held itself rigid, anticipating the explosion of pain that the implement invariably delivered. Beside her, she heard Chelsea gasp twice. An ear-piercing shriek of ecstasy escaped her lips and she threw her head back.

Holly teased Ken's balls with a little more pressure from her fingertips as she worked her mouth on his cock. She felt the explosion begin in his sac and then his entire cock was rigid. The first spurt of come hit the back of her throat in a hot spray.

They groaned in unison. Holly wasn't sure if she was experiencing her own mild orgasm, or simply delighting in the joy of having won the competition. Whatever the source of her elation, she found she was grinning triumphantly. Even when Ken held her head against his length, forcing her to accept the remainder of his come, she felt her lips smiling around his pulsing length. The taste of his seed in her mouth was the distinctive flavour

155

of success. She rolled her tongue greedily against his member, savouring the pleasure of her victory.

The whip cracked again.

Chelsea moaned loudly and Holly turned to stare at her.

'You can stop that now, Chelsea,' Corinne murmured. 'Holly has won.'

Chelsea shook her head, seemingly unwilling to accept this news. 'No. I need to spend the night with you. I have nowhere else to . . .' Her voice trailed off when she realised Corinne was glaring angrily at her.

'I don't care,' she growled at Chelsea. 'You can sleep anywhere you damned well please; just don't go troubling my horses.' She turned her back on the submissive, as though she had dismissed the topic. 'Holly, get dressed,' she growled. 'You're coming back to my van.' With an angry about turn, Corinne glanced at Ken. 'Did you enjoy having your cock sucked?'

He hesitated before replying. The expression on his face showed that he didn't know how she wanted him to respond. Eventually, after a moment's stammering, he seemed to decide that honesty was the best policy. He nodded and said, 'Yes. I enjoyed it very much.'

Corinne nodded. 'It wasn't much of a humiliating punishment, though, was it?' She glanced at Joey's raging hard member and smiled thoughtfully to herself. 'Finish what you started, Ken,' she decided. 'Suck Joey off, then I'll consider you properly dealt with.'

Holly saw the flicker of rebellion burning in the back of Ken's eye. She thought he was about to say something; a word of protest or an outright refusal. Then she saw the commanding glare in Corinne's eyes. The cold black orbs stared defiantly at Ken, almost daring him to disobey her order. Beneath that fearsome stare, Holly wasn't surprised to see the man acquiesce.

As she watched, Ken lowered himself to his knees and put his mouth to Joey's cock.

Corinne distracted her view by barking another order. 'Holly, go to my caravan. I'll be along shortly. Chelsea, get out of my sight. I'm growing tired of seeing you now.'

'I need to spend the night with you,' Chelsea insisted. Her tone was a beseeching sound, begging Corinne to reconsider. 'I have a secret,' she said suddenly. 'I have a secret, and I'll share it with you if you let me stay the night. Please, Corinne.'

Corinne hesitated for a moment.

Holly watched the woman toy idly with her keys. It was an infuriating habit and she wished she could stop herself from focusing on it. Every time she saw the woman playing with the bunch, Holly found her thoughts returning to their obvious importance. Listening to the plaintive tone of Chelsea's words, she tried to dismiss the keys from her mind and focus on what the submissive had to say.

'You have a secret,' Corinne repeated softly. 'What on earth makes you think I'd be interested in it?'

Chelsea exercised a confident smile. It sat uneasily on her pale face and looked like an expression she seldom got to wear. 'It concerns your brother and that girlfriend of his,' she began, speaking so smugly she appeared almost arrogant. 'Let me spend the night with you, and I'll tell you what she told me.'

Corinne's reactions were so fast Holly was stunned. She saw the woman's hand begin to move, but it seemed as though her mind had only just registered that fact when the woman was holding Chelsea's hair.

Chelsea squealed and then fell to her knees.

Corinne pressed the woman's face close to her pussy, then pulled her back sharply. 'You'll tell me your secret anyway, Chelsea,' she said, speaking with a cold detachment that was more chilling than any threat she could have used. 'You'll tell me your secret, or you'll be very, very sorry.'

Chelsea drew a shuddering sob and tried to nod. It was an impossible gesture to attempt but fear seemed to have robbed her of the ability to think rationally.

Smiling darkly, Corinne knelt down beside Chelsea. 'I'm glad you see it my way,' she said kindly. Her voice was a whisper, barely audible to Holly. She realised the exchange between the two women would remain unheard by the men. Holding her breath, she strained to hear what Chelsea had to say.

'What's your secret?' Corinne urged gently. Her fingers remained tightly pulling the brunette's hair. 'What did Georgia say?'

Chelsea spoke in the same hushed tone, her words interspersed with shuddering tears. 'She's been looking into the fairground's accounts,' Chelsea explained carefully. 'That's why Curtis brought her here.'

'That's not his only reason, I bet,' Corinne said with a knowing smile. 'And that's hardly a secret. What else do you know, Chelsea? I'm rapidly losing patience with you.' As if to prove this point, she tugged harder on the submissive woman's hair.

Holly cast a black look at Corinne's back. The woman's bullying manner and threatening behaviour were really beginning to irk her, and she longed for the opportunity to revolt. Knowing that now was neither the time nor the place for such thoughts, she checked her rising temper. Whatever Chelsea's secret was, she wanted to hear it. Desperately, she concentrated on the whispered conversation.

Chelsea moaned and shook her head as Corinne pulled her hair. She spoke quickly and rushed the words, all the time keeping her voice in a low whisper intended only for Corinne's ears. 'Curtis is streamlining the fairground. He's getting rid of the non-productive rides and attractions.'

'So?' Corinne pressed.

Holly guessed that Corinne had already worked out

what was coming. Her back was tense and the muscles at the nape of her neck were furiously stiff. Seeming determined to hear the words regardless of how unhappy they would make her, Corinne shook Chelsea's head again. 'Tell me what's been said, Chelsea,' Corinne demanded angrily. 'Or so help me I'll rip every fucking hair from your head before I'm finished.'

'She says the circus isn't profitable,' Chelsea said quickly. 'Georgia's going to recommend that Curtis gets rid of the circus.'

Corinne snatched her hand away from the woman. Holly could see the fury of her outrage in the thinned lips and narrowing eyes. 'The hell she is,' Corinne said firmly. 'Georgia and I are about to be reacquainted, and when that happens . . .' Her dark smile softened as she pictured the moment in her mind's eye. 'When that happens,' she repeated, 'closing the circus will be the last thing on Georgia's mind.'

Eight

As the hands of her wristwatch moved past midnight, the crowds began to seep slowly out through the fairground's gates. Georgia watched the stalls grow quiet, aware that the rides and attractions were still running at the same brisk pace they had maintained all evening. She stood by the hall of mirrors, watching the faceless couples snuggling close together as they ambled aimlessly through the dwindling excitement of the fairground. Turning her attention deliberately away from them, she glanced at the roller-coaster. She watched a brightly lit car swoop down one frantic descent before rushing up another steep incline.

Wearily, she shook her head. 'Who needs a roller-coaster?' she whispered. The way her life had treated her to ups and downs over the past two days, she thought the ride looked rather tame. Compared with the things that had happened to her, the roller-coaster was closer to a steady walk across a bowling green.

At first, she had to admit, she hadn't been happy to find herself in Curtis's fairground. Comparing it to the roller-coaster, she realised that it had been one hell of an unwanted plunge into the unknown. But straight after that, she had found herself rushing up to new heights of happiness as she remembered how much he meant to her. The morning in the hall of mirrors had been the equivalent of reaching the peak of a roller-coaster's summit. Then, this afternoon, she had found him with Chelsea, and dressed the way he was . . .

She drew a shaky breath, trying to brush the image from her mind. That had been an unexpected plunge if ever she had endured one.

'Georgia. There you are. We have to talk.'

She glanced up from her silent reverie, not surprised to see Curtis bearing down on her. His imposing presence no longer intimidated her and she found it easy to treat him to an expression of rank disdain. 'Find Chelsea and talk to her,' she said tiredly. 'I'm busy.'

He was standing close to her, glaring down at the top of her head. 'I want to talk to you,' he repeated.

She shrugged. 'Too bad. I don't want to talk to you.'

'You're my employee and around here that means you do as you're told,' he reminded her. 'Don't try testing my patience, Georgia.'

She dared to glare up at him. His mention of employment rankled when she thought how he had made her accept the job. She found the emotion fuelled her determination to make a stand. 'I might work for you during the day but as of now I've clocked off for the evening. Go away and annoy someone else.'

'You're not going to make this easy for me, are you?' He asked the question as though it were directed at himself, rather than her.

Before Georgia could decide whether or not to reply, she felt him grab hold of her wrist. He held her firmly and pulled hard, dragging her along with him.

'Let me go, you bastard,' she demanded hotly. 'You have no right to treat me like this and I won't . . .' She stopped, aware that he wasn't listening to her and wouldn't have heeded her words even if he had been. 'Where the hell are you taking me?'

'We need to talk,' he told her, calling the words over his shoulder as he walked. 'I'm taking you somewhere quiet, where we can talk.'

161

Shaking her head, Georgia dug the heels of her shoes into the soft ground. With a determined effort, she managed to hold herself against the relentless strain of Curtis's powerful march. 'I'm not going to spend another second in your bloody caravan,' she told him earnestly. 'I don't care what you threaten to do to me, or what you think of me, I'm not going there.'

'We're not going to my caravan,' he said, speaking through clenched teeth. 'I'm taking you somewhere discreet and we're going to talk.' He took a step closer to her side, his lips curled into a dark sneer. 'And you're going to start walking as though you're pleased to be with me, or so help me, I'll fucking carry you.'

She stared into the uncompromising depths of his dark eyes and realised this wasn't an idle threat. The thought of having him lift her in his arms was simultaneously frightening and exciting. Georgia didn't want to give in to either of those emotions at the moment, so, with a heavy air of reluctance, she nodded. She was still dragging behind Curtis as he led her purposefully towards the Ferris wheel, but she made no attempt to stop him from leading her there.

Because it was so late, the Ferris wheel was on the point of closing. The bright lights along its huge spokes still illuminated the black sky and, although it was no longer turning, the empty carriages rocked idly in the cool night's breeze. A solitary couple climbed from an open carriage, arms linked and dewy-eyed smiles gracing one another. Curtis pushed rudely past them. He marched up to the operator and barked a harsh instruction at him.

With an eager nod, the operator agreed to the instruction he had been given.

Curtis pushed Georgia into the nearest carriage and climbed in alongside her. Slamming the metal gate closed, he sat down and nodded at the operator.

The Ferris wheel rocked lethargically into life. A dull

162

whirr filled the air as its motor began to roll and Georgia was pushed back into her seat by the carriage's sudden jolt forward.

'We have to talk,' Curtis told her. He released her wrist and placed his fingers beneath her chin. Slowly, but with the latent threat of force, he turned her head so that she was facing him. 'We really have to talk,' he repeated.

Georgia glared defiantly at him. The world began to disappear below as they were gradually transported higher. 'So talk,' she declared coldly. 'You never know, I might even listen.'

The slap seemed to come from nowhere. She felt the stinging blow of his hand strike her cheek and her head rocked backward. Glaring furiously at him, she stood up and made for the gate of the carriage. It was only when she felt the carriage come to a slow halt that she realised he had managed to trap her. The Ferris wheel had stopped with them at the top. She was alone with Curtis and, from bitter experience, she knew that only he would be capable of getting them down.

It wouldn't matter how much she shouted and bawled at the operator down below – he would be oblivious to everything but Curtis's command.

She glared morosely at the horizon. The bright lights of the fairground were laid out beneath her, like a shimmering oasis in the desert of blackness. On the horizon, the twinkle of distant street lights sparkled like stars. It was a picturesque view, and she fervently wished she could be a part of it rather than a witness to it.

'In a way,' Curtis began softly. 'I'm glad that you saw what you saw today.'

Georgia turned towards him. There was a curious softness to his voice that she had never heard before. She tried to study his face but found the bright lights below and beyond the Ferris wheel didn't cast their rays into the carriage. Dark shadows held him from her vision.

'I'd been wanting to tell you about my fetish for a while,' he whispered. 'But it's a difficult subject to bring up in conversation. It's not that I don't get pleasure from being masculine and dominating sexually, because I do. But I get a real buzz from exploring my feminine side. Wearing clothes like the ones you saw help me to indulge that side of my sexuality.' He paused, still and silent in the darkness for a moment. In a heavy voice, he said, 'From the moment we first met, I thought you could help me to explore. I just couldn't find the right way to ask.'

Georgia drew a deep breath. 'We were together for six months,' she said stiffly. 'We tried everything in that time. Didn't it occur to you that you could have told me then?'

She saw his shadow nod. 'As lame as it sounds, I was going to. The night you left, I'd dressed myself in some beautiful lingerie and I was going to show you.'

Georgia had no difficulty casting her mind back to the evening he was referring to. Every detail was still etched painfully in her memory. 'You tied me up that night,' she reminded him. 'You tied me up and . . .' She stopped quickly, not sure what she had been about to say. The thought of accusing him of complicity in the events of that evening suddenly seemed wrong. She had no proof that he knew what had happened. Thinking about the way he had treated her over the past two days, she felt a growing certainty that he knew nothing about the humiliation she had been forced to endure.

The silhouette of his head was held to one side. 'And?' he prompted. 'You never did tell me why you left. One minute you were tied to the bed, waiting for my return. The next minute, the bed was empty.'

'It was more than a minute,' Georgia reminded him sharply.

He nodded. 'It was more than a minute,' he agreed. 'It was probably closer to an hour. I got called out of

164

the van to deal with a problem in the circus. But you knew I'd be coming back, didn't you? You didn't think I was just going to leave you there?'

With a determined effort, Georgia shut the whole memory from her mind. 'This is talking about the past,' she told him. 'You didn't bring me up here to take me on a Ferris wheel ride down memory lane, did you?'

She could hear the inflection of a bitter smile in his words. 'Shrewd as ever,' he noted. 'I only mentioned the past because, back then, I thought we were starting a relationship that was going to last forever.'

Georgia closed her eyes, trying not to feel warmed by the sentiment.

'I thought at the time that I'd gone too far with you, that my demands had proved too much, and I'd left it too late to show you my softer side.'

Thinking back to the passion they had shared, Georgia couldn't honestly say that she had found any of his demands too much. She thought of saying this, then decided they had already used too many words. Moving carefully towards him in the gently rocking carriage, she placed her mouth over his.

Their tongues met and she drew a deep sigh of pleasure, knowing that they were taking the first steps towards reconciliation. His hands were cupping her breasts and, as she leant against him, she could feel the tips of his fingers stimulating the ardent thrust of her nipples. Above the sound of the whispering breeze, she had no difficulty hearing his breath deepen. 'Show me your softer side tomorrow,' she urged him. 'Tonight I want to take a last look at your domineering nature.'

It seemed as though her words were the impetus his passion needed. His teasing hands, which had been caressing her breasts so deftly, now kneaded her flesh with unfettered brutality. Rather than stroking and caressing her, the tips of his fingers squeezed and pulled at her eager nipples through the fabric of her blouse.

165

Georgia gasped excitedly. She tried to stroke her fingers through his hair, and felt him push her hands roughly away. He grabbed hold of her blouse and tore it open. In the silence, she heard the soft sound of buttons striking the metal floor of the carriage.

A cool wind caressed her exposed breasts. The blouse was pulled from her shoulders and hurled over the side of the Ferris wheel. She made a small sound of protest as she watched the garment fall down through the night.

'You want to see my domineering nature for a final time?' he growled.

Georgia nodded, excitedly. With a shuddering breath, she told him, 'One last time. We'll talk tomorrow.'

His mouth fell against her breast. The warmth of his lips and tongue against her flesh sent shivers through her body. She was aware that his hands were working on her skirt. His rough manhandling had inspired an arousal that demanded satisfaction. With an animalistic grunt, he snatched the short length of material from her hips.

Georgia felt her legs treated to the same breath of cool wind that was teasing her upper body. And then she saw the skirt tumbling through the air, away from the Ferris wheel, towards the ground. There were no thoughts for the moment when the carriage reached the bottom of the Ferris wheel. The notion that she would be naked down there, and faced with the long walk back to her caravan, was as far away and unimportant as the twinkling lights on the edge of the horizon.

Placing a hand between her legs, he snatched at the gusset of her panties. With an effortless flick of his wrists, he tore the skimpy garment from her body. The torn pants disappeared over the side of the carriage and fluttered down to join the rest of her clothes.

Georgia was completely naked now and knew that he would do whatever he pleased with her. The thought sent her pulse racing like a roller-coaster carriage. She smiled at him in the darkness, wondering if he was as blind in this environment as she was.

His hands traversed her body. The rough, callused palms stroked her smooth, cool flesh, concentrating on the swell of her breasts and the arc of her waist. She felt his fingertips tease between the cleft of her legs and then he was pushing roughly into her. There was no thought given to her feelings – she realised his exploring fingers were merely acting for his own selfish purpose.

Her breathing deepened. She could feel her nipples tightening as one hand brushed carelessly against them. He pulled her towards himself and she lurched into his arms gracelessly. The carriage began to rock and she was treated to a disorienting glimpse of the horizon as it rose and fell dramatically.

Under other circumstances she would have found the unsettling view exhilarating. But this time there were other things to occupy her mind. Curtis placed his mouth against her flat stomach and pressed his warm lips against her.

As she struggled excitedly within his grasp, he moved his mouth slowly downward. She could feel his breath warming the pale patch of downy blonde hairs covering her sex. The contrast of his heated breath and the cool night air was darkly invigorating. While the rest of her body tingled with goose-flesh, she felt the heat between her legs intensify. Her need for him was greater than she would have imagined, and as the desire increased she arched her back and thrust her hips towards his face.

Moving his mouth lower, she heard him chuckle against her warm flesh. His hands were holding her buttocks, squeezing the orbs with callous disregard for her pleasure. At the same time, he flicked his tongue against the heated nub of her clitoris.

Elated by an intense thrill of pleasure, Georgia squealed. She pushed her hands on to his head and buried her fingers in his hair. He continued to lap at the warm haven of her pussy. His rough hands were hard and uncompromising against the soft peach-like cheeks of her backside.

In an instant, he had changed position. He was suddenly holding her waist with one arm and pressing his mouth over the taut pulsating bud of one nipple. His other arm was away from her, moving with quick, determined actions. She could only guess that he was undressing himself and she trembled, imagining his naked body being revealed to her.

As his lips teased the sensitive flesh of her areola, she felt his teeth threaten the tip of her nipple. He tormented her breast with tiny, delicate nips that had her shivering and sweating in the same moment.

The heated passion of his kisses was the perfect antidote to the chill night. Her entire body had been cooled by the combination of a light breeze and their modest altitude. With his warm lips brushing against her chilly flesh, Georgia felt the magnitude of her response heightening. Every time his mouth touched her skin, she felt a furious response that left her panting.

Stepping out of his jeans, he pressed his lean, hard body against hers. The pulse of his cock pressed against her cool skin as he held her tightly in his arms. Georgia could feel his length between them. The urgency of his erection had heated his shaft beyond boiling point. It felt as though he were wielding a branding iron and she could feel it searing her ice-cold flesh as it brushed against her.

He lurched forward in the tight confines of the carriage.

As Georgia stepped back, she felt the carriage dip and saw the horizon behind him fall from view. For an instant, she was convinced that the carriage was going to tip over and spill them the hundred feet to the ground. As soon as the tilt reached its apex, she chastised herself for being so foolish. She would have continued berating herself if Curtis hadn't been pleasuring her so efficiently.

The cold metal rail of the carriage pressed against the small of her back and her upper half dangled dangerously over the perilous drop below. With her eyes wide open, she could see the stars tilting drunkenly above her, but her concentration was devoted to the pleasure that Curtis was giving her.

He held her safe in one broad, strong arm. The other stroked her body with rough, exploring fingers. She could feel the urgent pulse of his length as it nuzzled between her legs and she tried to push herself against him.

He moved his mouth over hers and they kissed. The passion of the moment was intoxicating. As his tongue entered her mouth, she could feel the tip of his cock pressing forcefully against the wet, eager lips of her pussy. A scream of euphoria welled in the back of her throat and when he gently bit on her lower lip, she released the sound. Her cry echoed sonorously into the endless night.

As his cock plunged into her, she felt herself being pushed back against the thin rail of the carriage. Outside her body, his length had felt like a poker, almost glowing with the furious heat of its burning warmth. When he entered her, she realised just how wrong she had been.

The chill night air had worked quickly on him. His rigid length was deliciously cold inside her. As he pushed his cock into her sodden hole, she shivered.

Before, she had thought her own body was cold. As his cock moved purposefully forward, filling her and thrilling her, she could feel her warmth being chilled by his icy length. The inner muscles of her pussy were feverishly hot and she felt them burning his shaft.

They continued to kiss as he began his slow egress from the tingling lips of her sex. Georgia drew excited sighs, the sounds deepening as he began to push back inside her.

Within moments his brutal lovemaking had developed a slow, languid rhythm. She realised distantly that the carriage was rocking to the same laconic tempo, and as she glanced at the world around them, she saw it too was rising and falling in time.

The shriek of her orgasm was inevitable. She felt the explosion begin inside the heated pulse of her pussy. As his length ploughed roughly and repeatedly into her, the delightful sensations began to well like waters at a dam. With his passionate kisses on her mouth, and the exploring fingers at her breasts, she found it impossible to fight against the irresistible moment. Clenching her hands against him, she pressed the tips of her nails against his bare flesh and threw her head back, frantically rocking her hips backward and forward against his cock. The climax began in the pulsating walls of her sex, quickly travelling to every nerve ending in her body.

As the depth of her passion took control, she buried her fingernails deeper into his bare skin. She heard him growl with the sullen enjoyment of discomfort, and her passionate response fuelled him to ride harder into her.

It was a beautiful spiral of responses. The harder he forced himself into her, the more she buried her nails into his flesh. The more passionately she clawed at him with her fingers, the harder he retaliated with forceful thrusts of his cock.

Instead of her climactic pleasure ebbing slowly away, she felt herself being transported to a plateau of hitherto undiscovered joy. The world around her continued to pitch and roll but that seemed trivial and unimportant. All that mattered was the cold length of his shaft in the burning wetness of her pussy.

It occurred to her that she was going to miss his dominant nature. The pleasure of being treated so brutally and forcefully was incredible. Regardless of how much joy Curtis was likely to get from exploring his feminine side, Georgia doubted it would be as satisfying for her as a moment like this.

His hands were on her sides and she felt herself being turned roughly around. His cock was snatched from the delicious haven between her legs and her pussy suddenly felt cold and empty. The euphoric delight of her orgasm was merely a memory.

Georgia gasped softly, surprised that the pleasure could have ended so abruptly. She was about to say a word of protest when he pushed her back against the carriage's rail. This time the metal bar was forced against her flat, smooth stomach.

The bulbous tip of his shaft pressed deliberately between her legs, but this time he used one hand to guide it. The other hand was pressed against her scalp. His fingers strove to find purchase in the short shock of blonde hair and when they found none, he gripped her head tightly with one large hand.

'Where do you want this?' he growled.

She didn't have time to puzzle over the question. The meaning was obvious. Holding his length firmly, he slid the tip of his cock against the lips of her pussy. Guiding it deliberately against her yielding flesh, he slid the purple dome of his shaft along her heated lips. Starting at the clitoris he worked the end over her labia and up to her perineum.

She felt the throbbing end of his length brush forcefully at the rim of her anus and in that moment she knew exactly where she wanted him. The fire of her passion had been stoked by his cock already – now she wanted him to fan the flames. She could feel the powerful yearning of her body's need and she knew that she would only have true satisfaction from one source.

'Fuck my arse,' she gasped. Passion bleached every nuance from her tone, save for the raw power of her urgent desire. 'Please, Curtis. Fuck my arse.'

He pressed the tip of his length against the tightly puckered rim and held it there for an instant.

Georgia stared at the deserted fairground below as the world rocked back and forth. She drew short, delighted breaths, anticipating the thrill of his entry. Her hands had fallen to the rails of the carriage, and she steadied herself in preparation for him.

His fingers pressed tightly against the pliant flesh of her hips as he held her. Pushing slowly, but with little concession to gentleness, he filled her arse with his cock.

This time Georgia didn't scream. Her cry of euphoria was close to a howl.

Each millimetre of his cock's entry sent a shiver of ecstasy coursing through her. She pressed back against him, determined to enjoy as much of him as her body would allow. She could feel her arsehole being stretched by his broad length and the discomfort was so erotic she felt her orgasm move even closer. Her breath came in snatched gasps and she struggled to suppress the monumental climax before it could tear through her.

The cock inside her was twitching with a familiar pulse and she sensed that Curtis was close to his own climax. The need to have him come inside her was so great she dared to squeeze the muscles of her arse against him. She had tried this variation of lovemaking with him before, but even then she had never dared to try to squeeze the muscles of her arse against his huge cock.

Her body was suddenly filled with sensations so sublime they felt spiritual. Her inner muscles clamped greedily around him and she felt his body respond with a fury that went beyond any pleasure she had ever enjoyed before.

They climaxed together, shouting their euphoria into the night. The Ferris wheel carriage rocked slowly to and fro, tipping the world around them on its axis.

When Curtis finally drew his spent cock from her

172

warmth, he turned Georgia around and kissed her. 'Was I domineering enough for you?'

She laughed happily at his question and pushed her body against his. Trembling in the aftermath of her orgasm, she pressed herself close to his warm chest. Not wanting to spoil the moment with words, she smiled up at him and nodded.

From the corner of her eye, she saw a small, solitary figure walking briskly through the deserted fairground below.

From her position, tied to the bed, Holly could see very little.

They were in the room that Corinne referred to as her 'little mobile dungeon'. It was a smaller caravan than the one she used for accommodation, and those members of staff who didn't know its true purpose believed that she stored her circus props there. Holly had only been with the fairground for a day, but she already knew that the mobile dungeon wasn't used for anything as mundane as storage. She tried to shut the thought from her mind, daring to study her surroundings. Aside from the bed she was tied to, there was little in the way of furnishings. The windows were sealed shut for some reason she couldn't begin to imagine. A cupboard near the foot of the bed seemed virtually redundant, save for the dusty CD player on its flat top. A handful of cracked CD boxes were scattered beside the black music box; one of them had been used as a coaster for an empty wine glass.

Holly took a tentative glance at the drab magnolia walls, then turned her attention back to the master.

Corinne seemed in a worse mood than ever and had sent Chelsea on an errand. Holly had no idea what the submissive was doing, but, as with Corinne's bad mood, she suspected it had something to do with Georgia and the circus's ailing finances.

173

Corinne had moved to a cupboard beneath the bedroom's dressing table. Raising her head slightly, Holly watched her open a door and reach for the keys at her waist. She held her breath when she caught a glimpse of the large steel safe behind the door. It didn't take much imagination to realise how much punishment she would receive for watching the woman in this way.

Seeing Corinne's head begin to move, she lay her head quickly back down on the bed. Aware that some movement might have been noticed, she made a pretence of pulling against her restraints.

'You're tied securely,' Corinne murmured, turning her attention back to the safe. 'Keep fighting it and I'll make you suffer.'

Holly raised her head again, realising that Corinne's interest was focused back on the safe. From over her shoulder, she could see the safe door swing slowly open. When she glimpsed the contents, it was difficult to suppress a gasp of surprise. She noted the familiar bunch of keys hanging from the keyhole and tried to stop herself from grinning. After spending the last day and a half wondering why the bunch was so important to Corinne, the secret was now revealed. Inside, beneath a shelf containing dusty papers, Holly could see her own skirt and blouse. They were tied in a loose bundle and she saw a handful of notes protruding from a loose corner of the package.

Excitedly, she realised she was looking at the possessions that had been stolen from her. She didn't care about the skirt and blouse. They were only clothes and now that she had other garments they were relatively unimportant. But the money was a different matter.

Corinne placed a neatly bound wad of notes on the shelf, beside Holly's possessions. As soon as she had finished, she started to close the safe door.

Holly lay back on the bed, as though she had never moved position.

Fastening the keys back on her belt, Corinne turned to her and smiled. 'You were demanding I return your things to you earlier,' she said thickly. 'If I remember correctly, you said you'd do anything to get them back. Would you care to prove that?'

Holly swallowed nervously. The tantalising glimpse of her possessions could have been calculated to have this effect on her, she thought cynically. Knowingly or otherwise, Corinne had allowed her to see the things she so desperately craved. Now that they had been snatched away from her view, Holly felt an irresistible impulse to yield. She was prepared to do anything to get her property back and she realised that Corinne knew this.

A sound to her right caught Holly's attention. She turned and saw that Chelsea had returned from the errand she had been sent on.

Corinne glanced at her. 'Did you put the ticket on the table, where I told you?'

As Holly watched, Chelsea nodded. She was holding a pair of toffee apples in one outstretched hand. On her face she wore a hesitant expression, as though she expected to be punished even though she had carried out the instructions perfectly.

Corinne snatched one of the toffee apples from Chelsea's hand and glared at her sullenly. 'You've surprised me,' she admitted. 'I didn't think you had the wit to do as you were told.'

Chelsea said nothing. She studied the caravan floor meekly.

'As a reward,' Corinne went on, 'you can eat that toffee apple while you watch Holly enjoying hers.'

Holly frowned. When she had told Corinne that she would do anything to get her possessions back, the last thing she had expected was to be tied to a bed and force-fed confectionery. She watched Corinne turn to

175

smile at her, brandishing the toffee apple as though it were a weapon. A wicked smile split her lips. Her gaze was fixed on the cleft between Holly's legs.

In that instant, Holly realised exactly what was about to happen. It had been facile to think that the woman was simply going to make her eat the apple. Perhaps she did intend that to happen at some point, but Holly knew it wouldn't be the first thing to occur. She struggled against her restraints frenziedly, trying to pull away from the brandished sweet. The bulbous apple was coated with a glass-like shell of smoky-brown toffee. As it neared her, its broad width gleamed dully in the muted light of the caravan.

Corinne pushed the smooth round apple against the lips of Holly's sex. Flashing her wicked eyes on Holly, she said softly, 'You'll let me do anything if I give you back your possessions. Is that right?'

Valiantly, Holly tried not to look at the safe behind the woman. She didn't want to let Corinne know that she was aware of her secret. Her heart was beating fast. The straps on her ankles and wrists were biting into her flesh as her body tried to pull free. Unable to meet the challenge of the woman's stare, Holly glanced down at the keys on Corinne's belt. Staring at them, she felt her confidence return. 'That's what I said,' she confirmed. 'Whatever you want.'

Corinne's wicked grin broadened. She pushed the toffee apple slowly forward.

Holly drew a startled breath. The glassy-smooth dome of the apple pressed firmly against the lips of her sex. The pressure against the throbbing pulse of her clit forced a shiver of excitement to steal over her. It seemed obvious that the apple was too large an object to be used as a dildo. However, she could see a determined glint sparking in the back of Corinne's eye.

'I've always wanted to try doing this,' Corinne whispered, confirming Holly's worst fears. 'Do you think this tight little hole of yours can manage all this apple?'

Holly bit back a scream of refusal, snatching gasps of breath as the fear washed over her. The shiny apple pushed hard against her and she felt her pussy lips respond excitedly to the unbidden threat of intrusion. The sensitive flesh of her labia was stretched wider than she had ever felt it stretched before. She moaned softly, unable to remain silent any longer.

'You look like you need exciting first,' Corinne observed, moving back and taking the apple away.

Holly breathed a deep sigh of relief, thankful for the moment's reprieve. She watched as Corinne snapped her fingers and summoned Chelsea. 'Make her good and wet,' Corinne barked. 'I want to see this sliding all the way up her, and I'll punish the pair of you if I don't see it.'

As Chelsea climbed on the bed and crawled towards her, Holly tried not to think about what lay ahead. Even if she had wanted to, she wouldn't have been able to escape the woman's intrusive tongue as it slid against the lips of her sex. Chelsea ran her tongue against the glistening lips of Holly's labia, teasing the tip purposefully against the pulsing nub of her clitoris. Holly realised that her own moan hadn't been a sound of desperation. She had made the noise with the knowledge that Corinne would get to witness that long-sought-after spectacle. Already Chelsea's tongue was exciting her enough to set the inner walls of her sex quivering. She knew it would only take a few moments more before her sex was wet enough to accept anything – even the toffee apple.

As though she had read Holly's mind, Corinne laughed darkly.

Holly glanced up at the woman and watched her lick the glassy toffee with her broad, wet tongue. Rudely, she pushed Chelsea out of the way and pushed the apple back between Holly's legs.

This time her determination seemed more resolute, her deliberate intention made clear in the forceful pressure she applied. Holly could feel her pussy lips spreading wide to accommodate the bulbous fruit. She stared at Corinne, wide-eyed and breathless as the impending threat of intrusion snatched the air from her lungs. Her pussy lips had never been spread so wide and she felt certain that her body wasn't built for something like this. Every sensitive nerve ending in the lips of her sex screamed in absolute protestation. Her body was coated with a thin film of sweat and she realised her heart was racing faster than ever.

Staring into Corinne's eyes, she saw the woman's smile widen.

Her pussy felt as though it had been stretched to its limit, the flesh between her legs shrieking with diabolical ecstasy. And in the same instant, she felt the toffee apple push firmly into the dark velvety depths of her sex.

The orgasm hit her like a fist.

Holly screamed with elation as the pain blended seamlessly with the euphoria. She tried to sit up on the bed, her body wanting to double over with the force of her pleasure. The restraints on her wrists and ankles held her in place and she struggled against them with her eyes squeezed tightly shut.

As the waves of pleasure began to subside, she became aware of Corinne's soft laughter. Numbly, she realised the sound was mixed with her own. Unable to contemplate the prospect of any more pleasure, she started to protest as the woman pushed the toffee apple deeper inside her.

'Too much,' she whispered. The words were so ragged they were almost indecipherable. 'No more. Please,' she begged.

Corinne ignored her. She pushed deeper into Holly, forcing the toffee apple to slide and stretch the inner walls of her sex just as it had the outer lips. Holly's sex was burning with the heat of her arousal. Because of this she could feel the toffee melting from the apple. The glass-like shell had softened to a thick, viscous smear that helped to lubricate the inner walls of her sex.

Arching her back, Holly fell against the bed, screaming words of praise and hatred in the same breath. She rolled her head from side to side, hating the bonds that held her there and loving them in the same instant. If the bonds hadn't been holding her, she knew she would have pulled away from Corinne and refused to accept any more of this brutal pleasuring. Because of those restraints, she was being forced to endure the most explicit delight she had ever encountered. A rush of joy swept through her, only to be replaced by another cataclysmic wave of ecstasy.

'Are you enjoying your toffee apple?' Corinne asked.

Holly's pleasure was complete, and she heard Corinne's voice as though she were speaking from miles away. She nodded, a dazed smile twisted her lips, and heard herself breathing the words, 'Yes, master.'

Corinne moved quickly. She pushed the toffee apple a fraction deeper, forcing a squeal from Holly. Then, with a swift flick of her wrist, she pulled it out.

In an instant, Holly felt delight and dismay wash over her in equal measures. The lips of her sex were stretched impossibly wide once again as the apple slid from her warmth. The thick lubrication of the melted toffee helped it slide easily from her pussy. The joy of the discomfort was tempered by the feeling of emptiness, as the toffee apple's swift exit left her inner muscles feeling hollow and wanting. She could feel a sullen frown forcing her jaw to drop and she turned the hurt expression on Corinne.

Smiling, Corinne leant forward. She placed three fingers against the lips of Holly's sex and teased her clitoris. Pushing the toffee apple into Holly's face, she whispered, 'If you're enjoying this so much, you can eat it.'

Holly didn't hesitate to obey. She could smell the musky fragrance of her own sex coating the sticky toffee. Greedily, she pushed her tongue forward. Aware that Corinne was grinning at her, she opened her mouth and bit through the moist, glassy shell. The flavour of her own sex and the sweetness of the toffee were a cloying combination, but she ate the apple dutifully. As her mouth stretched wide to bite it, she felt a distant thrill. It seemed incredible to think that something so broad had managed to fit inside her tight little pussy. The memory of that forceful entry was still fresh enough to hurt, but the recollection of pain brought with it a dirty pleasure that made it more than worthwhile.

Swallowing pieces of pussy-scented toffee apple, she shivered uncontrollably.

Corinne continued to smile at her, holding the slender stick of the apple as Holly bit chunks from it. 'You like that flavour?'

Holly nodded in reply, unable to think of words that would express her enjoyment of the flavour. She could tell by the woman's voice that she intended to do something else, but she no longer cared whether she was giving the right or wrong answer. Her appetite for pleasure was stronger than she could ever have anticipated. She needed to suffer more of Corinne's peculiar treatment.

Corinne snapped her fingers, summoning Chelsea back to her side.

Holly glanced up from the bed as her lips worked greedily on the apple. She could see that Chelsea was now naked and her hand appeared to have been busily working at the wet lips between her legs – the tips of her fingers glistened with the unmistakable dew of pussy juice. In the other hand, she held the untouched toffee apple Corinne had allowed her to keep.

Corinne snatched the apple away and pushed Chelsea down. She fell next to Holly on the bed with a moan of protest.

Holly tried to ignore the excitement that the woman's body gave her. Tied to the bed and unable to properly join in with the others, every inch of her flesh had become ultra-responsive. The threat of another orgasm quickly welled within her. Her resistance wasn't helped by the tentative pressure of Chelsea's sticky fingers against her nipple.

Corinne slapped Chelsea hard across the face. 'Untie her,' she growled.

Chelsea shifted suddenly, obeying Corinne as soon as the words were spoken.

Holly felt a brief moment's regret as the exquisite pressure of the woman's body was snatched away. The sadness was short-lived as she realised that her hands were being untied. The ache in her arms, legs and back had been forgotten as the waves of pleasure washed over her. But now, on the brink of release, she felt each torturous twinge in her body.

Trying to dismiss the discomfort, she glanced at the woman above her. Chelsea held her gorgeous nudity tantalisingly close to Holly's face. One pale pink nipple brushed at her cheek as the woman worked on the wrist straps.

Squirming from side to side, Holly tried to resist the urge to kiss the nub. The impulse was sudden and strong; the need to feel that tiny pulse of pleasure between her lips so fierce that Holly knew she couldn't take the torment a moment longer. Unwittingly, she pushed her tongue out and flicked the tip at the woman's nipple.

Chelsea groaned excitedly, pausing as she worked on the restraints.

Holly lifted her head higher and placed her mouth around the peak of the inviting orb. She sucked gently, thrilling to the giggling sounds of excitement made by the woman above her.

A slap struck hard against her leg.

Holly groaned as the explosion of pain burnt her flesh

and she quickly lay back on the bed. She didn't need to be told that she had been acting without Corinne's permission. Already aware of the rules of this caravan, she knew she should have expected nothing more than such sharp, swift punishment.

It came as no surprise when she heard an apology tumbling from her lips. Distantly, she realised she had already learnt the basic rules of being Corinne's submissive. It was a sickening realisation and she fervently hoped that a little of her own willpower remained.

After freeing Holly's hands, Chelsea turned to release her ankles.

Again, Holly was painfully aware of the woman above her. The cleft of her sex, glistening wetly with the spilt juices of her arousal, begged to be kissed. Able to move, Holly fought the irresistible impulse to push her mouth against the cleft and tongue the sweet-scented musk. Her leg was still stinging from the slap she had been given and Holly knew better than to incur Corinne's wrath again.

Chelsea pushed herself back as she moved to work on the last restraint. The lips of her sex were held unnervingly close to Holly's face.

Unable to resist the urge any longer, Holly pushed her face forward and buried her tongue against the woman. Her nostrils and mouth were filled with the heady scent of Chelsea's pussy juice and she relished the ambrosial taste.

Chelsea squealed excitedly.

Holly pressed her face hard against the woman's sex, pushing her tongue firmly inside. She could feel her own excitement mount as she tasted the eager flavour of Chelsea's sex. It seemed unreal to be extracting such enjoyment from this, but Holly could feel the thrill of climax building swiftly inside her.

A second explosion of pain on her inner thigh was

enough to remind Holly of Corinne's rules. Without another thought she moved her mouth away and lay back on the bed.

Chelsea finished unfastening her restraints and Corinne barked a command for the pair of them to switch places.

Holly swiftly tied the submissive with the same restraints that had held her only moments earlier. Glancing down at Chelsea's nubile feminine form, Holly tried to ignore the feelings of excitement she was experiencing. It was a difficult impulse to suppress. Chelsea's naked body looked so inviting that Holly longed to use her.

When Corinne pushed her abruptly to one side, Holly realised miserably that this had never been an option.

'Lick my hole while I fuck her,' Corinne snapped abruptly. She still held a toffee apple in one hand and her intention was painfully obvious. Chelsea was staring at her with a wide-eyed refusal of the plan but Corinne ignored her. She turned a threatening glare on Holly and said, 'Make sure you do it well.' The malice in her words was unmistakable.

Holly lay down on the bed as Corinne knelt above Chelsea. She pushed her head between the woman's legs, using her mouth on the wet lips of Corinne's sex. Staring up, she could see the silver sparkle of Corinne's keys.

As her tongue worked against the slippery flesh, and her mouth filled with the syrupy sweet juice, Holly stroked her fingers against Corinne's thighs.

'That's good,' Corinne murmured.

Holly smiled softly to herself. Slowly, she moved her fingers dangerously close to the key's dog-leash fastener.

Georgia stepped into the caravan's lounge, not sure whether the shivers that racked her body were caused by the cool night or the remnants of the joy she had just

183

discovered. Tomorrow she knew they would talk, and she supposed she ought to think about that before going to sleep. But her mind was still a maelstrom of hedonistic pleasure, and she couldn't find the enthusiasm to think about the future after experiencing such bliss. She glanced at a card on the lounge table, and wondered if Curtis had left it there for her.

When she read the printed words on the front she realised it was a circus ticket. She smiled, finding herself looking forward to the simple pleasure of the circus. Her thoughts turned to the roller-coaster she had been watching earlier and she grinned ruefully at her own cynicism. This evening, her roller-coaster had just taken her to new, unimagined heights. She felt certain that this time it wasn't going to plummet downward, as it had always done in the past.

Clutching the circus ticket close to her chest, oblivious to the fact that Chelsea had left it there on Corinne's instructions, Georgia relished the feeling that things were finally going right.

Nine

Holly glared at the cup of coffee as though it were the source of all her problems. A dark frown furrowed her brow and her lips were set in a cold, determined line.

'Corinne,' Georgia said abruptly.

Holly glanced up, treating the blonde woman to an antagonistic expression. ''Scuse me?'

Georgia grinned into her threatening glare. 'I said "Corinne". I was guessing why you looked so miserable, and she's the main reason for anyone in this fairground being unhappy.'

Holly exercised a tight, humourless smile and returned her attention to the mug of coffee. 'Corinne's a fucking bitch,' she murmured.

Georgia nodded. 'You're not the first person to voice that sentiment.'

For an instant, Holly considered telling Georgia about the torturous night she had just endured. The marks on the cheeks of her arse were raised and they burnt whenever she brushed against them. Following Corinne's trick with the toffee apple, Holly could still feel a tingle of discomfort in her pussy lips. Her arms ached from the bondage and her neck felt stiff from the position Corinne had kept her in afterwards. Corinne hadn't allowed her to leave until the early hours of the morning and now Holly felt drained, exhausted and used. Worse than that, she still hadn't had her possessions returned.

At the beginning of the evening, Corinne had made a veiled promised to return Holly's things if she did as she was told. By the time Holly was eventually dismissed from the caravan, the woman seemed to have forgotten that promise. When Holly had boldly asked about them she had been treated to a slap across the face and the threat of more punishment.

Holly was tempted to tell all these things to Georgia, but she didn't. The remnants of a tension headache were making themselves known to her as she sipped her morning coffee and none of these memories were helping.

She considered telling Georgia about Corinne's threat of retribution. The ringmaster was determined to keep her circus going at all costs. On learning Chelsea's piece of gossip, Corinne believed that Georgia was equally determined to close her down. Her obvious rage was only tempered by her plans for revenge, and Holly felt certain they could prove perilous for Georgia.

But still she remained silent.

She had other plans. Fondling the stolen key in her pocket, Holly allowed a bitter smile to twist her lips. Because of Corinne's behaviour, she was tempted to clean the bitch's safe out. She was already intent on reclaiming her property now that she had the means. She could do that little bit extra without so much as a single qualm. By the time Holly had finished with the safe, Corinne's revenge on Georgia would be the least of her worries.

'Do you want to talk about it?' Georgia asked, settling herself beside Holly at the breakfast table. She picked up a slice of toast and bit delicately at one corner.

Holly shook her head. She didn't want to talk – she wanted to make her move. It was only the thought of Corinne still using the mobile little dungeon that stopped her. Thinking logically, Holly knew she would have to plan to make her move during the evening's performance of the circus. It was the only time when she could be guaranteed that Corinne wouldn't suddenly appear.

'What about money?' Georgia said suddenly. 'I can give you a little and you'd be able to make a break from here. Would that help you?'

For the first time, Holly glanced up from her coffee and studied the woman properly. She had been so lost in her own world of bitter revenge and reprisals that she hadn't even noticed how Georgia was dressed. Her ample breasts were threatening to burst over the top of a tight ivory basque. The lacy frills of the garment not only accentuated her femininity but also hinted at the darker flesh of the barely concealed areolae.

Wishing that her eyes weren't drawn to the sight, Holly tried to snatch her gaze away from the ardent thrust of Georgia's nipples. They were pressing against the stiff lace just below the neckline of her basque. Her obvious arousal seemed so wholly inappropriate that Holly wondered if she had missed something.

Unable to stop herself, she glanced beneath the table and took a look at Georgia's legs. Although they were cast in shadows, she realised the stockings were the same colour as the basque. She also realised she was staring at the fluffy thatch of Georgia's naked pubic triangle.

Startled by the sight of the woman's solicitous appearance, Holly straightened up and fixed Georgia with a puzzled frown. She wanted to ask her why she was dressed like that, then realised it was none of her business. Remembering she had just been offered money, Holly tried to focus her thoughts on that. 'What did you just say?'

Georgia repeated the offer, grinning inanely. She appeared completely at ease and unembarrassed by the way she was dressed. Looking at her faraway smile, Holly could have believed she started every morning dressed like this.

187

'I asked if some money would help,' Georgia reiterated. 'I've got a couple of hundred in my purse. Would that be enough to help you get away from Corinne?'

Holly studied her with a suspicious frown. 'Why would you do that for me?' Her pale brown eyes had narrowed into untrusting slits. 'Why are you offering me money? Is this some sort of trap?'

Georgia shook her head. 'I'm not trying to trap you. I'm trying to help,' she said quietly. 'I don't like seeing anyone having to suffer and if I can . . .'

'But you're offering me your own money,' Holly broke in. 'Why would you do that? You barely know me.'

Again, Georgia shrugged. 'I know you're getting it pretty shitty at the moment and no one deserves what you're going through.' She reached for her bag from a nearby chair and withdrew her purse. The movement caused one nipple to force its way above the lacy fabric of her basque.

Holly turned her gaze deliberately away from the sight. There were enough complications in her life at the moment and she didn't need to add to them with lascivious thoughts about Georgia. The woman was the closest thing to a friend Holly had known in a long time and she didn't want to spoil that relationship by making a pass at her.

She had rarely found herself having such thoughts about another woman before, but Georgia appeared so fresh and enticing it was difficult not to. The eager thrust of her nipple above the ivory basque inspired an excitement in Holly so poignant that she felt uncomfortable. Suddenly, she found herself wondering what it would be like to take the nipple between her lips and tease the tip of it with her tongue. Her body still ached from the previous night and the thought of indulging in any sort of lovemaking was unsettling. She shut the erotic thoughts from her mind with a deliberate effort and tried to concentrate on the wad of notes Georgia was retrieving from her purse.

As Holly watched, Georgia counted a crisp pile of tens from her purse, emptying it completely.

'I don't really need any money while I'm here,' Georgia explained. 'And if I do, I can get Curtis to drop me near a cashpoint machine.'

Holly glared at her. All thoughts of sexual excitement were suddenly gone from her mind. 'I don't want your money,' she said brusquely.

Georgia shrugged, unoffended. She placed the money on the table next to her empty purse. 'I'll leave it there for now, in case you change your mind,' she explained patiently. Reaching back into the purse, she removed a small strip of card. Although Holly wasn't watching closely, she was distantly reminded of the used circus tickets she had seen fluttering around the fairground.

'I won't be changing my mind,' Holly assured her. She spoke with her gaze fixed on the money.

'Whatever,' Georgia said simply. 'It's there if you need it. I'm sure it will still be there if you don't.' She eased herself from her chair and snatched a second slice of toast from the rack.

Holly tried not to look at the offered glimpse of Georgia's bare sex. She turned her eyes deliberately away, aware that the woman was shrugging her arms into the sleeves of a full-length raincoat. When she felt confident that the distraction of Georgia's body was no longer on view, Holly turned back to face her.

Fastening the belt on her coat, Georgia grinned. 'If I see you later, we can talk some more then. If I don't, then good luck.'

Frowning, Holly watched the woman step cheerfully from the caravan. As soon as the van door was closed, she snatched the wad of notes from the table and leafed through them with a scrupulous eye for detail. The paper seemed the correct weight and thickness; the watermarks and security strips were all present and intact and she could discern no visible markings on any of the notes. To her well-trained eye, she could see no obvious trick. Leafing through the tens, she felt certain that this wasn't a set-up or trap instigated by Corinne.

Quickly, she pushed the cash back on the table. The idea of taking Georgia's money was unthinkable. She had refused the offer of a reward the previous evening when she had taken the wallet belonging to the captain. Back then the idea had seemed worse than stealing. Taking what Georgia offered seemed even worse than that.

She slid from her chair and went to the caravan window, determined to see where Georgia was heading. There was no way on earth she was going to take the money from her. Holly intended to get her own money back, and possibly take enough to make Corinne suffer. But that was all. She had stopped thieving for ever now, and she was also determined that she wasn't going to live off other people's charity. As though she were trying to prove her own resolve on this matter, Holly pushed her hand into her pocket and squeezed the comforting weight of the key she had stolen.

Staring through the caravan window, she watched Georgia walking cheerfully through the rows of caravans. It was obvious the woman was in more than just a good mood. Holly would have been able to guess that much even if she hadn't seen and spoken to her that morning. But all the time she kept wondering why.

What could there possibly be about the fairground to make someone so happy? Holly asked herself. She tried to work out an answer but nothing sprang to mind.

Watching Georgia step buoyantly through the vans, she was mesmerised by the swing of her handbag as it bounced lightly to and fro with each step. Her head was held back and she stared defiantly up at the clear blue sky. Her lips were pursed into an expression that went beyond a smile.

'I'll bet she's whistling,' Holly decided, with rueful cynicism. Closing her eyes, she tried to rid herself of the mental image of Georgia standing virtually naked beside her in the caravan. It was too arousing a picture for her to allow herself to dwell on it.

She took a final glance at the woman's back and shook her head, wondering what could cause someone to be so intolerably bloody happy.

It was almost as though Georgia was in love.

'So this was your big secret,' Georgia murmured.

Curtis stood before her dressed only in a basque, panties and stockings. He looked remarkably good as a woman. His chest was broad, but not so much that it looked ridiculous in the tight confines of the ivory silk basque. His slender waist was accentuated by his narrow, feminine hips.

Georgia caught herself admiring his long shapely legs, encased in ivory white stockings that matched his basque and panties perfectly. She could see the eager bulge of his erection pressing at the front of his panties, but that was the only real giveaway as to his true gender. Aside from the tell-tale thrust of his shaft, she would have defied anyone to guess that he was a man.

'My big secret,' he grinned. He studied her with a peculiar expression in his eyes. Reaching a hesitant hand towards her shoulder, he asked, 'Are you shocked?'

Georgia shrugged the raincoat from her shoulders and revealed herself to him. Her ivory basque and matching stockings were identical to the ones he wore. 'Look at us,' she grinned. 'We're a matching pair.' She took a step closer to him, pressing her body against his. With tentative lips, she placed a delicate kiss against his cheek. 'Why do you ask if I'm shocked?' she asked.

His grin had a trace of embarrassment in it. 'You seemed pretty shocked yesterday,' he reminded her.

She had the good grace to blush. 'Yesterday I was surprised,' she admitted. 'Surprised, and a little bit annoyed when I saw that you had Chelsea in here.'

He nodded his understanding. 'You never did say why you'd come looking for me.'

Georgia remembered her discovery about the circus's poor finances and realised she hadn't mentioned them to Curtis. She shook her head and dismissed the topic, knowing it would spoil his mood. The circus's finances were relatively important but she didn't believe they needed to be tackled at this particular moment. 'Just business,' she told him, trying to inject a firm tone of reassurance into her voice. 'It was nothing that won't wait a while longer. We can talk about it later.' Tracing a finger down his chest, she whispered, 'We have other things to do first, don't we?'

The bulge at the front of his panties twitched purposefully. With a delicate finger, he reached out and caressed the soft flesh of her neck.

Georgia sighed. The tenderness of his touch was soft and subtle. His fingers seemed to excite an electric charge that made her body shiver with its desperate need for him. Slowly and almost hesitantly, he moved his fingers towards her breast.

She was struck by the marked contrast between this delicate, sensitive creature before her and the brutal lover who had buggered her the night before. It didn't seem like the same man, and in a way she supposed it wasn't. During normal day-to-day work at the fairground, Curtis needed to be hard, ruthless and uncompromising. It was a way to deal with those around him and a way to stay on top and in control.

But this, she thought, studying his delectable, slender figure, this was an outlet for his more sensitive, caring side. The indulgence of his feminine nature was a luxury he had allowed himself in his search for true happiness. Judging by the way his erection pushed so fiercely at the front of his ivory white panties, she felt certain that he had no more searching to do. She remembered the way he had spoken to her in the hall of mirrors, asking her about what she saw reflected in the glass. The memory brought a smile to her lips as she realised he had been close to telling her his secret then. She had only been seeing the reflection of his physical form; she hadn't seen the identity he so desperately aspired to.

Georgia stroked the bulge that strained at the front of his panties and rocked her bare crotch against his stocking-clad leg. The pulse of her arousal was beating forcefully and she longed for Curtis to satisfy her craving. Thinking about the contrast between this man and the lover she had known him as previously, she wondered if it would be so great a difference. It seemed ridiculous to think of him as a different person, but studying his feminine figure and stylish lingerie she could see no trace of the rough-and-ready Curtis she had known before.

Puzzled by his hesitant touch, she pressed her mouth over his and kissed him.

His response was instantaneous. He held her lightly in his arms, his hands gently stroking her waist and caressing her hips.

'You don't seem as willing to take control today,' she observed.

He smiled demurely. 'Why don't you try being the dominant one?' he suggested. Grinning at her, he added, 'I always got the impression that you liked to get your own way.'

Georgia considered the idea before nodding her agreement. 'If that's the way you want it,' she told him firmly, 'get down on your knees.' For a moment, she thought he was going to refuse. In the past they had tried role-playing games but those had always involved Curtis taking the lead. This was so totally different that Georgia wasn't sure how he would respond. She studied his dark eyes, surprised to see his smile widen as he watched her.

With his gaze fixed on hers, Curtis lowered himself to his knees.

She stared down at him, amazed by the thrill of excitement his willing submission inspired. The pulse of her arousal had been beating like a drum before. Now it thumped like the backing beat on the fairground's waltzers.

Reaching her fingers down to the lips of her pussy, she spread them wide. The tip of one finger accidentally brushed against the pulsing nub of her clit and she was surprised by the explosion her touch created. Forcing herself to hold the lips of her sex open, she said firmly, 'Lick my hole, Curtis.'

He moved slowly forward on his knees and bent his head awkwardly against her. His hands, still tender and gentle, cupped the cheeks of her backside. Caring fingers caressed the moon-like orbs of her arse as he nuzzled his tongue against the wetness of her sex.

Georgia felt a shiver of ecstasy rack her body. She couldn't tell if it was caused by Curtis's tongue or her power over him. Whatever the source, she couldn't deny the effect.

His tongue slid wetly against the heated lips of her sex. Rather than concentrating on the pulsing tip of her clit, he teased his tongue against the juicy folds of flesh, exciting every pore of her labia as he lapped at her hole.

Georgia kept the fingers of one hand against the glistening lips of her pussy. He was quickly licking her into a frenzy and she was determined to enjoy every second. Using a gentle rocking motion, she swayed her hips backward and forward, making Curtis work harder in order to please her. With her other hand, she began to toy with the tingling tips of her nipples. Shockwaves of pleasure rippled through her as she squeezed roughly on the hard nubs.

Although his hands were cupping and caressing her buttocks, he made no attempt to hold her still. She continued to rock and sway, guiding her pussy away from him, then forcing the delicate lips against his nose and tongue so he could satisfy her ferocious appetite. Rather than holding her steady, or overpowering her with his capable strength, he let her take command of where and how he tongued her.

'Enough,' Georgia said, smiling down into Curtis's upturned face.

His lower lip jutted forward in a soft pout. She could see the shimmer of her own wetness coating the lower part of his face. The expectant expression in his dark eyes reminded her that she was in control.

'Lie down,' she told him stiffly.

He obeyed instantly.

Grinning broadly, Georgia knelt to the floor and straddled his prone body. The basque had pulled down slightly and she could see the dark brown circles of his areolae. Leaning forward, she placed her mouth over one tiny, erect nipple and sucked hard.

Curtis released a shuddering sigh.

Encouraged by the response, Georgia dared to let her teeth nibble playfully against him.

Unable to deal with the exquisite torture she was administering, he rolled his head from side to side, as though he were trying to deny himself the pleasure.

Georgia moved her mouth away. She considered teasing his other nipple with the same brand of punishing pleasure she had just been using. It was only the eager pulse of her own urgency that stopped her. His tongue had performed beautifully against her sex and the heat of her arousal was so fantastic she couldn't tolerate it a moment longer.

She reached for his panties and began to pull them down. As she slid the garment from his body, her hands traversed the cool silk of his stocking-clad legs. She allowed the tips of her fingers to brush against him. An electric frisson tingled beneath her fingertips as she slid the panties down. She moved them slowly, relishing the electric charge as she pushed his feminine underwear over his knees, along his calves and past the heels of his ivory stilettos.

The hunger of his erection had forced his cock to stand up and beg. Staring at it, Georgia licked her lips lasciviously. She stroked a warm palm against the throbbing length of flesh and guided it towards her sex. With the cock still in her hand, she teased the swollen end against the moisture of her pussy lips.

As Curtis groaned, she heard herself laughing. It would be nice to prolong his enjoyment, she thought wickedly. He was extracting a good deal of pleasure from the thought of having his cock inside her, and her deliberate teasing was only adding to his torment. But her own needs were increasing at a maniacal rate and she was getting no satisfaction from the delicate pressure of his erection against her outer lips. She needed to feel him inside her and because she was in control, nothing was going to stop her.

She rubbed the tip against her exposed sex one last time, coating her pussy lips with his pre-come. Finally she placed his cock at the entrance to her hole and with one leisurely movement, lowered herself on to him. Georgia felt his length slide purposefully into her. The sensations of fullness and satisfaction were so powerful that she could feel a rush of adrenaline coursing through her body.

He stared up at her, a grimace of joy twisting his lips.

Aware that he was resisting the urge to come, Georgia grinned down at him. She began to raise herself from him slowly, enjoying the slow egress of his cock from her pussy lips. When she felt the tip of his shaft touching the tingling folds of her outer labia, she lowered herself quickly back on to him.

They cried out together, unmindful of the noise their enjoyment was causing.

Georgia continued to ride him in the same fashion, amazed that he was fighting so well against the threat of his climax. Staring down at his feminine body, she felt a thrill of excitement. He looked so pretty that it was just like making love to another woman.

The memory of what she and Chelsea had enjoyed yesterday seemed irrelevant. Then she had been allowing the submissive woman to satisfy her needs, and, because it happened in those circumstances, she didn't consider it to be important. The earlier memory of her bondage, and the unknown woman in the dark, didn't even occur to her. The mental scars of that ordeal were almost healed and she was too involved with the moment to even contemplate trying to reopen them.

Placing a hand behind herself, she reached down to his balls and kneaded them gently with the tips of her fingers. The sac was so tight she could feel he was on the verge of exploding. How he had managed to hold off for this long was a mystery. The excitement of his underwear and the thrill of their lovemaking should have sent him beyond the point of no return. 'You're holding back quite well, aren't you?' she whispered.

His smile was tinged with the bitterness of effort. 'I'm waiting for your permission to come,' he told her.

Georgia smiled broadly, intrigued by the concept. 'You won't come until I tell you to?' she confirmed.

Gritting his teeth, he nodded bravely and said, 'I'm trying not to.'

She eased herself off him and turned around so that she was facing his legs. His words seemed like a challenge and for a moment she couldn't decide how best to deal with it. At first, she contemplated pushing the lips of her sex against his face and sucking greedily on his cock. Georgia knew she would be able to force him to come that way, but the situation seemed to merit something more than that.

His length stood proudly before her and she could see the silver sparkle of her pussy juice slickly coating him. The desire to taste him was strong, but she reminded herself that there would be plenty of time for that later.

Straddling him again, she rubbed the swollen end of his length against her pussy lips three times before easing him into her velvety warmth. As before, she lowered herself quickly on to his rampant shaft, squealing with pleasure as he filled her.

She heard no sound from behind, and wondered if he was still struggling to contain his joy. Glancing over her shoulder, she saw the tortured expression of resistance straining his face. His obvious torment brought a broad smile to her lips.

In this position her pussy seemed fuller than ever. Moving on to her haunches, she eased herself up from him, then lowered herself quickly back down.

This time, Curtis allowed himself the indulgence of a soft moan.

Georgia barely heard the whispered sigh, lost in a world of euphoria as her pussy was filled with his cock. It was the second climax to wash over her in as many minutes and she felt her inner muscles tremble with joy. She realised that there was only one thing she now needed, to make her pleasure complete. The thrill of having Curtis explode inside her was going to be the perfect end to this morning's entertainment.

Briefly she considered telling him that he could come, but that seemed too easy.

To extract full enjoyment from the moment, Georgia knew that she had to make him come against his will.

She sat quickly on him again.

Curtis groaned, but continued to fight against the release of his orgasm.

Moving her hand beneath his balls, Georgia traced the tip of one finger against the sensitive flesh of his anus. She could feel his cock stiffen inside her and she felt the body beneath her turn hard with concentrated resistance.

'No,' Curtis groaned. The sound seemed to be torn from his lungs.

Georgia slipped the tip of her finger inside him. His puckered rim resisted at first, the tightly clenched muscles allowing her no purchase. But with a firm, forward thrust she penetrated him.

With a howl, Curtis bucked his hips forward.

Georgia could feel the furious pulse of his climax, distantly aware that she was revelling in her own orgasm. Her body was ablaze with the fire of the climax that tore at every nerve ending.

Together their cries of fulfilment echoed against the caravan walls and beyond.

Impatient as ever, Holly hid behind the caravan. She was watching the door of Corinne's little mobile dungeon, wondering if she had seen it move or if it was just her imagination.

Her natural instinct was to barge into the van, snatch the remainder of her possessions, and then run as fast as she could. But over the past two days she had learnt several lessons in the necessity of caution. If Corinne was there, Holly knew she wouldn't get far. Similarly, if Corinne had left Chelsea, or anyone for that matter, tied to the bed, they would surely raise the alarm before she could make her escape.

Holly felt sure she could put up a fairly good fight against someone of Corinne's skill, but she doubted she would be successful. The bitch wasn't simply athletic and powerful – she also had a penchant for causing people pain.

A movement glimpsed from the corner of her eye made Holly hold her breath. She felt sure she had seen something. Silently, she cursed the caravans. The slightest murmur of a breeze and the damned things shook as though they were hosting an acid-house party.

The need to get her money back was so strong she realised it was making her nervous. She knew it would be sensible to go back to the fairground and make her move this evening. Her hiding place, standing by the side of an adjacent caravan, wasn't the most secure spot, and she knew someone would eventually be bound to notice her.

Yet she was reluctant to let the mobile dungeon out of her sight. A caravan wasn't like a normal home, she reminded herself. With an ordinary house, you could feel safe that it wouldn't move away once you left it. With a caravan, it simply needed tying to the back of a car and it was off.

Not that Holly believed Corinne would take the caravan away, but the uncertainty niggled at her. It was a fairly safe bet that the vehicle wasn't going to move but Holly didn't gamble, even on safe bets. She was particularly loathe to gamble her four thousand pounds on the prospect.

Trying to take her mind away from the nerve-racking thoughts of her money, she considered the offer Georgia had made that morning. The woman had to be out of her mind to make such a proposition. The more Holly thought about it, the crazier she thought Georgia actually was. If the tables had been turned, Holly knew she wouldn't have been trying to give her own money to a relative stranger.

Casting her thoughts back to Georgia, she felt the peculiar sensation of arousal she had experienced earlier. In her mind's eye, she was struck by the vision of the blonde in her ivory basque. It was a daring outfit, made more adventurous by the fact that it was all she wore beneath her raincoat.

Remembering that, and the way Georgia had been acting with such a distinctive spring in her step, Holly wondered if the woman really was in love. It was an intriguing thought, and it distracted her from the worry of her vigil. She toyed idly with the question of who Georgia's lover might be. It was a ridiculous guessing game, but it kept her mind occupied and away from the worry of her possessions.

The sound of an opening door snatched her thoughts back to the moment's main priority. Glancing warily from her hiding place, Holly watched Corinne appear in the doorway. As usual the woman was glowering with unconcealed rage.

Corinne turned her head back into the caravan and called loudly, 'You'll bloody stay there until your first performance tonight, do you hear me?'

Holly felt a frown crease her brow as she glared at the woman. Whoever she was speaking to had obviously heard her. Half the fucking fairground could hear Corinne when she started shouting.

Corinne was still staring back into the caravan. 'Try and remember where you left them, you stupid little bitch,' Corinne shrieked. 'I have more important things to deal with tonight than you.' With an angry lurch, she stepped out of the caravan and slammed the door closed behind her.

For an instant, Holly thought she could hear the muffled sound of muted sobs, but she supposed that could have been her imagination. Once the door had slammed shut, she realised she could no longer hear the sound anyway. She slid behind the caravan and pushed herself to safety, out of Corinne's view.

Quickly she went over the woman's words in her mind, aware of each repercussion. There was no chance of her getting her things back until the circus started this evening. Even then, she would have to be careful; Corinne would come back to the dungeon during the intermission. But if there was someone in there now, Holly didn't dare try to make a move.

Miserably, she stared at the closed caravan door and began to wish the remainder of the day away. She wondered what the woman was looking for, thoughtfully stroking the stolen keys in her pocket as she tried to guess what it might be. It wasn't much of a distraction from her vigil outside the door, and eventually she turned her mind on to other, more tangible things.

The sooner the circus began this evening, the sooner she would be able to make her bid for freedom. Because the prize was so great, Holly realised the afternoon was going to be longer than ever.

Surprisingly, Georgia found herself thinking about the roller-coaster again.

The day had been going so well she should have guessed something like this was going to happen. The morning with Curtis had turned into an afternoon. Before she realised so much time had passed, the evening darkness had begun to fall outside the caravan. She had wanted to spend the rest of the night with him but he had work to do and Georgia felt weary after a day of relentless pleasure.

The idea of spending a relaxing night at the circus had seemed like the ideal tonic after such a brilliant day. She realised the evening would have been fun, if it hadn't turned out this way. Mentally, she could picture herself in a roller-coaster carriage hurtling downward at breakneck speed. She could feel the wind blowing through her hair as she plummeted purposefully towards the bottom of an endless descent.

The circus audience roared and cheered all around her. The noise of their laughter seemed inappropriate and unkind. She knew they were only enjoying the antics of the tumbling clowns but that thought did little to appease her terror. The miniature troupe of entertainers were making the audience laugh as Corinne tied Georgia to the knife-thrower's wheel.

'Do you want to know what happens to little sluts

who try and close my circus down?' Corinne growled menacingly. She could have bawled the words in the hearty euphoria of the circus ring and still the audience wouldn't have heard. Nevertheless she kept her voice low. Her black eyes glinted wickedly in the brilliant lights of the big top. 'If you don't know what happens, you ought to stick around for a while. You're about to find out how bad things can get.'

Georgia stared unhappily at her. She wanted to say she didn't know what Corinne was talking about but that would have been a lie. Chelsea was helping the ringmaster to fasten Georgia against the wheel. She kept her eyes held low as she worked on the clasps, making sure that she didn't have to meet the blonde woman's gaze.

Unable to blame Chelsea for repeating the gossip she had told her, Georgia ignored the woman. She had tried to ignore the clowns who had brought her out here as well. Initially she thought they had mistaken her for another member of the audience, rather than one of the fairground staff. When they had insisted on dragging her out of her seat she had gone with them, unwilling to cause a scene in front of a large, cheering audience.

As soon as they had started tugging her towards the knife-thrower's wheel, she had known something was wrong. But by then it was too late. She had seen Corinne bearing down on her with a ferocious expression blazing in her eyes. In that instant, Georgia had realised she was trapped.

'I thought you'd have more to say for yourself,' Corinne said coolly. She raised her hand and cupped the swell of Georgia's breast. It was a disturbingly intimate gesture and she was shocked to think that the woman dared to be so obvious in front of such a large audience. She supposed that the distraction of the clowns was enough to make Corinne's action go unnoticed, but that was just a passing thought.

More worrying was the sparkle of excitement that Corinne's touch inspired.

'Curtis won't be happy if he hears about you threatening me,' Georgia said quickly. 'You know bloody well that he'll . . . ouch!' Her exclamation came as Corinne tightened her grip on the hard nub of Georgia's nipple. The combination of pleasure and pain was so intense she couldn't stop herself from crying out.

Corinne was staring at her with a cold smile. She dropped her hand away from Georgia's breast and glanced questioningly at Chelsea. The dark-haired submissive nodded and stepped away from the wheel.

Corinne turned her gaze back to Georgia. 'You shouldn't have threatened me with Curtis,' she whispered quietly. Her words were clear beneath the hollow roar of laughter surrounding them. 'My hands might shake now,' Corinne explained, with an evil smile surfacing on her lips. 'And if my hands start shaking, you don't know what sort of trouble you might be in.' With a nasty laugh, she took a handful of blades from Chelsea, then turned her back on Georgia and began to walk away.

Georgia watched the woman move smoothly to the centre of the circus ring. As she watched, she was casting daggers of hatred at Connie's back with every flicker of her eyelid.

It didn't help that Corinne had such a beautiful body. Georgia's look of malice felt inappropriate, being hurled at someone so enticing. Corinne wore a pair of long dark stockings that went all the way up to the high-cut line of her silver, sequinned leotard. The split sides of her bright red ringmaster's costume revealed the gorgeous expanse of her lithe, muscular legs with each purposeful step.

Georgia groaned softly with mounting frustration. The manacles around her wrists and ankles were tight enough that she didn't bother struggling against them. It would have been a futile waste of energy.

A hushed silence had fallen over the circus audience. The clowns had hopped back into their comedy car and driven out of the ring. The lights dimmed around her and Georgia saw that both she and Corinne were held in the brilliant glare of two separate spotlights.

From the small orchestra, she heard the distant trill of a drum roll. The rapid beat of the timpani mimicked her heartbeat's flurry. Beads of nervous sweat trickled down her face.

'Ladies and gentleman, boys and girls, you've witnessed a lot of fun and excitement already this evening but now it's the turn of your ringmaster.' Amplified through a small microphone, Corinne's clear, sonorous voice echoed musically around the big top.

Georgia swallowed and stared timidly at the woman. She could see the dark gaze of the woman's eyes smiling malevolently at her.

'Make yourself comfortable on the edge of your seat as you prepare to see knife-throwing like you've never seen before.'

She held one long, menacing blade casually in her hand. The metal glinted like a shard of evil in the glow of the spotlight.

As Georgia watched, Corinne raised the blade and hurled it effortlessly. The lethal length of silver turned head over heels as it sped directly towards her.

Unable to stand the threat for a moment longer, Georgia closed her eyes.

Ten

Eventually Holly realised it was time to make her move. She had been watching the caravan all day. When she saw Corinne lead Chelsea from the door towards the circus, she knew that her moment had finally arrived.

Night was threatening to fall on the fairground. The shadows were so long that they stretched into infinite blackness along the distant fields, almost touching the silhouetted hills on the horizon. Loud music and flashing lights from the adjacent fair worked hard to banish the gloom around her, but they didn't quite manage it.

Holly slipped stealthily into the shadows as Chelsea and Corinne walked by her hiding place. She could hear the bitter words of Corinne's furious tirade as the woman got closer. Corinne was still angry, and threatening Chelsea with all kinds of retribution. Each deliberate step across the field's thin grass was punctuated by a sharp curse. The word 'keys' was repeatedly mentioned and Holly realised she had been the cause of Chelsea's miserable day.

The thought didn't bother her.

After she had seen the easy way Chelsea told tales behind Georgia's back, she felt no prick of conscience. It seemed only fair that the submissive woman should suffer something after having placed Georgia in such an invidious situation. Holly knew nothing about the machinations of the feud between Corinne and Georgia, but she knew that Chelsea's contribution wouldn't have helped.

Besides, during the introspective hours of her long day, she had come to realise that there was no percentage in having ethics. Perhaps those people who had friends and families needed such internal moral guidance, but Holly had neither, and believed she could cope quite well without. The pangs of guilt she had experienced over the past two days proved how little use she had for a conscience.

Once the two women had disappeared from sight, Holly took a final, nervous glance from her hiding place, then started towards the caravan. The electric taste of excitement filled her mouth as she ran quickly towards the little mobile dungeon. By the time she reached the door, her pulse was racing furiously.

Trying to find the right key for the caravan door, she cursed herself for not having done this during the day. All the hours she had spent watching the caravan had been wasted time. If she had troubled herself to find the right key earlier, Holly knew she could have saved valuable minutes getting inside.

When she finally slid the right key into the lock, Holly released a heartfelt sigh of relief. She turned the key, and realised she had just secured the door. The thought struck her like a fist and she spent a moment hating herself for being so idiotic.

Of course Corinne couldn't lock the door, Holly told herself. The woman didn't have her keys. Twisting the lock open again, Holly eased the door from the jamb. She cast a final, nervous glance over her shoulder, then disappeared into the caravan. Carefully, she closed the door behind her.

It took a few moments for her eyes to get used to the darkness and she cursed every one of the long, tiring seconds. Outside, the night was illuminated by a fading twilight. There were also the multicoloured rays of the fairground neons banishing the darker shadows from the moody encampment of caravans.

But in Corinne's little mobile dungeon, there was only darkness.

Holly didn't contemplate turning the light on. She was too well practised in the art of stealing to do something that foolish. Instead, she counted the long drawn-out minutes as her eyes adjusted to the poor light.

Kneeling in front of the safe, she blindly tried to find the keyhole in the caravan's gloom. It only took a moment before she had placed the right key in the safe's sturdy lock. With one effortless twist, the heavy metal door fell slowly open.

Holly drew an excited breath.

She snatched her bundle of possessions from the safe, their unusual shape making them distinctive even in the shadows. After quickly rifling through the clothes, Holly found her hand buried in an unmistakable sheaf of paper. It was still too dark for her to be able to see anything, but her dextrous fingers worked their way through the haphazardly bundled notes. She wasn't a hundred per cent certain, but she felt sure that none of her four grand was missing. Her grin was so brilliant she was surprised it didn't give off its own light in the darkness.

'Time to pack your trunk and say goodbye to the circus, Nellie,' she whispered cheerfully to herself.

Her fingers reached out for the safe door, and she was about to push it closed when a thought struck her. Her eyes were becoming more used to the poor light now and she could make out the shapes of neatly bundled cash and important-looking paperwork on the safe's shelves.

Hesitating, she toyed with the idea of really paying Corinne back.

The bitch had done more than make her suffer over the past two days. Now that the opportunity for revenge was in front of her, Holly found the temptation almost irresistible.

She reached into the safe and snatched two crisp bundles of notes. Each one was a stack of tightly packed fifties, and she guessed that with the total of the two bundles added together she was holding close to ten thousand pounds. Instead of dropping them into her makeshift bundle of clothes, she pushed them back into the safe.

Despising the unwanted conscience that troubled her, she turned her attention to the important-looking paperwork. Obviously it wasn't just important-looking, she reminded herself. No one stored things in a safe as secure as this unless it was either cold hard cash or an irreplaceable document.

In the unlit gloom, she squinted at the words on the front sheet but darkness didn't allow her to read it. Not that it mattered to Holly. Without giving the theft a second thought, she dropped the paperwork into her clothes bundle. She had no idea what she intended to do with it. She supposed she would simply burn it, or toss it in a bin. Her intention was to cause Corinne inconvenience rather than loss. It somehow seemed appropriate to return the woman's gift of unhappiness in such a way.

Making a sudden decision, she reached into the safe and snatched the money. 'What the hell!' she told herself softly. Corinne was bound to get over a little inconvenience. The loss of ten grand would take a lot longer to recover from.

She stood up, her decision made, then paused again. The prick of her conscience was infuriating and annoying. As much as she wanted to ignore it, Holly realised she couldn't. Her mind insisted that she was wrong to even try to take Corinne's money. Despising herself for listening to such a weak internal voice, she knelt down in front of the safe again and returned the documents and the two bundles of notes. It seemed ridiculous to give money back in such a way and she loathed her new-found morals for insisting that she do so. But she put it all back where she had found it, all except for her own bundle of possessions.

She had pushed the safe door closed, and tied her bundle into a knot, when she heard something. The whispered voices outside the caravan door sounded dangerously close.

Holding her breath, Holly took a tentative step towards the door and listened intently.

'. . . because Corinne says so.'

It was Chelsea's voice and Holly wondered who the woman was talking to.

'Can I wait inside?'

That was Joey, she realised.

'Corinne said to guard the door. She didn't say which side of it but I don't think Corinne would be happy if she found someone inside there without her specific say-so.'

Holly closed her eyes and cursed wordlessly. She was trapped in the caravan with no means of escape. As she had noticed before, the windows were sealed shut. The only way out was past Joey and she didn't think he would be as obliging this evening as he had been on her first night at the fairground.

Chelsea's words echoed through her mind as she tried to think what to do for the best. 'I don't think Corinne would be happy if she found someone inside there without her specific say-so.' If Holly was any judge of character, that had to be the greatest understatement she'd ever heard. She knew that if Corinne found her in the caravan now, her anger would be uncontrollable.

The thought left her cold with fear. She couldn't imagine being in a worse situation.

* * *

Georgia tried to recall if she had passed out for a moment. She remembered the knife hurtling towards her and she knew she had closed her eyes and screamed, but after that her mind seemed peculiarly blank. She was still secured to the knife-thrower's wheel, but now she was out of the ring and was being held in some desolate area backstage at the circus. She guessed that if she had passed out, it hadn't been for long. The circus audience was still laughing and cheering loudly.

'Did I scare you?' Corinne's voice was filled with mirth when she asked the question, and there was no concern in her tone. She placed her fingers against Georgia's face, holding her mouth steady. Moving slowly forward, Georgia watched helplessly as the woman kissed her.

She tried to close her mouth but Corinne's merciless grip held her tight. She felt the unwelcome intrusion of the woman's tongue and heard Corinne sigh happily.

Glancing out of the corner of her eye, Georgia saw a long blade still embedded in the wheel. It was so close she was able to see the reflection of her own frightened eyes staring back at her.

With her other hand, Corinne began fondling Georgia's leg. She could feel the woman's brutal caress as she stroked her inner thighs.

'Well?' Corinne asked, taking a step back and smiling excitedly. 'Did I scare you?'

Georgia dared to glance at the woman, not trusting herself to answer the question. She could still taste Corinne's kiss on her mouth and her thighs felt disturbingly warm where she had been touched. In all honesty, Corinne hadn't just scared her – she had terrified her. And the worst part was that they both knew that the night wasn't over yet.

In her act, Corinne had hurled seven knives. The first two had landed on either side of Georgia's face. The second pair had gone just below her armpits, on either side of her breasts. Glancing down at them, Georgia could see that they were frighteningly close to the jacket she was wearing. Two more blades had been thrown at the outside of her thighs and the final one had gone between them. This had to be the most terrifying blade, Georgia thought. The razor-sharp tip was buried in the fabric of her short skirt, pinning the garment securely to the pock-marked wooden wheel.

She watched Corinne grab this knife and begin to lever it to and fro from the wood. It came free with a sigh and the woman whirled the blade effortlessly in front of Georgia's face. 'Tell me honestly, Georgia darling,' Corinne insisted. 'Did I scare you?' She grasped the handle of the blade and pushed it towards Georgia's chest.

Struggling against the restraints at her hands and feet, Georgia tried to back away from her. She watched with growing fear as Corinne casually sliced the buttons from her jacket. When the last button was cut away from the fabric, the jacket fell open.

Corinne moved closer. The corners of her lips twitched upwards as she smiled approvingly at Georgia's breasts. The lacy bra emphasised their ample swell and revealed the dark circles of her areolae through a gauze of delicate white.

Corinne eased the tip of her blade against Georgia's flesh and pushed it up so its edge was resting between the two cups. With one casual flick of her wrist, the bra was cut in two.

Georgia felt her breasts being released into the chill air backstage. She gasped as though the blade had cut her and turned her head deliberately away. Her cheeks were reddening madly. Knowing that the woman was still expecting an answer, she whispered, 'Yes, you scared me. You're still scaring me.'

The sound of Corinne's nasty laughter greeted her ears. She moved forward again and pressed her lips against one of Georgia's exposed breasts. At the same time, she allowed the fingers of her free hand to toy with the other exposed nipple.

Georgia's mind reeled as she tried to adjust to feelings of excitement and terror in the same instant. Her traitorous body seemed delighted to have Corinne touch her in such a way, despite her mind's revulsion. Struggling at the unrelenting restraints of the wheel, she realised she was only exciting herself more as she gyrated against her tormentor. The dull pulse of her fear beat a rapid tattoo in her ears.

Corinne stepped back, a satisfied smile broadening her lips. They were no longer as thin and cruel as Georgia remembered them. Her arousal seemed to have added a dark, excited lustre to the lips. 'You say you're scared,' Corinne's words were broken by her mounting excitement. 'You haven't begun to know about scared, yet,' Corinne told her firmly. Her smile widened as she studied Georgia's shocked expression. 'But I think you may understand the meaning by the end of the night.'

Holly tested the toilet window for one final time before giving up. She had been trying to prise it open with one of the spare knives Corinne had left in the little mobile dungeon, but it had done no good. She had simply bent the tip of the blade and she could see she wasn't going to do any more than that with such an inadequate implement.

It wasn't that she thought the small lavatory window would be more easy to climb from. In all honesty, she didn't think she would have been able to squeeze through it even if she could have opened it.

But as she turned away from the secured frame, she realised it was all just speculation. The toilet would have been the ideal window to climb from. It was the furthest one from Joey, and on the opposite side of the caravan to him. If she had been able to force it open, then squeeze through it, she knew she could have made a clean break.

'Bastard,' she whispered softly.

For a moment, she thought she had cursed too loudly. At the same instant that she broke the room's silence, the caravan door flew open. Unable to stop herself, Holly tumbled back into the bathroom. She caught her heel against the door and watched it glide shut. A thin line of light shone underneath the toilet door and she realised how close she had come to being discovered. Admittedly, her hiding place was probably not the securest in the world, but she knew she could look forward to a brief reprieve before the inevitable discovery.

Trying to comfort herself in the face of rising panic, she struggled to think of an alternative plan of action. Her possessions were in a bundle at her feet and she was prepared to make her break for freedom as soon as the opportunity arose. All she needed to do now was sit back and wait for the right moment.

'No! Don't! I mean it now, Corinne. I don't want this.'

Holly recognised Georgia's voice through the thin wall. She quickly stifled the feeling of concern that washed over her, knowing it wouldn't help.

'Tie her down,' Corinne barked.

Holly guessed there were at least three of them in the room if Corinne was barking instructions to someone, and possibly more. Dismissing Georgia and her predicament from her thoughts, Holly tried to gauge a suitable plan of action. It wasn't going to be easy. She couldn't see what was happening but she was certain of one thing: Corinne was in a vile mood.

Georgia was certain of one thing: Corinne was in a vile mood. She stared up at the woman as Chelsea and Joey tied her down. They were using two pairs of discarded stockings which had been lying beside the bed. Judging by their worn look, Georgia guessed this wasn't the first time the stockings had been employed in such a way.

She didn't feel ashamed or embarrassed by her nudity; she was well past that sort of emotion. Her concentration was fixed on the menacing figure of Corinne as the woman towered over her. In one hand she held a shorter version of the bull whip she had been wielding in the circus ring. Georgia guessed this one was shorter because the full-size version wouldn't have the room to operate in the restricted confines of the caravan. It was a peculiar thought, she decided. It seemed too detached and clinical considering her predicament.

Corinne barked her instructions at Joey and Chelsea in a hostile tone, allowing neither of them the opportunity to answer back. Then she turned her attention to Georgia and scowled darkly. The malevolence of her expression was exaggerated by a wicked glint in her eyes. Georgia found that evil light more intimidating than anything else.

'You were trying to get my circus closed down,' Corinne snapped.

Georgia shook her head, trying to refute the allegation, but it was no use. The small whip cracked through the air and struck her inner thigh. An explosion of pain erupted against the bare flesh. She shrieked unhappily as the fire of discomfort burnt her leg.

'Don't bother trying to deny it,' Corinne growled. 'I have no doubt it's true. I just want you to know what happens to people who cross me.'

Georgia stared fearfully up at her, but Corinne was turning away.

'Joey, Chelsea. Fuck off,' she snapped. 'This is between Georgia and me.'

The pair obeyed her without question, and suddenly Georgia felt the familiar fingers of terror clutching at her chest. Before, she had been able to view this scene with a cool air of detachment. But back then she hadn't been alone with this sadistic woman.

Not only was she alone, she realised, but she was tied firmly to the bed and escape wasn't an option. The mounting terror inside her chest began to give way to panic. She had a moment's relief when she watched Corinne place the whip down and wondered if the threat of danger had suddenly passed. It was a foolishly optimistic thought, she realised. Corinne had simply placed the whip down so that she could undress.

Georgia was forced to lie on the bed and watch as Corinne revealed her body.

Despite her loathing of the woman, Georgia had to admit that Corinne was blessed with a beautiful figure. Her long athletic legs weren't just shapely; they were defined by artistically sculpted muscles that emphasised her obvious strength. Her breasts were voluptuous, tipped with dark areolae and long, thrusting nipples.

Georgia turned her head to one side, trying not to look at Corinne's body. She could feel an unsettling arousal beginning to warm her and in these circumstances the sensation was abhorrent.

An explosion of red-hot pain erupted in her thigh, rekindling the glowing embers of the previous fire.

'You'll fucking watch me while I undress,' Corinne said, making no attempt to disguise the menace in her voice. 'You'll fucking watch me, or I'll start to get cruel.'

Georgia was too scared to defy her.

Corinne smiled tightly. 'Don't worry too much,' she said pleasantly. 'You won't have to watch me for long. I'll be turning the light off soon, and then it'll be just like old times.'

Georgia didn't understand what Corinne was alluding to and her feverish thoughts wouldn't allow her to dwell on the curious remark. Her gaze was caught by the sight of Corinne teasing a finger through the thick swatch of dark pubic hair above her shaved pussy lips. The hairs had been shaved into a line like an exclamation mark, with her sex as the dot beneath it.

'If you untie me now, I won't tell Curtis about any of this,' Georgia said suddenly. 'I can pretend that it never happened and . . .'

'You won't be telling Curtis anything,' Corinne replied confidently. She smiled cruelly into Georgia's puzzled frown and said, 'When I've finished with you, you'll simply slink off to your caravan, collect your things and say goodbye to the fairground forever.'

Even though she was tied to the bed and terrified beyond belief, Georgia dared to sniff dismissively at this suggestion. 'You'd have to do an awful lot to make that happen,' she said haughtily.

Smiling, Corinne nodded. 'I intend to do a whole lot to you,' she said, her menacing whisper giving the words a dark meaning. 'I intend to do a whole lot to you, and then some more.'

Georgia swallowed thickly, suddenly very frightened.

Corinne teased a carefully manicured fingernail through the forest of hairs, smiling broadly as she touched herself. All the time, she kept her gaze fixed on Georgia. She reached for the whip and licked the rounded end salaciously with her broad tongue. The gesture was unsettlingly lewd.

As Georgia watched, Corinne guided the end of the whip down towards the shaved lips of her sex. She pressed the bulbous tip against the yielding flesh, and then she pushed it deep inside herself.

Georgia heard Corinne sigh and realised she had released her own soft sound when the whip penetrated the woman's pussy.

Corinne grinned at her as she forced the whip deeper. Using both hands, she began to fuck herself gently with the short handle. Sliding it in and out of her tight hole, she growled words of soft appreciation as the pleasure took over.

Not for the first time, Georgia wished she didn't find the situation so damnably arousing. The urgent pulse of her own sexual excitement was a quickening tempo and she wished she could fight against it. The sight of Corinne's naked body had been a thrilling overture. Now, as she watched the woman pleasuring herself, Georgia felt her excitement building at an alarming rate.

It seemed wrong to be enjoying herself in these circumstances. She was tied to a bed with the threat of punishment hanging over her like the sword of Damocles. It was clear that Corinne was going to make her suffer, and possibly hurt her worse than she could imagine. But all her body seemed to care about was the eroticism of the situation.

With her teeth clenched together, Corinne pushed herself effortlessly beyond the brink of orgasm. She came with a guttural roar, tugging the whip from the tight lips of her pussy in one decisive, fluid motion. Her eyes were shining brightly with devilish glee as she stared down at Georgia.

'Did you see how much pleasure that whip gave me?' she asked, her breathing broken by the remnants of her excitement.

Georgia nodded fearfully.

'Let's see if it can please you as much,' Corinne said quickly. She moved on to the bed with the lithe grace of a stalking cat. Still holding the whip, she pushed it forward until the tip brushed against the lips of Georgia's pussy.

'No,' Georgia whispered. 'Please don't,' she urged her.

Corinne was deaf to her pleas. She pushed the bulbous tip of the whip's handle against Georgia's sex and eased it to and fro over the labia.

Georgia heard her breath quicken as she tried to find

218

the right choice of words to stop the woman. Threats of retribution from Curtis were having no effect and blithe promises to forget the entire incident were proving just as futile. The more she tried to think of the right thing to say, the more she realised that nothing would come.

The pressure of the leather handle against her sex was delectable. It was far too intoxicating for her to want it to stop, and she could feel herself giving in to the demands of her libido. Restrained by the straps at her wrists and ankles, she found it difficult to move on the bed. Nevertheless, she writhed against the teasing tip, wishing she could feel it slide inside.

Surprisingly, Corinne allowed it to part her pussy lips. The gentle pressure of the tip slid into the warm velvety depths of her sex and Georgia shivered. She stared at Corinne, puzzled by the effort the woman was putting into pleasing her. With a deft hand, Corinne eased the length of the handle into Georgia's tight hole, gently filling her. Explosions of joy erupted inside her as the solid length of leather made its slow entry.

'Why . . .' Georgia paused and swallowed, suddenly breathless. 'Why are you pleasing me like this?' she asked quickly.

Corinne grinned down at her, sliding the handle slightly deeper before beginning to pull it out. 'I'm doing it for a very good reason,' she whispered, her husky voice making the words enticing. 'The more you enjoy this at the start, the more you'll feel the pain when I begin to punish you.'

Trapped inside the toilet cubicle, Holly couldn't help hearing the woman's words. She felt a cold shiver touch her as she realised the danger that Georgia was in. Thinking of her introspective hours that afternoon, she tried to remember why she didn't need a conscience. She could think of a lot of reasons against having one right now. Most of them were sitting in the tied-up bundle of clothes at her feet and she felt a poignantly strong attachment to each one of them.

Outside, Georgia's cries of pleasure were growing louder in intensity. Her enjoyment was obvious in each roar of pleasure and Holly felt a pang of annoyance that she couldn't witness the scene. It was stimulating enough to overhear what the pair were saying, but to have had the chance to see it would have been so much better.

She could hear Georgia gasp as an orgasm washed over her. Her euphoric cry was tinged with sobs of gratitude and refusals of any more pleasure.

In the toilet cubicle Holly shook her head sadly, knowing that such refusals would go unheeded. Corinne would go on pleasing Georgia until she chose to stop. When that happened, Holly knew the woman would start with the punishment. By that time, she expected Georgia to have given up all hope of having the woman listen to her.

Again, her annoying conscience raised its ugly head and demanded to know what she was going to do to help the woman. That morning, she had realised Georgia was her only friend in the world. The idea of leaving her to suffer Corinne's peculiar brand of punishment didn't bear thinking about.

Outside, Georgia screamed passionately a second time. No longer bothering to refuse the pleasure that was being administered, she growled heated words of encouragement for Corinne to continue. Her guttural demands were so low they sounded positively bestial.

Holly stared down at her feet, wishing she could think of a way of helping. Perhaps Georgia was being pleasured at the moment, but Holly knew it would soon end. Holly would be powerless against Corinne's formidable strength, and that thought seemed to vanquish every idea that sprang into her mind. A sliver of moonlight flickered through the marbled window of the toilet. In the brief gleam of light, Holly saw the glint of silver on the floor. Her heart began to beat a little faster as she allowed herself a moment's hope. The knife she had been using to try to open the window was still in the cubicle with her. She wondered if she could dare to use it to threaten Corinne. She doubted she could properly frighten someone as powerful and domineering as the ringmaster, but if she could unsettle her for a moment, it might be long enough.

As Holly reached for the knife, the lights in the caravan disappeared. The thin beam of light that had been shining beneath the cubicle door suddenly winked out. And then there was the deafening sound of an unearthly scream.

Georgia had been startled when the light went off. Like Holly, she too thought the deafening sound was a scream. A moment later, as her ears grew attuned to the familiar lilt and cadence of the voice, she realised exactly what she was listening to. It wasn't a scream. It was a soprano singing a high 'C'. She had barely noticed the CD player when she was dragged into the caravan, but now she remembered having seen it sitting on top of a dusty old work surface.

The music was more familiar. This was *Madame Butterfly*, she thought, and the scream was simply the opening sigh to *un bel di vedremo*, played at an ear-shattering volume.

Georgia felt an icy cold hand clutch her heart. She hadn't heard this piece of opera in the past two years. The last time she had listened to it had been while she was tied to the bed in Curtis's caravan on that final fateful night. She hadn't been able to tolerate the thought of listening to it since then.

She knew Corinne had picked this piece of music deliberately and it wasn't difficult to guess her reason. Despite the darkness and the stocking she now wore as

221

a semi-useful blindfold, Georgia could see things with perfect clarity. She saw exactly what Corinne was doing and she understood why.

On that night, two years ago, it had been Corinne who had crept into the caravan. Corinne was the one who had excited her, then treated her to that unforgettable golden shower. She had done it then to get rid of Georgia and her plan had worked.

Shivering, Georgia realised this was exactly what Corinne intended to do now. Terrified by the thought of having to endure such humiliation again, Georgia knew that the punishment would have the same effect. If Corinne abused her in the same way tonight, she would never dare to stay on at the fairground. It didn't matter what was happening between Curtis and herself. Having to share the same working environment with a woman who could do that to her would be more than she could tolerate.

Corinne's body was next to hers on the bed. The swell of her voluptuous breast rubbed excitingly against Georgia's bare flesh. The unmistakable thrill of pleasure it evoked was difficult to deny, and she struggled against its intoxicating impulse.

The woman pressed her lips close to Georgia's ear. Warm breath tickled the cool flesh of her neck as she spoke. 'This is just like old times,' Corinne giggled, stroking a finger against Georgia's bare breast. 'Don't you find that exciting?'

'You bitch,' Georgia gasped. 'It was you, wasn't it? Why?' With the screeching rise of Butterfly's aria ringing in her ears, Georgia could barely hear her own voice when she asked the questions. She felt sure that despite the woman's nearness, her words had been lost.

Nevertheless Corinne leant forward on the bed, placing her mouth ever closer to Georgia's ear. 'I did it for three reasons,' she said quietly. The sultry threat of her voice was far more distinct than the deafening singing. 'I did it to get you away from Curtis,' she began. 'And I did it to make you suffer. But most importantly, I did it because I wanted to.'

Georgia felt a cold wave of panic chilling her body. The terror she had experienced before was nothing compared to the ice-cold rush of fear that coursed through her veins. Corinne was still fondling her breast and the tingle of pleasure was suddenly magnified by the contrasting sensation of dread. Vainly, she pulled her arms and legs against the stockings that tied her to the bed. There was no give in them and she could only feel the sheer fabric cutting tightly against her wrists. An anguished groan escaped her throat and she tried to turn away from the woman.

Corinne leant over her, pressing her naked body firmly against Georgia's.

The tactile stimulus of her smooth silky flesh, rubbing purposefully against her own, was too much for Georgia to fight against. She wanted to be away from the woman; away from the fairground if that was what it took. She was about to say this much when Corinne kissed her.

Thrusting her tongue into Georgia's mouth, Corinne kissed with the brutal passion of a wild animal. Her hands squeezed and kneaded the tender flesh of Georgia's sensitive breasts. At the same time, her tongue was exploring the silken lining of Georgia's mouth. The allusion to the lovemaking she was about to administer didn't go unnoticed and Georgia felt torn between a need to submit and a desire to escape.

'How did we start, two years ago?' Corinne wondered idly.

As soon as she moved her mouth away, Georgia snatched a huge gasp of air. She was shivering so fiercely that she was sure her teeth were chattering. She didn't know if her body's tremors were caused by fear or arousal. The only thing she did know was that she no longer wanted to be in the caravan, alone with Corinne. She hadn't wanted to be there from the beginning, but now she sensed the woman was building up to something darker. Fear of what might be about to happen increased Georgia's yearning to escape.

'I started by eating your pussy, didn't I?' Corinne whispered. There was a smile in her voice when she asked the question. She took no umbrage from Georgia's lack of response. In the dark, poised over her body like an impatient vulture, she continued to smile. 'I don't particularly like eating pussy,' she remarked absently. 'I've always felt it was the act of a submissive, rather than something I should be doing. Wouldn't you agree?'

Georgia remained silent.

'I'll take that as a yes,' Corinne told her. 'We can start tonight in a different way,' she said shifting position on the bed. 'Lick my pussy, Georgia,' she demanded firmly. 'And if you don't lick it well . . .' Her voice trailed off into a chuckle of dark laughter. 'If you don't lick it well, I'll make this the most memorable night of your entire life.'

Georgia stared through the sheer denier of the stocking over her eyes. She could see the moon-like orbs of Corinne's arse moving towards her and smell the excited fragrance of her sex. The musky scent was sweet, thrilling and exhilarating. She realised that a part of her was actually enjoying this torture and she dared to give in to that submissive nature for an instant.

Pushing her tongue forward, she felt the electric touch of her mouth against the intimate flesh of Corinne's labia. The sultry sweet flavour of the woman's juice moistened her lips.

Corinne uttered a low moan. With careless disregard for the blonde beneath her, she pushed herself down on to the deftly squirming tongue at her hole.

The pussy lips threatened to suffocate her but

Georgia continued to roll her tongue against them. She could feel the tip of her nose pressing against the puckered rim of Corinne's arsehole and her chin was brushing against the clitoris.

Corinne's low moan turned into a satisfied growl. Her hands were stroking Georgia's thighs, moving purposefully upwards. She brushed the soft inner flesh at the top of Georgia's leg with cruel, uncaring fingers.

Georgia shivered excitedly and made her tongue work harder. Perhaps this wouldn't be as bad as she was anticipating, she told herself. Perhaps Corinne just wanted to play a little. If this was the sort of game she was into, then Georgia knew she could tolerate it. She could even enjoy it if it didn't slip back into the dark realms of punishment, torture and malevolence.

Remembering Corinne's earlier threats, she realised she was only fooling herself by clinging to such a hope. Whatever Corinne had in store for her, Georgia was certain that it wouldn't be for their mutual pleasure.

'You're very good at that,' Corinne muttered. She teased a fingertip against the swell of Georgia's pouting sex.

If Georgia's face hadn't been pressed so firmly against the woman's pussy lips, she would have sighed heavily with the depth of her arousal.

'Mind you,' Corinne observed. 'You were very good at it the last time, right up until the moment when I did this.'

Georgia detected the subtle change in the woman's scent a moment before it happened. She tried to pull away but the pressure of Corinne's backside against her face held her firmly. As the woman released a spray of hot golden liquid over her face, Georgia felt the first dousing drench her tongue, and then the back of her throat.

She wanted to scream with revulsion. She wanted to shout, curse and get away from the loathsome creature above her.

But at the moment when she released herself, Corinne teased her finger against Georgia's pussy hole. The tip brushed softly but deliberately against the pulsing nub of her clit.

Instead of screaming words of abuse and hatred, Georgia heard herself calling out with joy as an intense and unexpected orgasm washed over her. Corinne continued to piss, soaking Georgia with a burning spray that was virtually chilled on contact. The floral scent of her water was everywhere. Its taste filled her mouth and its cool wetness drenched her sweat-soaked body.

Purposefully, Corinne stroked soft, tiny circles against the undulating pulse of Georgia's clitoris.

Georgia growled with bitter elation as wave after wave of euphoria coursed through her. The feeling of being abused was still prevalent but the delight of her orgasm seemed to make that sensation unimportant. She knew that afterwards she would feel different. Later on, when she was washing the smell of the woman's golden shower out of her hair, she wouldn't find the thought so liberating.

She pushed her tongue into the burning stream of Corinne's piss and began to gulp the amber fluid down. Her tongue lapped carelessly against the lips of her tormentor's sex and she realised Corinne was nearing the brink of her own orgasm.

As though it was a way of retaliating, Georgia pushed the tip of her tongue against the woman's clitoris. With delicate flicking motions, she treated the pearl of pleasure to a staccato burst of pure pleasure.

Corinne screamed as the climax tore through her. She pushed herself harder on to Georgia's face, laughing giddily. The flow of her water had begun to taper off but as the orgasm ripped its way through her, Georgia felt a sudden spray of liquid splash wetly against her sodden cheeks and lips. The taste and scent was different to the insipid, lightly florid taste of her piss. This was a climactic explosion of Corinne's cloying, rich pussy honey.

'Very good,' Corinne said, climbing off the bed. She was still laughing softly but her mood seemed to have changed into one of a darker, more menacing nature. After switching the light on, she snatched the makeshift blindfold from Georgia's eyes. She stared impassively down at the blonde, the remnants of her smile fading fast.

'Not just very good,' Corinne said sternly. 'If we're being honest, that was a little too good.'

Now it was Georgia's turn to frown, lack of understanding apparent on her face. 'How can it . . .' she stopped herself, aware that the question would have been too challenging. 'Why was it too good?'

Corinne was shaking her head. 'You got off on that, didn't you?'

If she could have turned away, Georgia would have. She would have done anything to avoid the accusatory stare of the woman's fearsome black eyes. Tied to the bed, all she could do was blush softly and nod.

Corinne aimed a punishing slap at her face.

Georgia's head rocked and she gasped meekly. For a moment, she was treated to the sight of exploding stars conjured up by the blow.

'You weren't meant to enjoy that,' Corinne told her abruptly. 'That was meant to terrify you, just like it did the last time.' The pensive frown on her brow deepened and she stroked a thoughtful finger against her pouting lower lip. 'I'll just have to make sure I really upset you,' she said suddenly. Her frown disappeared and a wicked grin replaced it. She snatched the whip from the side of the bed and raised it into the air. 'When I've finished with you tonight, I bet that even I feel sorry for you.'

Georgia stared fearfully at the whip as Corinne held it high. She didn't know where it was going to land and she supposed it didn't really matter. Wherever Corinne hit her with it, it was going to hurt. The strains of *Madame Butterfly* still filled the caravan at a raucous volume and she knew that no matter how loudly she screamed, her cries would go unheard. Sobbing softly, she felt the first helpless tears begin to pour down her piss-stained cheeks.

As though a guardian angel had suddenly appeared, she heard the shouted words, 'Stop right there.'

'I said stop right there.'

Holly tried to inject venom into the words but she found that she didn't have the acting capabilities. Rather than trying to intimidate Corinne with her manner, she simply brandished the knife.

Corinne's expression was dark and threatening. 'Get out of here now, pickpocket,' she growled. 'Get out of here now, or so help me, when I next get my hands on you, I really will cut your fingers off.'

Never before had Holly sensed more sincerity in a threat. It was difficult not to be intimidated by the woman, but she held her ground. From the corner of her eye she could see Georgia staring at her meekly, but she didn't dare look at the woman. She knew that it would be fatal to let her gaze leave Corinne.

'I'm going to get out of here,' Holly said calmly. She sounded far more confident than she actually felt. 'But I'm taking my friend with me.'

Corinne snorted. 'Over my dead body.'

Holly studied her with a blank gaze. She twisted the knife slightly so that it caught the light and glinted wickedly. 'That can be arranged,' she said flatly. 'Put the whip down and step away from the bed.'

For a moment Corinne didn't move and Holly didn't think she was going to. She saw how ugly the whole incident could turn and she felt repulsed by the thought of what she might have to do. Hurting Corinne wasn't a course of action she wanted to take. However, she knew it might come to that. She realised from the vehement glare on the woman's face that she was no longer angry; she was outraged.

Corinne had been formidable before, and that was when she was keeping a tight rein on her temper. Judging by the anger that sparked in the dark depths of her eyes, Holly guessed the woman's mood was now close to being murderous.

When Corinne tossed the whip on the bed, Holly breathed a sigh of relief.

'Take her,' Corinne snapped sharply. 'Take her, but make sure you never cross my path again.'

Holly moved calmly to the bed and cut the stockings free from Georgia's wrists and ankles. All the time, she kept her gaze fixed on Corinne. 'Here,' she said, handing her own jacket to Georgia. 'Take this.'

Corinne was gracing her with a ferocious expression that silently shouted threats of repercussions. It took all of Holly's willpower not to cower away from the angry gleam in the woman's eye. 'You can kiss goodbye to your possessions now,' Corinne hissed angrily.

Georgia opened the caravan door and stepped out into the cool night air. Holly felt the soft breeze brush against her face as the chill air rushed into the room. The fresh fragrance of the night was like the sweet scent of freedom and she knew that escape was finally within her grasp. It was only Corinne's mention of her possessions that stopped her from running out into the night to join her friend.

When the realisation struck her, she felt like crying. Unhappily, she realised that she had left her possessions bundled together in the toilet cubicle. Not only had she left her clothes and money, but she also remembered that Corinne's filched keys were sitting on top of the bundle. Holly considered turning back to get them, then stopped herself, aware that it would be a catastrophic mistake.

Trying not to think of how hard she had worked to build up that small fortune, Holly kept her gaze fixed firmly on Corinne. Every muscle in her body wanted her to turn back to the toilet and retrieve the possessions. For the past two days, they had been symbolic of freedom and success.

The rational voice in her mind insisted she would be stupid to attempt to get them back. But it was only a whisper compared to the frantic screams of her natural greed. In her heart, she knew there was only one option available to her, but she was loathe to accept it.

Staring glumly at Corinne, she said, 'I've left my things in your toilet. You can keep them as a memento.' With that said, she walked cautiously past the woman, and out into the freedom of the night.

Eleven

'Georgia? Are you OK?'

She had only just stepped out of the shower and was still considering the answer to that question. The evening had been a revelation and she wasn't sure it was over yet. Her mind was a chaotic whirl of thoughts and ideas and she still felt as though she was reeling from her punishing ordeal with Corinne.

Curtis was glancing at her with a concerned frown creasing his brow. Holly stood next to him, her lips pursed together unhappily. 'I told him what happened,' she explained.

Curtis nodded. He cast an appreciative glance at the deep cleavage she was revealing from her fluffy white bathrobe, then frowned again. 'Holly's told me everything,' he confirmed. 'And if it's true, I'll make sure Corinne never comes near this fairground ever again.' The menace in his voice was barely controlled.

Georgia smiled at him and shook her head. 'Close the door and sit down,' she said quietly. 'I don't doubt Holly's told you the truth, but I'll be damned if I'll have you go to Corinne's caravan and enjoy my revenge.'

He studied her doubtfully, then cast a curious expression at Holly. The dark-haired woman shrugged uncertainly.

'Close the door, Curtis,' Georgia said firmly. 'Come in, sit down and listen. What I have in mind might be beneficial for us all.'

Dutifully, he closed the door and settled himself, facing her across the table.

Holly remained standing beside the door. She had no idea what Georgia was planning but judging by the contemplative smile on her lips, it looked as though she had some thoughts of her own.

'Corinne treated me to an evening of her vitriol earlier,' Georgia began carefully.

'I'll kill her,' Curtis said, standing from his seat.

'You'll sit down and listen to me,' Georgia instructed him sharply. 'You'll sit down and listen, or Holly and I will be out of here so fast you could blink and miss it.'

Chewing thoughtfully on his lower lip, Curtis settled himself back down in the facing chair. 'I'm sorry,' he said quietly. 'Please go on.'

'Corinne had a damned good reason for bullying me this evening,' Georgia went on. 'She'd heard about your streamlining plans and then learnt that the circus wasn't pulling its weight financially. I guess she wanted me to get out of the picture before I could tell you that last little fact.'

Curtis nodded thoughtfully. 'How great a loss?'

Georgia shook her head. 'It's a fairly negligible amount if we're being honest,' she assured him. 'I've studied the books a lot since I first glanced at them and it comes closer to breaking even than running at a loss. If you compare the circus's loss with the profits that the fairground reaps in excess custom . . .' She broke off and smiled at Holly. 'Is this going too fast for you?'

Holly shook her head. 'I said I was uneducated, not brain-dead. Punters from the circus pour the remainder of their night's cash into the fairground before they go home. Yeah?'

Georgia turned her attention back to Curtis. 'All of which makes the circus a very viable asset. And that means you can't just get rid of Corinne the way you wanted to. We'll have to go forward with my plan.' She paused and smiled warily at him. 'That is, if you're willing.'

He shrugged, a noncommittal gesture. His shrewd black eyes were studying her as though he didn't know how to treat her. It was as though he was looking at a woman he had never met before.

Georgia wasn't surprised by his questioning expression. After the evening she had just endured, she felt like a different woman.

'Let's hear what you're planning,' he urged her. 'Then I can decide.'

Georgia shook her head. 'You'll agree with me, Curtis,' she said confidently. 'We'll discuss it all afterwards. For now, we need to establish some ground rules. Doesn't Holly look pretty in a skirt?'

Curtis looked as though he were about to say something in reply, then paused. He graced Georgia with a quizzical expression, then turned to consider Holly.

She was wearing the stark navy business suit that Georgia had worn when she arrived at the fairground. The tailored cut of the jacket emphasised her slender waist and the short skirt revealed her long, stocking-clad legs.

Curtis turned away, careful not to study her for too long. With a cursory nod, he said, 'Yes, I suppose she does look very pretty. Does that have any bearing on your plans?'

Georgia smiled. 'Perhaps.' She stood up and moved gracefully around the table so that she was standing beside Holly. 'Holly got me away from Corinne this evening and because of that I'm very grateful.' She placed a hand around Holly's waist and kissed her softly as she gave her a reassuring squeeze. 'I'm very grateful to her indeed and I want my revenge to incorporate a token of gratitude to my friend here.'

Grinning happily, Holly slid her arm around

Georgia's waist and squeezed tightly. 'That is so sweet,' she whispered.

Georgia smiled and turned back to face Curtis. 'There's a paradox to this situation that I think you might find amusing. While Holly looks very pretty dressed like this, I think you'll find she looks even better out of these clothes. And at the same time, while you're a very handsome and attractive man, I think you might look better if you were wearing them.'

The colour drained from Curtis's face as though he had been slapped. He snatched his gaze from Holly's tempting figure to the challenge in Georgia's eye. 'I thought that was our little secret,' he hissed with dull anger.

Georgia shook her head. 'I'm in charge now, Curtis,' she said decisively. 'I'll decide what secrets you're allowed and I'll tell you who you can share them with. Challenge me on this, and Holly and I will be out of here forever. And I mean that.'

There was no doubting her sincerity and Curtis simply nodded. He glared at Holly and pointed a warning finger, 'Tell a living soul about this and so help me, I'll . . .'

Georgia didn't allow him to get any further. 'Stop with the blustering machismo and start doing as you're told,' she snapped. 'I want you to see how good Holly looks naked, and I want Holly to see how good you look in those clothes.'

The tension in the air was thick, but Georgia knew it wasn't caused by antagonism. Her suggestion had excited Curtis and she knew he was going to do as she had asked. His need for her was desperate and she realised he would do anything she told him. Yesterday, a part of her mind would have balked at the idea of such exploitation. Right now, it seemed like the most appropriate weapon in her armoury.

She could tell that Holly was also in a mood to enjoy

herself. The young woman had seemed inordinately touched by Georgia's use of the word 'friend'. She had acted as though that was the first time she had been addressed in such a way. Still in a cynical frame of mind, Georgia decided that if that was what had earnt her loyalty, then she was quite willing to exploit the relationship to its fullest.

'Undress, Curtis,' Georgia snapped sharply. 'You weren't so slow to obey my orders this afternoon.'

He treated her to one last puzzled glance, then began to unbutton his plaid work shirt. The fumbling haste of his clumsy fingers revealed his obvious excitement.

Holly was reaching for the buttons on her jacket but Georgia stopped her with a cool hand. Placing her lips over the young woman's, she kissed her passionately. Their tongues intertwined and as the excitement between them intensified, they pressed their bodies against one another with a feverish urgency.

Georgia could feel her near-naked body rubbing eagerly against Holly's. The swell of the young woman's breasts through the barrier of their clothes wasn't the most profound stimulation she had ever experienced. But in the current situation, it served as an intoxicating appetiser.

'Don't undress,' Georgia whispered, breaking their kiss for an instant. 'I have a special surprise in store for you.'

Holly smiled excitedly, her brown eyes shining. The hand that had been reaching for her own buttons moved purposefully towards Georgia's breast. She eased her hand inside the fluffy fabric of the bathrobe and brushed warm fingers against the tingling circle of Georgia's areolae.

Sighing happily, Georgia closed her eyes and revelled in the pleasure of Holly's careful touch. Her nipple was taut and aching for the woman's caress. When Holly traced the tip of her finger against the pulsing nub, Georgia felt her excitement swell dramatically.

'Do you want me to take everything off?' Curtis asked.

His question intruded on her enjoyment of Holly but Georgia didn't mind too much. There was a lifetime of such pleasures ahead if she handled this situation properly, and she was determined to experience all of them. She smiled warmly at him and nodded. He had already removed his shirt and his fingers were paused tentatively over the first button at his fly.

'Everything,' she told him. 'Holly and I want to see you stark naked. I trust you won't disappoint us.'

In Georgia's arms, Holly giggled.

Curtis was still studying Georgia with a doubtful expression but it seemed as though he had finally accepted her new, more confident persona. He stood up and began to ease the buttons from their holes.

'Curtis has a gorgeous cock,' Georgia said conversationally. 'Have you tried him yet, Holly?'

Holly shook her head, watching Curtis with an avaricious smile. 'Not yet,' she replied.

Curtis pulled his boots off before attempting to remove his jeans. When he stepped out of them, he was naked save for a pair of light cotton boxer shorts. His erection pushed the crotch out of shape and a dark circle of pre-come had stained the fabric where the tip of his cock lay.

Smiling at his helpless expression, Georgia shook her head. 'Everything,' she insisted.

Blushing furiously, Curtis reached down and stepped out of his shorts. When he stood up again, he was completely naked. His huge length pushed forward, standing proud beneath the inspection of the two excited women.

'He's big,' Holly said, desire apparent in her voice.

Georgia took a step over to Curtis and placed a tentative fingertip against the red-hot flesh of his pulsing shaft. 'Thank you,' she told him sincerely. She kissed him, holding his cock tight in one hand as she pressed her mouth against his lips. When her tongue slid into the warmth of his mouth, she could feel the shaft between her fingers stiffening.

'Why don't you put Holly's clothes on?' Georgia suggested. 'Then we can start to have some real fun.'

Curtis cast a shy glance in Holly's direction. Whispering in Georgia's ear, he said, 'Holly's still wearing her clothes.'

Georgia laughed softly and shook her head. 'She won't mind if you take them off her,' she replied calmly. 'Just make sure you're gentle.' She gave him a last kiss and then led him to Holly. Circling her arm back around the woman's waist, Georgia placed a kiss on her new friend's cheek and stared expectantly at Curtis.

With hesitant fingers he reached out and began to unfasten the buttons at her jacket. They fell open to reveal her blouse and he slid the jacket from her shoulders.

'Put the jacket on the chair,' Georgia snapped. 'The same goes for the blouse and the skirt.'

Curtis nodded, his concentration fixed on the buttons and zips of Holly's clothes. By the time he had stripped her of the suit and blouse, Holly was shivering. His erection was still raging furiously and the bulbous end was leaking a stream of pre-come. Occasionally, as he rubbed against her, the tip brushed at her bare flesh. Each time this happened, his cock left a dewy trail of his arousal on her naked skin.

'You still have to take her underwear off,' Georgia reminded him. 'But as you take it off Holly, I want you to put it on.'

His impassive gaze would have looked calm and cool under other circumstances. Because she was able to see the furious twitching of his cock, Georgia wasn't impressed by the stoical expression on his face. She stroked her fingers against his length and smiled

237

indulgently at him. 'Do it now, Curtis. Your sister has taught me a lot about how to control people and her ways aren't half as pleasurable as mine.'

It wasn't surprising that his erection was so hard, Georgia thought. She took a discreet glance at Holly and felt her own longing heighten. The lacy black basque was the perfect complement to her mild tan. It exaggerated the swell of her breasts and clung to her sleek frame like a second skin. The black stockings on her legs looked just as good. The sheer denier was stretched taut against her flesh, the glassy fabric glistening with a dull, wet lustre in the caravan's light. The lacy tops darkened to a thick opaque ebony, contrasting with the sun-kissed flesh of her upper thighs.

Acting quickly on Georgia's instructions, Curtis moved his hands to the front of Holly's basque. He was about to open the lacy bows that fastened it when Georgia stopped him.

'The stockings first,' she said.

Curtis glanced down at Holly's long, slender legs and then reached for the clasp of the basque's suspenders.

Georgia slapped his fingers away firmly. Staring into his startled expression, she said, 'Kneel down to do it, Curtis.'

For a moment, she thought he was going to refuse. He looked on the verge of ignoring the instruction, a defiant flicker appearing in the back of his dark eyes. It was gone before she could decide whether she had seen it or not, and then he was kneeling down in front of Holly.

His fingers stroked against the silky flesh of her inner thighs as he tried to release the stockings from their clasps. Holly shivered as he touched her and Georgia felt the thrill of her pleasure as the woman in her arms trembled. She dared to kiss Holly again as Curtis teased the fastener free.

Holly's tremors of enjoyment made her body

undulate delightfully as their tongues explored one another. She felt the young woman move slightly, allowing Curtis to roll the sheer fabric down the smooth length of her leg.

Curtis stood up and began to put the stocking on. His cheeks were burning crimson, in spite of the fact that neither of the women watched him. As soon as he was finished, he knelt down again and began to remove Holly's other stocking.

'What's your plan, Georgia?' Holly asked quietly.

Georgia shook her head. 'I can explain it later,' she said. 'But you'll like it.'

Holly frowned sceptically. 'Are you sure?'

Nodding, Georgia reached a hand down to the crotch of Holly's panties. She eased the gusset to one side and traced a finger against the moist lips of the woman's sex.

Holly loosed a soft sound of pleasure.

'Curtis,' Georgia snapped. 'Tongue this for a moment.' There was no question, or allowance for his desires. She was giving an instruction and he was allowed no chance of refusal.

Without hesitating, Curtis pushed his tongue toward the haven of Holly's sex. He drew slowly against the delicate pink lips, concentrating the tip on the throbbing nub of her clitoris.

Holly panted coarse words of encouragement, unable to silence her obvious enjoyment. Georgia's fingers still held the gusset of her panties to one side, while Curtis worked his tongue lovingly against her warm flesh.

'This is why I'm sure you'll like it,' Georgia whispered. 'You're enjoying this. I'm certain you'll enjoy the rest of my plans.' Reluctantly, she moved her fingers from Holly's panties and pushed Curtis away. 'Lick this, then carry on undressing her,' she snapped. As she gave the instruction, Georgia tugged the cord free from her bathrobe and teased her fingers through the pale thatch of blonde pubic hairs.

Curtis nuzzled affectionately against her sex, before brushing his tongue along the lips. He drew the tip repeatedly over her labia, inspiring waves of pleasure that were more than just physical. Georgia couldn't deny that his tongue felt divine as it licked at her pussy lips, but that wasn't the only source of her pleasure. The young woman holding her waist and occasionally kissing her was helping to make the situation even more memorable. But again, Georgia knew that Holly wasn't the principal source of her pleasure. The most arousing part of this moment, Georgia thought, was the fact that she was finally in control. This was how she had always wanted to be and the thrill of commanding two lovers, and instructing them on how to please her, was far more exciting than any single aspect of the night.

She pushed Curtis's mouth away reluctantly and told him to get Holly's clothes on. He worked with the same slow deliberation he had employed before, removing the stocking slowly, then pausing to stroke it on to his own leg.

This time Holly and Georgia watched him, smiling their approval when he glanced up at them.

'I'll remove Holly's basque,' Georgia said firmly. 'You can take off her panties.'

Curtis knelt down again to do as he was told.

'I want you to lick me while you're doing it,' Holly said suddenly.

Curtis cast a wary glance up at her and then directed questioning eyes at Georgia.

She nodded sharply and said, 'Do as the lady asks, Curtis.' Then, deliberately ignoring him, she started to unfasten the series of bows that tied Holly's basque. The task was made more difficult as Holly began to squirm and writhe beneath the combined talents of Curtis's tongue and her touch. Laughing and shrieking helplessly as the intensity of her pleasure increased, Holly struggled to remain motionless as Georgia unfastened the bows.

Eventually, with a concentrated effort, she managed to remove the garment.

Holly was suddenly revealed to Georgia in all her splendid naked glory. The swell of her breasts was an enticing sight, making an unspoken offer that Georgia couldn't refuse. Dismissively, Georgia pushed the basque at Curtis and mumbled an instruction for him to put it on. As soon as he had hold of it, she placed her hands against the heaving orbs of Holly's breast and gently caressed the sensitive flesh.

The two women kissed and began to explore one another with furious intent. Georgia revelled in the sensation of the sensitive flesh of her own breasts being touched and fondled. She shrugged the bathrobe from her shoulders and pressed her naked body hard against Holly's. An electric charge of sheer passion surged through her as their naked bodies met.

Unable to resist the temptation, Georgia lowered her lips to the urgent thrust of Holly's nipple. She kissed it softly, feeling the rigid flesh beneath the pouting jut of her lower lip, then took it into her mouth.

Holly drew jagged breaths of pleasure. Her hands had been caressing Georgia's waist but, as the euphoria caught hold, she dug talon-like nails into the woman's bare flesh.

Unmindful of the mild discomfort, Georgia continued to suck at the nipple. She allowed her other hand to tease Holly's ignored breast, brushing against the hardened nub, then concentrating on the dark brown cap of her areola.

'Too much,' Holly gasped. The words were strained with emotion. 'Too much, too much,' she hissed.

Georgia laughed softly against her skin. 'Not enough, yet,' she said decisively. Moving her lips to the other breast, she lowered her hand to the warm, wet cleft between Holly's legs.

This time, Holly shrieked. She rocked her head back

and released a cry of ecstasy that shook the paper-thin walls of the caravan. Her orgasm was sudden, swift and earth-shatteringly powerful.

For a single instant, Georgia felt envious of the pleasure the woman had received. She felt a splash of warm liquid douse her fingers and realised that Holly hadn't just climaxed, she had physically ejaculated.

Giggling happily, Holly nuzzled her face against Georgia's neck.

Georgia's envy quickly evaporated. She could feel a rush of excitement overwhelm her as Holly clutched her tightly. Her body trembled with a whole series of after-tremors from her climax.

'Now what to do you want from me?' Curtis asked quietly.

Georgia turned her broad smile on him. She realised that Holly had glanced at him at the same time because she heard the woman's soft cry of surprise. It was difficult not to release her own exclamation. Standing in the dark lacy basque and black stockings, Curtis looked stunning.

'I want an awful lot from you,' Georgia grinned. The smile didn't reach her eyes as she allowed him to hear the sincerity in her words. 'I want an awful lot, but first, I want us all to have fun.' She turned to Holly. 'What would you like to do to him?'

Holly seemed to consider the idea for a moment, a playful smile toying with her broad, sensuous lips. 'He looks very good dressed like that,' she remarked. 'And he's very skilled with his tongue.'

Georgia nodded. 'He's just as skilled with his cock,' she said. 'He won't come until he has permission.'

Holly raised a sceptical eyebrow. She reached her hand forward and stroked the bulging front panel of Curtis's panties. The shape of his erection was clearly defined by the flimsy material and her fingers caressed it idly as she spoke to Georgia. 'I wouldn't mind trying that,' she conceded. 'But won't you feel a little left out?'

Smiling happily, Georgia shook her head. She snapped her fingers and pointed at the bedroom. Curtis turned and led the way.

Holly held Georgia back for a moment and cupped her hand against the blonde's ear to whisper something he wouldn't hear. 'You've got him eating out of the palm of your hand,' she said softly.

Georgia smiled darkly. 'It's not the palm of my hand where I want him to start eating,' she said.

Laughing, Holly shook her head. 'How much control do you have over him?'

Georgia shrugged, trying not to let the frown of consternation appear on her brow. 'We're about to find out,' she said uncertainly. 'I only hope it's enough.'

They followed Curtis into the bedroom and Georgia resumed her command with a vengeance. She pushed Curtis on to the bed and told him to lie still. Turning to Holly, she grinned easily. 'If you want to try out his cock, then feel free to enjoy yourself.' Glancing down at Curtis, she added, 'Remember, I don't want you coming until you've been given proper permission.'

He nodded sullenly, his eyes studying her with a mixture of uncertainty and adoration. Staring at the expression, Georgia realised she had little to worry about with the question of his servility. She suddenly felt sure he would do everything she asked.

Holly was climbing on to the bed, her eagerness to enjoy Curtis obvious in every frantic gesture. She didn't bother to remove the panties from his crotch. Her urgency was so paramount she simply eased his length from the side.

Georgia smiled at the sight. The gusset was stretched to a taut wire that pulled tightly between his balls. She supposed he was enduring some discomfort from the sensation but it didn't seem to be hampering his erection. Over the past two days she had learnt her own lessons regarding the combination of pain and pleasure.

243

If things went according to her plans, Curtis had a lot more lessons to learn.

Holly held his shaft firmly in one hand, teasing the tip of his cock against the slippery wetness of her pussy lips. With a sigh, she guided him against the opening of her cleft, then lowered herself heavily on to him.

As Georgia watched, she teased a finger against her sex and played idly with the lips. When she realised what she was doing, she stopped herself sharply. She was in control now, she reminded herself. She was in charge of the situation and she had others to do this for her.

Climbing on to the bed, facing Holly, she straddled Curtis's face. Pushing herself down forcefully, she placed her pussy lips over his mouth.

Without needing to be instructed, Curtis began to lap at her wet hole. Tremors of excitement shivered through her body, and for an instant she was swept away by the pleasure. His tongue slid against her flesh, teasing the sensitive nub of her clit, then concentrating on the inner flesh just inside the velvety depths of her sex.

Groaning with mounting pleasure, Georgia opened her eyes and smiled. She was staring at Holly, enjoying the sight of her naked body bouncing happily up and down on Curtis's shaft. Her fulfilment was so complete she felt the rush of an orgasm building swiftly inside. Without hesitating to think about what she was doing, Georgia leant forward. She placed one hand against Holly's breast and teased the hard nipple that stiffened beneath her touch. Her other hand encircled Holly's neck and she pulled the woman close to her.

Together, as they both enjoyed the man beneath them, Holly and Georgia kissed.

It was a euphoric moment and Georgia couldn't stop the blistering release of a climax from scorching through her body. She trembled with passion as the orgasm ripped a scream from her. As the tremors began to subside, she felt Holly shaking against her, enjoying her own climax. She was still kissing Georgia but her lips were pulled back in a tortured grimace of elation. The muscles of her neck were strained with her struggle against some exceptional internal tension.

'Let me,' Georgia insisted. She pushed her hand down between Holly's legs. The tips of her fingers brushed against the thick cock that penetrated Holly but she ignored it. She was briefly aware of the slippery coating of pussy-honey that lubricated Curtis's length but that wasn't where she wanted to put her hand. Tracing gently upwards, she teased her fingertips against the stretched flesh of Holly's folds.

Holly pushed herself down on to the wriggling fingers and squirmed against the rapture she found there. Her hands moved up and she cupped Georgia's breast as the woman tickled a finger against the pulsing flesh between her legs.

Unable to contain her excitement a moment longer, Georgia writhed herself against the wriggling tongue at her sex. The strength of her orgasm was surprising and she felt herself being transported away from the tiny caravan to a world where there was nothing but pleasure and satisfaction. Even with her eyes open the universe was clouded a by a bliss-filled red mist. Her plans and schemes were forgotten, as were the injustices she had suffered over the past two days. The only thing that existed was the burning delight of her joy.

When the waves of passion began to subside, Georgia found herself grinning at Holly. The woman was returning her smile, but beneath the expression there was something more. Georgia realised that in the moment of their mutual climax something had happened between her and Holly. There was a determined gleam in the woman's eye, its meaning made clear by the set of her smile.

Without needing to be told, Georgia realised that

Holly was just as willing to do her bidding as Curtis was.

She grinned at her new ally, touching grateful kisses against her neck and cheek. Curtis was still stroking his tongue against the cleft of her sex, evoking delicate thrills of joy. Georgia could also see that his stiff length was rigid between the lips of Holly's pussy. She wondered idly how he had managed to fight off his own climax, then remembered that he hadn't had a choice.

Admittedly he had been drinking the plentiful juice from her pussy and his cock had been treated to the slippery friction of Holly's sex, but she knew orgasm would have been impossible for him. Georgia remembered that she hadn't allowed him to have his climax yet.

'You still haven't told me what your plan is,' Holly prompted.

Georgia laughed softly, wondering if the woman had been reading her thoughts. 'My plan is simple,' she said quietly. 'And all I need to start putting it into action is one small gift from Curtis.' She eased her sex away from his probing tongue and grinned down at him. 'That's all I need,' she repeated, not sure if he could hear her with her legs around his ears and her sex over his face. 'Just a small gift from Curtis.'

His features were contorted from an obvious struggle against the threat of his own climax. He glanced up at her, beseeching her with his expression. Holly was still riding slowly up and down on his cock and Georgia suspected that his resolve was on the verge of weakening. She didn't know if she could have held off from coming if she had been enjoying the same sort of treatment. However, it was important to her plans that Curtis be in this state of desperate need when she explained what she wanted.

'Anything,' he gasped. 'You know that already. Whatever you want.'

Georgia smiled down at him. She was aware of Holly's puzzled frown but she ignored the expression, concentrating on Curtis. 'I want your fairground, Curtis,' she said firmly. 'I want absolute control and ownership of your fairground but I don't expect you to make a decision like that instantaneously.' Treating Holly to a knowing smile, she told him magnanimously, 'Take a minute to think it over while you lick me some more.'

With a languid motion, she slipped her pussy lips back against his face.

Holly stared at her with unfettered admiration.

Georgia grinned back and then glanced down at the cleft between Holly's legs. 'Let's both lick this for a while, while Curtis makes up his mind,' Georgia said.

Holly eased herself from the cock and knelt between the man's stocking-clad legs. Together, she and Georgia lowered their mouths against the glistening, slippery wetness that coated his shaft.

Georgia drew her tongue lovingly against the rigid flesh, enjoying the taste of Holly's pussy juice. The cock pulsed to the combined touch of their tongues. Georgia felt her excitement mount as she realised that she and Holly were occasionally kissing as they tried to work simultaneously on him. She watched the woman lower her mouth to the tight sac of Curtis's balls and heard him groan softly beneath her. His cock twitched furiously and she felt every nerve in his body tighten as he struggled not to climax.

Casually, she moved her sex away from his mouth and glanced curiously back at him. 'Made any decisions yet?'

His words came in a ragged burst, the closest that his excitement would allow to a normal voice. 'You're asking a hell of a lot.'

Georgia laughed and pushed herself back against his face. 'I know I'm asking a lot but I'm giving a lot in return. Put me in control, Curtis, and this sort of pleasure will be a daily occurrence.'

To emphasise her promise, she lowered her lips over the swollen end of his glistening cock and sucked gently. As she sucked, she moved her mouth slowly down. She grinned at Holly around the shaft and watched the woman lick the tight sac beneath his length.

Daringly, Holly pushed her tongue against the rim of his arsehole.

Curtis growled, fighting furiously to contain himself. The sound was muffled as Georgia pushed her sex against his face. As though he were retaliating, she felt him thrust his tongue forcefully between her legs. The stimulus sent her reeling with excitement and she felt the onset of another burst of pleasure threatening to pulse through her body.

'Keep tonguing his arse,' she growled, smiling at Holly as she gave the instruction. With the command given, Georgia turned to face Curtis and smiled sweetly at him. At the same time, she guided his cock between her legs and lowered her pussy on to him.

A tortured expression of pained pleasure twisted his features as he stared up at her. 'You're asking too much,' he gasped. 'Far too much.'

She shook her head. 'I'm not asking for anything you don't want to give me. Let me have the fairground, and I'll allow you to come.'

She knew that he would have glared angrily at her if the circumstances were different. But they weren't. He wanted to, she could see that in the dull sparkle of his eyes, but as she made the offer Georgia squeezed the inner muscles of her sex tightly around his cock.

His face contorted and he pushed himself back on to the bed.

Glancing behind her, Georgia saw that Holly was pushing her tongue deliberately into the puckered rim of his arse.

'Tell me it's mine, and I'll let you come,' Georgia whispered. She moved her mouth closer to his and kissed him tenderly.

He closed his eyes so tightly she could see the tears of consternation squeezing from the corners. His lips were drawn back from his teeth in a scowl of defiance but she knew that he wasn't trying to defy her.

'It's yours,' he whispered.

Georgia smiled. 'Say that a little louder, would you? I'm not sure I heard.'

With his teeth clenched and his gaze fixed balefully on her, he shook his head from side to side, as though he were trying to take back what he was saying. 'It's yours,' he gasped. 'It's all yours.'

'Yes,' Georgia whispered triumphantly. She lowered herself on to him and squeezed the inner muscles of her sex tightly around his shaft. The thrill of her climax welled and she drew a deep breath of elation. Her entire body was shaking with the sudden feeling of power she was enjoying. 'Permission granted, Curtis,' she whispered softly. 'You may come.'

His cock pulsed on command.

Georgia heard Holly gasp behind her. The sound could have been surprise or pleasure but she couldn't tell which. As she felt the huge cock inside her pulsing furiously, she was taken over by the bliss of her own climax. Her pussy tingled electrically and she heard herself roar with a furious groan of satisfaction.

Sliding herself from Curtis's spent body, she turned to face Holly.

The woman was grinning broadly back at her.

'Holly,' Georgia began, a triumphant smile splitting her lips. 'There's been a change of management here at the fairground and once we've sorted out the paperwork, I'd like – no, I insist, that you help me get things running the way they should be.'

Holly frowned uncertainly. 'The way they should be?'

Georgia turned to smile at Curtis and gave him a knowing wink. 'The way they should be,' she reiterated. 'Or to put it a little more succinctly, my way.'

Twelve

Corinne was in a vile mood and she felt perfectly entitled to take it out on someone. As if the previous evening hadn't gone badly enough, now she was being summoned to her own circus tent straight after a show. She had wanted to relax and chill out a little, perhaps vent some of her frustrations on Chelsea's backside.

But after the show Chelsea had been nowhere to be seen and when she finally arrived at the caravan, she was only there to carry a message from Curtis. He wanted to see her in the big top, immediately.

Corinne guessed it had something to do with Georgia and she was prepared for a fight. To be totally honest, she was more than prepared for a fight. She was ready to draw blood. Her anger was so great she didn't see the young woman who bumped into her.

' 'Scuse me,' the woman muttered.

'Fuck off,' Corinne growled, marching deliberately past the waltzers. She was dressed in a pair of black leather jeans, a black leather waistcoat and a brilliant white T-shirt. Because she was six-foot tall and broadly built, she was surprised anyone had been foolish enough not to see her and get in her way.

But obviously someone had.

She paused and glanced over her shoulder, a frown of uncertainty crossing her brow. Night had fallen thickly over the fairground and the crowds were bustling.

Whoever she had bumped against was no longer in sight and even though their voice sounded unnervingly familiar, Corinne couldn't see a face she could recognise. Dismissing the notion that had crossed her mind as being ludicrous, she carried on towards the big top. Every step she took was a thunderous march that hinted at the threat of violence for anyone who dared get in her way. Whatever Curtis had to say to her, he could be damned sure she wasn't going to be bullied.

She marched angrily past the attendant on the ticket booth, treating him to a contemptuous glare when he asked her how she was this evening. If she had stopped to tell him exactly how she was, he would never have dared speak to her again.

Inside the big top, she stopped and glared angrily into the centre of the ring. The spotlight was shining on a solitary figure centre-stage. Corinne recognised her instantly and wondered what the hell she was still doing here.

Collecting her thoughts quickly, Corinne decided it didn't matter. She would take on Curtis and his stupid girlfriend if she had to. Whatever the problem, whatever the situation, Corinne was in no doubt that she would be in control.

Alone and scared in the centre of the ring, Georgia could hear Corinne approaching her. The woman's impatient footfalls echoed dully against the wooden benches, chilling her with the forceful power in each step. Her heart began to beat a little faster as nervousness ate away at her confidence.

'What the fuck are you doing here?' Corinne asked tersely, marching over to the edge of the ring. 'I thought Curtis would be here.'

'The fairground is under new management, Corinne,' Georgia said coolly. 'I thought you might want to be one of the first to hear that.'

Corinne frowned. 'Since when?' she demanded. 'What new management?'

Georgia dared to grin. 'You're looking at it.'

A deathly silence filled the big top, loud enough to be heard in every corner.

'I don't believe you,' Corinne decided after a moment's thought. 'I don't believe you for a fucking moment. Where's Curtis?'

Georgia snapped her fingers and Curtis stepped into the spotlight beam beside her. He was dressed in a pair of pale jeans and a plaid shirt. His face was serious as he stared through the veil of the blinding light into Corinne's questioning expression.

'She's telling the truth, Corinne,' he confirmed flatly. 'Georgia now owns the fairground and circus. A solicitor finalised the details this afternoon. She's owned them since this morning.'

'The fuck she has,' Corinne declared dramatically. 'Why wasn't I consulted?'

Curtis held her gaze. 'You weren't consulted because that would only have been a matter of courtesy and I didn't think you merited such consideration. It was my fairground, I owned it and I was free to do whatever the hell I wanted with it. I've given it to Georgia.'

Corinne stared at him with slack-jawed amazement.

Georgia could see questions and threats lurking at the back of Corinne's eyes and she wondered which the woman would choose to use first. There would be no sense in her arguing over the practicalities of the fairground's ownership. It was hers now and a day with a helpful solicitor had secured that. All that remained now was to deal with Corinne.

'Go back to your van and wait for me, Curtis,' Georgia said firmly. 'Corinne and I can talk about the rest of this without you.'

He seemed reluctant to move, but eventually relented

and walked out of the circus. The two women remained in silence until he had left them alone.

'What's it going to be, Corinne?' Georgia asked. 'Do you want to work for me, or are you going to leave?'

'You manipulative bitch,' Corinne growled angrily. 'I should have really laid into you last night when I had the chance.'

Georgia shrugged as she considered this. 'Perhaps,' she said. 'But that might have made me even angrier than I already am. Right now, you can look forward to working for me if you just come over here and kiss my feet.'

'Kiss your feet!' Corinne grunted. 'Kiss my arse. Fuck you,' she snapped sharply. 'I can manage my life without my idiot brother and his tacky piece of pussy.' She turned her back on Georgia and started to leave the circus.

'If you go now,' Georgia called, 'then you lose everything.'

Corinne paused and stared back unhappily at her. The anger in her face was fighting for a predominant position but the flicker of unease in her eyes was growing noticeably larger.

Georgia cleared her throat. 'The circus is mine, the props are mine, the livestock and the acts are mine. You leave now, and you'll be leaving everything.'

Corinne snorted sourly. 'The circus is yours, the props are yours and the livestock and the acts are yours. And if you want to keep them, then you can shove them all the way up your arse.' Determinedly, she turned away and began to march towards the circus exit.

' 'Scuse me,' a voice called.

Corinne turned and glanced at the spotlight.

Once again, Georgia was no longer alone. This time she had Holly standing beside her. The two women were both grinning and Holly was holding up a set of keys that she jangled musically. An infuriatingly cheeky grin split her lips.

Corinne snatched a hand against the belt-loop on her waist and discovered that her keys were missing. Even from ten metres away, she could see that the pickpocket was holding them. 'You bitch,' she growled, unable to mask the note of admiration that tainted her words.

Holly laughed. 'I hope that doesn't spoil your plans too much,' she said sweetly. 'I suppose you were planning to make use of those five grand bundles you store in your safe,' she said quickly. 'Not having the keys to the van and the safe might make it a little difficult to get your hands on them.'

Georgia glanced curiously at Holly and saw the wicked glint in her eyes. She could feel a malicious glee emanating from the woman and wondered if she had tapped an unplumbed reserve of sadism in Holly's soul. If that was the case, then tonight would be the night when she found out about it.

'I'll tell you what,' Holly went on, obviously enjoying herself. 'You come over here and kiss my feet instead of Georgia's, and I might think about giving them back to you.' She began to laugh darkly to herself.

'You pair of bitches think you've won, don't you? You think you have me just where you want me, don't you?' Corinne hissed.

'I know I've won and I know I've got you,' Georgia agreed. 'But I'm not sure I particularly want you. Come over here and kiss my feet. Then we can start discussing your new role in the circus.'

Reluctantly, Corinne took a step towards the two women. 'You can't have thought of everything,' she whispered. 'What if I decided to react physically and take my keys back by force?'

Georgia shook her head, a rueful smile twisting her lips. 'Joey and Ken and a couple of the other boys are lurking around here in the shadows,' she explained. 'Since the change of management, they're acting on my instructions.'

Corinne shook her head. 'You conniving bitch.'

'Spare me the insults and kiss my feet,' Georgia snapped. 'I don't intend to waste much more time on this conversation. If you haven't done it in the next minute, I'll assume you're not going to. If that's the case, I'll just have you thrown off the fairground. It's up to you, Corinne.'

Glaring angrily, Corinne stepped into the spotlight. They stood face to face, glowering defiantly at one another. Corinne was taller by a good six inches and staring threateningly down, but Georgia didn't appear intimidated by the woman's menacing posture or her angry scowl.

'What would you do if I chose to defy you?' Corinne asked sharply.

Georgia smiled softly but she tempered the expression with steel. 'I wouldn't recommend you try it,' she said calmly. 'You wouldn't suit life penniless and outside the fairground. You've been left with one remaining option. Bend down and kiss.'

Corinne didn't move. She stood where she was, still glaring defiantly at Georgia, her frown deepening. Every muscle in her body seemed to vibrate with a mounting tension and the threat of attack crept closer with each passing second.

'How's that minute going, Holly?' Georgia asked quietly.

'It's going quickly,' Holly said cheerfully. She jangled the keys unnecessarily as she glanced at her wristwatch. The sound caused Corinne to flinch, and she cast a dangerous glance in the woman's direction. Holly ignored the glare. 'I'd say we were down to the last ten seconds, and counting.'

Georgia nodded and turned her glib smile back on Corinne. 'What's it going to be?'

Wordlessly, Corinne lowered herself to the floor. She bent her head down and placed her lips against Georgia's feet.

Georgia felt a soaring thrill of triumph erupt inside her. 'Good girl,' she whispered softly. 'Very good girl.' She saw that Corinne was preparing to stand up. Casually, she raised a foot and placed it firmly on the woman's shoulder. 'Stay down there until you're told otherwise,' she said flatly. Moving her fingers to the hem of her skirt, she raised the fabric, revealing the bare lips of her pussy. 'When you've finished kissing my feet, I want you to kiss this,' she whispered. 'And after that, perhaps Holly and I can take you back to your little mobile dungeon, and we can all listen to an opera together. I rather fancy hearing *Madame Butterfly* tonight.'

As Corinne moaned, Georgia began to laugh darkly to herself.

Two weeks later the fairground had settled on a new pitch. The rides, stalls and attractions had been assembled during the night. For the first time, dawn was breaking on the fresh paint of a newly erected sign. Over the entrance to the pitch, in garish yellow letters on a red background, were the words, WELCOME TO GEORGIA'S FAIRGROUND. The early morning world was silent, save for the sound of birdsong and an angry, shouting voice.

'Move faster, you stupid bitch! Faster!'

Corinne almost stumbled in her hurry to obey. There was a chain between her ankles and the combination of stilettos and uneven ground were threatening her with catastrophe. Her long dark hair flew carelessly about her face as she tried to move more quickly. Holly was in a foul mood and she didn't want to worsen it; not until they got back to the caravan, anyway.

'What the hell is wrong with you?' Holly demanded angrily.

Corinne mumbled an apology and tried to quicken her pace. She was risking tumbling and hurting herself, but a slower gait would have meant she was risking a damned sight more. She reached the door of the booth without incident and began to nail the sign into place.

The whip whistled through the fresh dawn air. An explosion of pain erupted on the exposed cheek of Corinne's arse. She drew breath, momentarily lost in a world of exquisite torment. The red-hot flare of the whip crack was so intense it left bitter tears stinging her eyes.

'Nail it good and hard,' Holly growled. 'Or I'll have you holding the fucking thing all day and all night.' She delivered another whip crack, scoring the other cheek this time. A red welt appeared in the wake of the whip's tip, adding to the collection of fresh and fading bruises that already covered the woman's bare cheeks.

Corinne groaned. The pulse of her arousal was beating so hard the hammer trembled in her fingers and the nail wouldn't stay still. The wetness between the lips of her sex was now so prevalent she could feel the slippery frisson with each step. The tips of her bare nipples were standing taut, tingling with excitement each time Holly cracked the whip against her exposed backside.

Eventually she managed to hammer the sign into position. She glanced over her shoulder to face Holly, praying that her handiwork would meet with the woman's approval.

Holly brought the whip across the cheeks of her arse with a final punishing blow. The impact echoed across the empty fairground.

Corinne stiffened against the pain, surprised and hurt. Her cowed expression showed that she couldn't understand why the blow had been delivered. 'Isn't it right?' she asked, her lower lip quivering nervously.

Holly shrugged, a wicked smile twisting her lips. 'It's OK,' she allowed. 'I just did that for the hell of it.'

'Having fun?' Georgia asked, joining the pair of them.

Corinne cast a suspicious glare at her, but kept the expression brief, not allowing Georgia to see it.

Holly grinned at Georgia and winked knowingly. 'Corinne's just erecting a sign for me,' she explained.

Georgia moved closer and stared at the SITUATION VACANT sign Corinne had nailed to the booth door. She glanced warily at Holly and said, 'Does this mean that you're leaving?'

Holly shook her head. 'I'm not leaving yet,' she explained. 'But I have plans for Corinne tonight and once I've finished, I don't think she'll be able to work for the next week or two.'

Smiling at Corinne's look of happiness, Holly and Georgia laughed loudly together.

NEW BOOKS

Coming up from Nexus and Black Lace

The Test by Nadine Somers
January 1998   Price £5.99   ISBN: 0352 33320 0
When Rachel starts working for Michael, a high-ranking Government minister, she doesn't realise exactly what kind of job training he has in store for her. She is to be initiated into a mysterious and perverse group of female devotees of discipline; total obedience is expected of new recruits, and bizarre and lewd demands are made of them. Will Rachel pass the test?

Exposing Louisa by Jean Aveline
January 1998   Price £5.99   ISBN: 0352 33321 9
Anton and Magdalena are brother and sister, separated at birth but reunited as teenagers. The forbidden nature of their love for each other only serves to intensify their passion for experimentation – for the darkest of sexual games. Working as dancers, they fall under the spell of the manipulative Sophie and the masterful Dieter, both of whom have secret and perverse plans for the couple. By the author of *Sisters of Severcy*.

There are three Nexus titles published in February

The Submission of Stella by Yolanda Celbridge
February 1999   Price £5.99   ISBN: 0 352 33334 0
Stella Shawn, dominant Headmistress of Kernece College, craves to rediscover the joys of submission. Her friend Morag suggests an instructive leave of absence, and enrols her at High Towers, a finishing school in Devon, whose regime is total submission of women to women. The strict rules and stern discipline at High Towers ensure that even Stella can learn once more how to submit to the lash. By the outher of *The Schooling of Stella*.

Bad Penny by Penny Birch

February 1999   Price £5.99   ISBN: 0 352 33335 9

Penny Birch is a very naughty girl. Not only has she shamelessly revealed her love of the bizarre world of pony-girl carting in *Penny in Harness*, but she has also let us know dark secrets about her best friend in *A Taste of Amber*, and has now, in *Bad Penny*, told us everything we ever wanted to know about her cheeky activities. Fans of Penny's writing will know what to expect from this collection of stories – the uninitiated are in for a treat.

The Image – A Nexus Classic by Jean de Berg

February 1999   Price £5.99   ISBN: 0 352 33350 2

The Image was first published in Paris in 1956, and was suppressed almost immediately. In this piece of classic erotica, the story is simple yet subtle, intriguing and very erotic. The narrator, Jean de Berg, is drawn to the delectable and apparently innocent Anne. But Anne is the sex slave of Claire, an icy beauty whom Jean knew years previously. He becomes involved in the women's games of ritual punishment – but who is seducing whom? This is the first in a series of Nexus Classics – a unique collection devoted to bringing the finest works of erotic fiction to a new audience.

BLACK
lace

A Feast for the Senses by Martine Marquand
January 1998   Price £5.99   ISBN: 0 352 33310 3
Claira Fairfax leaves her innocent life in Georgian England to
embark on the Grand Tour of Europe. She travels through the deca-
dent cities – from icebound Amsterdam to sultry Constantinople –
undergoing lessons in perverse pleasure from the mysterious and
eccentric Count Anton di Maliban.

The Transformation by Natasha Rostova
January 1998   Price £5.99   ISBN: 0 352 33311 1
Three friends, one location – San Francisco. This book contains three
interlinked and very modern stories which have their links in fairy
tales. There's nothing innocent about Lydia, Molly and Cassie, however, as one summer provides them with revelatory sexual experiences
which transform their lives.

Mixed Doubles by Zoe le Verdier
February 1999   Price £5.99   ISBN: 0 352 33312 X
Natalie takes over the running of an exclusive tennis club in the
wealthy suburbs of Surrey, England. When she poaches tennis coach,
Chris, from a rival sports club, women come flocking to Natalie's
new business. Chris is skilled in more kinds of adult sport than tennis,
though, and the female clients are soon booking up of extra tuition.

Shadowplay by Portia da Costa
February 1999   Price £5.99   ISBN: 0 352 33313 8
Daniel Woodforde-Ranelagh lives a reclusive but privileged existence,
obsessed with mysticism and the paranormal. When the wayward and
sensual Christabel Sutherland walks into his life, they find they have
a lot in common. Despite their numerous responsibilities, they
immerse themselves in a fantasy world where sexual experimentation
takes pride of place.

NEXUS BACKLIST

All books are priced £4.99 unless another price is given. If a date is supplied, the book in question will not be available until that month in 1998.

CONTEMPORARY EROTICA

THE ACADEMY	Arabella Knight		
AGONY AUNT	G. C. Scott		
ALLISON'S AWAKENING	Lauren King		
AMAZON SLAVE	Lisette Ashton	£5.99	
THE BLACK GARTER	Lisette Ashton	£5.99	Sept
THE BLACK ROOM	Lisette Ashton		
BOUND TO OBEY	Amanda Ware	£5.99	Dec
BOUND TO SUBMIT	Amanda Ware		
CANDIDA IN PARIS	Virginia Lasalle		
CHAINS OF SHAME	Brigitte Markham	£5.99	July
A CHAMBER OF DELIGHTS	Katrina Young		
DARK DELIGHTS	Maria del Rey	£5.99	Aug
DARLINE DOMINANT	Tania d'Alanis	£5.99	Oct
A DEGREE OF DISCIPLINE	Zoe Templeton		
THE DISCIPLINE OF NURSE RIDING	Yolanda Celbridge	£5.99	Nov
THE DOMINO TATTOO	Cyrian Amberlake		
THE DOMINO QUEEN	Cyrian Amberlake		
EDEN UNVEILED	Maria del Rey		
EDUCATING ELLA	Stephen Ferris		
EMMA'S SECRET DOMINATION	Hilary James		
FAIRGROUND ATTRACTIONS	Lisette Ashton	£5.99	Dec
THE TRAINING OF FALLEN ANGELS	Kendal Grahame		
HEART OF DESIRE	Maria del Rey		

ANCIENT & FANTASY SETTINGS

THE CLOAK OF APHRODITE	Kendal Grahame		
DEMONIA	Kendal Grahame		
THE DUNGEONS OF LIDIR	Aran Ashe		
THE FOREST OF BONDAGE	Aran Ashe		
NYMPHS OF DIONYSUS	Susan Tinoff		
THE WARRIOR QUEEN	Kendal Grahame	£5.99	Dec

EDWARDIAN, VICTORIAN & OLDER EROTICA

ANNIE	Evelyn Culber	£5.99	
ANNIE AND THE COUNTESS	Evelyn Culber	£5.99	
BEATRICE	Anonymous		
THE CORRECTION OF AN ESSEX MAID	Yolanda Celbridge	£5.99	
DEAR FANNY	Michelle Clare		
LYDIA IN THE HAREM	Philippa Masters		
LURE OF THE MANOR	Barbra Baron		
MAN WITH A MAID 3	Anonymous		
MEMOIRS OF A CORNISH GOVERNESS	Yolanda Celbridge		
THE GOVERNESS AT ST AGATHA'S	Yolanda Celbridge		
MISS RATTAN'S LESSON	Yolanda Celbridge	£5.99	Aug
PRIVATE MEMOIRS OF A KENTISH HEADMISTRESS	Yolanda Celbridge		
SISTERS OF SEVERCY	Jean Aveline		

SAMPLERS & COLLECTIONS

EROTICON 3	Various		
EROTICON 4	Various	£5.99	July
THE FIESTA LETTERS	ed. Chris Lloyd		
NEW EROTICA 2	ed. Esme Ombreux		
NEW EROTICA 3	ed. Esme Ombreux		
NEW EROTICA 4	ed. Esme Ombreux	£5.99	Sept

NON-FICTION

Please send me the books I have ticked above.

Name   ....

Address   ....

              ....

              ....

              .... Post code........................

Send to: Cash Sales, Nexus Books, Thames Wharf Studios, Rainville Road, London W6 9HT

Please enclose a cheque or postal order, made payable to **Nexus Books**, to the value of the books you have ordered plus postage and packing costs as follows:

UK and BFPO – £1.00 for the first book, 50p for the second book and 30p for each subsequent book to a maximum of £3.00;

Overseas (including Republic of Ireland) – £2.00 for the first book, £1.00 for the second book and 50p for each subsequent book.

If you would prefer to pay by VISA or ACCESS/MASTER-CARD, please write your card number and expiry date here:

....

Please allow up to 28 days for delivery.

Signature ....